"A CHILLING LITERARY EXPERIENCE"

—*Time* Magazine

"A collection of seventeen short stories that show a remarkable variety . . . Some, like THE TUNNEL (to my mind one of the best) are closeups . . . One feels one has lived through the experience. Others, such as the title story which describes the almost automatic affairs of an elderly man who cannot help falling in love, are more extended and tentative . . .

"On the whole, a very distinguished collection."

—L. P. Hartley,
Spectator

DORIS LESSING
THE HABIT OF LOVING

POPULAR LIBRARY • NEW YORK

To my friend
Joan Rodker

Contents

1

The Habit of Loving

In 1947 George wrote again to Myra, saying that now the war was well over she should come home and marry him. She wrote back from Australia, where she had gone with her two children in 1943 because there were relations there, saying she felt they had drifted apart; she was no longer sure she wanted to marry George. He did not allow himself to collapse. He cabled her the air fare and asked her to come over and see him. She came, for two weeks, being unable to leave the children for longer. She said she liked Australia; she liked the climate; she did not like the English climate any longer; she thought England was, very probably, played out; and she had become used to missing London. Also, presumably, to missing George Talbot.

For George this was a very painful fortnight. He believed it was painful for Myra, too. They had met in 1938, had lived together for five years, and had exchanged for four years the letters of lovers separated by fate. Myra was certainly the love of his life. He had believed he was of hers until now. Myra, an attractive woman made beautiful by the suns and beaches of Australia, waved goodbye at the airport, and her eyes were filled with tears.

George's eyes, as he drove away from the airport, were dry. If one person has loved another truly and wholly, then it is more than love that collapses when one side of the indissoluble partnership turns away with a tearful goodbye. George dismissed the taxi early and walked through St. James's Park. Then it seemed too small for him, and he went to the Green Park. Then he walked into Hyde Park and through to Kensington Gardens. When the dark came and they closed the great gates of the park he took a taxi home. He lived in a block of flats near the Marble Arch. For five years Myra had lived with him there, and it was here he had expected to live with her again. Now he moved into a new flat near Covent Garden. Soon after that he wrote Myra a very painful letter. It occurred to him that he had often received such letters, but had never written one before. It occurred to him that he had entirely underestimated the amount of suffering he must have caused in his life. But Myra wrote him a sensible letter back, and George Talbot told himself that now he must finally stop thinking about Myra.

Therefore he became rather less of a dilettante in his work than he had been recently, and he agreed to produce a new play written by a friend of his. George Talbot was a man of the theater. He had not acted in it for many years now; but he wrote articles, he sometimes produced a play, he made speeches on important occasions and was known by everyone. When he went into a restaurant people tried to catch his eye, and he often did not know who they were. During the four years since Myra had left, he had had a number of affairs with young women round and about the theater, for he had been lonely. He had written quite frankly to Myra about these affairs, but she had never mentioned them in her letters. Now he was very busy for some months and was seldom at home; he earned quite a lot of money, and he had a few more affairs with women who were pleased to be seen in public with him. He thought about Myra a great deal, but he did not write to her again, nor she to him, although they had agreed they would always be great friends.

One evening in the foyer of a theater he saw an old friend of his he had always admired, and he told the young woman he was with that that man had been the most irresistible man of his generation—no woman had been able to resist him. The young woman stared briefly across the foyer and said "Not really?"

When George Talbot got home that night he was alone, and he looked at himself with honesty in the mirror. He was sixty, but he did not look it. Whatever had attracted women to him in the past had never been his looks, and he was not much changed: a stoutish man, holding himself erect, gray-haired, carefully brushed, well-dressed. He had not paid much attention to his face since those many years ago when he had been an actor; but now he had an uncharacteristic fit of vanity and remembered that Myra had admired his mouth, while his wife had loved his eyes. He took to taking glances at himself in foyers and restaurants where there were mirrors, and he saw himself as unchanged. He was becoming conscious, though, of a discrepancy between that suave exterior and what he felt. Beneath his ribs his heart had become swollen and soft and painful, a monstrous area of sympathy playing enemy to what he had been. When people made jokes he was often unable to laugh; and his manner of talking, which was light and allusive and dry, must have changed, because more than once old friends asked him if he were depressed, and they no longer smiled appreciatively as he told his stories. He gathered he was not being good company. He understood he might be ill, and he went to the doctor. The doctor said there was nothing wrong with his heart, he had

9

thirty years of life in him yet—luckily, he added respectfully, for the British theater.

George came to understand that the word "heartache" meant that a person could carry a heart that ached around with him day and night for, in his case, months. Nearly a year now. He would wake in the night, because of the pressure of pain in his chest; in the morning he woke under a weight of grief. There seemed to be no end to it; and this thought jolted him into two actions. First, he wrote to Myra, a tender, carefully-phrased letter, recalling the years of their love. To this he got, in due course, a tender and careful reply. Then he went to see his wife. With her he was, and had been for many years, good friends. They saw each other often, but not so often now the children were grown-up; perhaps once or twice a year, and they never quarreled.

His wife had married again after they divorced, and now she was a widow. Her second husband had been a member of Parliament, and she worked for the Labor Party, and she was on a Hospital Advisory Committee and on the Board of Directors of a progressive school. She was fifty, but did not look it. On this afternoon she was wearing a slim gray suit and gray shoes, and her gray hair had a wave of white across the front which made her look distinguished. She was animated, and very happy to see George; and she talked about some deadhead on her hospital committee who did not see eye to eye with the progressive minority about some reform or other. They had always had their politics in common, a position somewhere left of center in the Labor Party. She had sympathized with his being a pacifist in the First World War—he had been for a time in prison because of it; he had sympathized with her militant feminism. Both

10

had helped the strikers in 1926. In the thirties, after they were divorced, she had helped with money when he went on tour with a company acting Shakespeare to people on the dole, or hunger-marching.

Myra had not been at all interested in politics, only in her children. And in George, of course.

George asked his first wife to marry him again, and she was so startled that she let the sugar tongs drop and crack a saucer. She asked what had happened to Myra, and George said: "Well, dear, I think Myra forgot about me during those years in Australia. At any rate, she doesn't want me now." When he heard his voice saying this it sounded pathetic, and he was frightened, for he could not remember ever having to appeal to a woman. Except to Myra.

His wife examined him and said briskly: "You're lonely, George. Well, we're none of us getting any younger."

"You don't think you'd be less lonely if you had me around?"

She got up from her chair in order that she could attend to something with her back to him, and she said that she intended to marry again quite soon. She was marrying a man considerably younger than herself, a doctor who was in the progressive minority at her hospital. From her voice George understood that she was both proud and ashamed of this marriage, and that was why she was hiding her face from him. He congratulated her and asked her if there wasn't perhaps a chance for him yet? "After all, dear, we were happy together, weren't we? I've never really understood why that marriage ever broke up. It was you who wanted to break it up."

"I don't see any point in raking over that old business," she said, with finality, and returned to her seat

11

opposite him. He envied her very much, looking young with her pink and scarcely lined face under that brave lock of deliberately whitened hair.

"But dear, I wish you'd tell me. It doesn't do any harm now, does it? And I always wondered. . . . I've often thought about it and wondered." He could hear the pathetic note in his voice again, but he did not know how to alter it.

"You wondered," she said, "when you weren't occupied with Myra."

"But I didn't know Myra when we got divorced."

"You knew Phillipa and Georgina and Janet and lord knows who else."

"But I didn't care about them."

She sat with her competent hands in her lap and on her face was a look he remembered seeing when she told him she would divorce him. It was bitter and full of hurt. "You didn't care about me either," she said.

"But we were happy. Well, I was happy . . ." he trailed off, being pathetic against all his knowledge of women. For, as he sat there, his old rake's heart was telling him that if only he could find them, there must be the right words, the right tone. But whatever he said came out in this hopeless, old dog's voice, and he knew that this voice could never defeat the gallant and crusading young doctor. "And I did care about you. Sometimes I think you were the only woman in my life."

At this she laughed. "Oh, George, don't get maudlin, now, please."

"Well, dear, there was Myra. But when you threw me over there was bound to be Myra, wasn't there? There were two women, you and then Myra. And I've never never understood why you broke it all up when we seemed to be so happy."

"You didn't care for me," she said again. "If you had, you would never have come home from Phillipa, Georgina, Janet *et al* and said calmly, just as if it didn't matter to me in the least, that you had been with them in Brighton or wherever it was."

"But if I had cared about them I would never have told you."

She was regarding him incredulously, and her face was flushed. With what? Anger? George did not know.

"I remember being so proud," he said pathetically, "that we had solved this business of marriage and all that sort of thing. We had such a good marriage that it didn't matter, the little flirtations. And I always thought one should be able to tell the truth. I always told you the truth, didn't I?"

"Very romantic of you, dear George," she said drily; and soon he got up, kissed her fondly on the cheek, and went away.

He walked for a long time through the parks, hands behind his erect back, and he could feel his heart swollen and painful in his side. When the gates shut, he walked through the lighted streets he had lived in for fifty years of his life, and he was remembering Myra and Molly, as if they were one woman, merging into each other, a shape of warm easy intimacy, a shape of happiness walking beside him. He went into a little restaurant he knew well, and there was a girl sitting there who knew him because she had heard him lecture once on the state of the British theater. He tried hard to see Myra and Molly in her face, but he failed; and he paid for her coffee and his own and went home by himself. But his flat was unbearably empty, and he left it and walked down by the Embankment for a couple of hours to tire himself, and there must have

13

been a colder wind blowing than he knew, for next day he woke with a pain in his chest which he could not mistake for heartache.

He had flu and a bad cough, and he stayed in bed by himself and did not ring up the doctor until the fourth day, when he was getting lightheaded. The doctor said it must be the hospital at once. But he would not go to the hospital. So the doctor said he must have day and night nurses. This he submitted to until the cheerful friendliness of the nurses saddened him beyond bearing, and he asked the doctor to ring up his wife, who would find someone to look after him who would be sympathetic. He was hoping that Molly would come herself to nurse him, but when she arrived he did not like to mention it, for she was busy with preparations for her new marriage. She promised to find him someone who would not wear a uniform and make jokes. They naturally had many friends in common; and she rang up an old flame of his in the theater who said she knew of a girl who was looking for a secretary's job to tide her over a patch of not working, but who didn't really mind what she did for a few weeks.

So Bobby Tippett sent away the nurses and made up a bed for herself in his study. On the first day she sat by George's bed sewing. She wore a full dark skirt and a demure printed blouse with short frills at the wrist, and George watched her sewing and already felt much better. She was a small, thin, dark girl, probably Jewish, with sad black eyes. She had a way of letting her sewing lie loose in her lap, her hands limp over it; and her eyes fixed themselves, and a bloom of dark introspection came over them. She sat very still at these moments, like a small china figure of a girl sewing. When she was nursing George, or letting in his many visitors, she put on a manner of cool

14

and even languid charm; it was the extreme good manners of heartlessness, and at first George was chilled; but then he saw through the pose; for whatever world Bobby Tippett had been born into he did not think it was the English class to which these manners belonged. She replied with a "yes," or a "no," to questions about herself; he gathered that her parents were dead, but there was a married sister she saw sometimes; and for the rest she had lived around and about London, mostly by herself, for ten or more years. When he asked her if she had not been lonely, so much by herself, she drawled, "Why, not at all, I don't mind being alone." But he saw her as a small, brave child, a waif against London, and was moved.

He did not want to be the big man of the theater; he was afraid of evoking the impersonal admiration he was only too accustomed to; but soon he was asking her questions about her career, hoping that this might be the point of her enthusiasm. But she spoke lightly of small parts, odd jobs, scene painting and understudying, in a jolly good-little-trouper's voice; and he could not see that he had come any closer to her at all. So at last he did what he had tried to avoid, and sitting up against his pillows like a judge or an impresario, he said: "Do something for me, dear. Let me see you." She went next door like an obedient child, and came back in tight black trousers, but still in her demure little blouse, and stood on the carpet before him, and went into a little song-and-dance act. It wasn't bad. He had seen a hundred worse. But he was very moved; he saw her now above all as the little urchin, the gamin, boy-girl and helpless. And utterly touching. "Actually," she said, "this is half of an act. I always have someone else."

There was a big mirror that nearly filled the end wall of the large, dark room. George saw himself in

15

it, an elderly man sitting propped up on pillows watching the small doll-like figure standing before him on the carpet. He saw her turn her head toward her reflection in the darkened mirror, study it, and then she began to dance with her own reflection, dance against it, as it were. There were two small, light figures dancing in George's room; there was something uncanny in it. She began singing, a little broken song in stage cockney, and George felt that she was expecting the other figure in the mirror to sing with her; she was singing at the mirror as if she expected an answer.

"That's very good, dear," he broke in quickly, for he was upset, though he did not know why. "Very good indeed." He was relieved when she broke off and came away from the mirror, so that the uncanny shadow of her went away.

"Would you like me to speak to someone for you, dear? It might help. You know how things are in the theater," he suggested apologetically.

"I don't maind if I dew," she said in the stage cockney of her act; and for a moment her face flashed into a mocking, reckless, gamin-like charm. "Perhaps I'd better change back into my skirt?" she suggested. "More natural-like for a nurse, ain't it?"

But he said he liked her in her tight black trousers, and now she always wore them, and her neat little shirts; and she moved about the flat as a charming feminine boy, chattering to him about the plays she had had small parts in and about the big actors and actresses and producers she had spoken to, who were, of course, George's friends or, at least, equals. George sat up against his pillows and listened and watched, and his heart ached. He remained in bed longer than there was need, because he did not want her to go. When he transferred himself to a big chair, he said:

16

"You mustn't think you're bound to stay here, dear, if there's somewhere else you'd rather go." To which she replied, with a wide flash of her black eyes, "But I'm resting, darling, resting. I've nothing better to do with myself." And then: "Oh aren't I a*wful*, the things wot I sy?"

"But you do like being here? You don't mind being here with me, dear?" he insisted.

There was the briefest pause. She said: "Yes, oddly enough I do like it." The "oddly enough" was accompanied by a quick, half-laughing, almost flirtatious glance; and for the first time in many months the pressure of loneliness eased around George's heart.

Now it was a happiness to him because when the distinguished ladies and gentlemen of the theater or of letters came to see him, Bobby became a cool, silky little hostess; and the instant they had gone she relapsed into urchin charm. It was a proof of their intimacy. Sometimes he took her out to dinner or to the theater. When she dressed up she wore bold, fashionable clothes and moved with the insolence of a mannequin; and George moved beside her, smiling fondly, waiting for the moment when the black, reckless, freebooting eyes would flash up out of the languid stare of the woman presenting herself for admiration, exchanging with him amusement at her posing, amusement at the world; promising him that soon, when they got back to the apartment, by themselves, she would again become the dear little girl or the gallant, charming waif.

Sometimes, sitting in the dim room at night, he would let his hand close over the thin point of her shoulder; sometimes, when they said good night, he bent to kiss her, and she lowered her head, so that his lips encountered her demure, willing forehead.

George told himself that she was unawakened. It

was a phrase that had been the prelude to a dozen warm discoveries in the past. He told himself that she knew nothing of what she might be. She had been married, it seemed—she dropped this information once, in the course of an anecdote about the theater; but George had known women in plenty who after years of marriage had been unawakened. George asked her to marry him; and she lifted her small sleek head with an animal's startled turn and said: "Why do you want to marry me?"

"Because I like being with you, dear. I love being with you."

"Well, I like being with you." It had a questioning sound. She was questioning herself? "Strainge," she said in cockney, laughing. "Strainge but trew."

The wedding was to be a small one, but there was a lot about it in the papers. Recently several men of George's generation had married young women. One of them had fathered a son at the age of seventy. George was flattered by the newspapers, and told Bobby a good deal about his life that had not come up before. He remarked for instance that he thought his generation had been altogether more successful about this business of love and sex than the modern generation. He said, "Take my son, for instance. At his age I had had a lot of affairs and knew about women; but there he is, nearly thirty, and when he stayed here once with a girl he was thinking of marrying I know for a fact they shared the same bed for a week and nothing ever happened. She told me so. Very odd it all seems to me. But it didn't seem odd to her. And now he lives with another young man and listens to that long-playing record thing of his, and he's engaged to a girl he takes out twice a week, like a schoolboy. And there's my daughter, she came to me a year after she was married, and she was in an awful mess, really awful . . . it seems to me your generation are very frightened of it all. I don't know why."

"Why my generation?" she asked, turning her head with that quick listening movement. "It's not my generation."

"But you're nothing but a child," he said fondly.

He could not decipher what lay behind the black, full stare of her sad eyes as she looked at him now; she was sitting cross-legged in her black glossy trousers before the fire, like a small doll. But a spring of alarm had been touched in him and he didn't dare say any more.

"At thirty-five, I'm the youngest child alive," she sang, with a swift sardonic glance at him over her shoulder. But it sounded gay.

He did not talk to her again about the achievements of his generation.

After the wedding he took her to a village in Normandy where he had been once, many years ago, with a girl called Eve. He did not tell her he had been there before.

It was spring, and the cherry trees were in flower. The first evening he walked with her in the last sunlight under the white-flowering branches, his arm around her thin waist, and it seemed to him that he was about to walk back through the gates of a lost happiness.

They had a large comfortable room with windows which overlooked the cherry trees and there was a double bed. Madame Cruchot, the farmer's wife, showed them the room with shrewd, noncommenting eyes, said she was always happy to shelter honeymoon couples, and wished them a good night.

George made love to Bobby, and she shut her eyes, and he found she was not at all awkward. When they had finished, he gathered her in his arms, and it was

19

then that he returned simply, with an incredulous awed easing of the heart, to a happiness which—and now it seemed to him fantastically ungrateful that he could have done—he had taken for granted for so many years of his life. It was not possible, he thought, holding her compliant body in his arms, that he could have been by himself, alone, for so long. It had been intolerable. He held her silent breathing body, and he stroked her back and thighs, and his hands remembered the emotions of nearly fifty years of loving. He could feel the memoried emotions of his life flooding through his body, and his heart swelled with a joy it seemed to him he had never known, for it was a compound of a dozen loves.

He was about to take final possession of his memories when she turned sharply away, sat up, and said: "I want a fag. How about yew?"

"Why, yes, dear, if you want."

They smoked. The cigarettes finished, she lay down on her back, arms folded across her chest, and said "I'm sleepy." She closed her eyes. When he was sure she was asleep, he lifted himself on his elbow and watched her. The light still burned, and the curve of her cheek was full and soft, like a child's. He touched it with the side of his palm, and she shrank away in her sleep, but clenched up, like a fist; and her hand, which was white and unformed, like a child's hand, was clenched in a fist on the pillow before her face.

George tried to gather her in his arms, and she turned away from him to the extreme edge of the bed. She was deeply asleep, and her sleep was unsharable. George could not endure it. He got out of bed and stood by the window in the cold spring night air, and saw the white cherry trees standing under the white moon, and thought of the cold girl asleep in her bed. He was there in the chill moonlight until the dawn came; in the morning he had a very bad cough and could not get up. Bobby was charming, devoted, and gay. "Just like old times, me nursing you," she commented, with a deliberate roll of her black eyes. She asked Madame Cruchot for another bed, which she placed in the corner of the room, and George thought it was quite reasonable she should not want to catch his cold; for he did not allow himself to remember the times in his past when quite serious illness had been no obstacle to the sharing of the dark; he decided to forget the sensualities of tiredness, or of fever, or of the extremes of sleeplessness. He was even beginning to feel ashamed.

For a fortnight the Frenchwoman brought up magnificent meals, twice a day, and George and Bobby drank a great deal of red wine and of calvados and made jokes with Madame Cruchot about getting ill on honeymoons. They returned from Normandy rather earlier than had been arranged. It would be better for George, Bobby said, at home, where his friends could drop in to see him. Besides, it was sad to be shut indoors in springtime, and they were both eating too much.

On the first night back in the flat, George waited to see if she would go into the study to sleep, but she came to the big bed in her pajamas, and for the second time, he held her in his arms for the space of the act, and then she smoked, sitting up in bed and looking rather tired and small and, George thought, terribly young and pathetic. He did not sleep that night. He did not dare move out of bed for fear of disturbing her, and he was afraid to drop off to sleep for fear his limbs remembered the habits of a lifetime and searched for hers. In the morning she woke smiling, and he put his arms around her, but she kissed him with small gentle kisses and jumped out of bed.

21

That day she said she must go and see her sister. She saw her sister often during the next few weeks and kept suggesting that George should have his friends around more than he did. George asked why didn't the sister come to see her here, in the flat? So one afternoon she came to tea. George had seen her briefly at the wedding and disliked her, but now for the first time he had a spell of revulsion against the marriage itself. The sister was awful—a commonplace, middle-aged female from some suburb. She had a sharp, dark face that poked itself inquisitively into the corners of the flat, pricing the furniture, and a thin acquisitive nose bent to one side. She sat, on her best behavior, for two hours over the teacups, in a mannish navy blue suit, a severe black hat, her brogued feet set firmly side by side before her; and her thin nose seemed to be carrying on a silent, satirical conversation with her sister about George. Bobby was being cool and well-mannered, as it were deliberately tired of life, as she always was when guests were there, but George was sure this was simply on his account. When the sister had gone, George was rather querulous about her; but Bobby said, laughing, that of course she had known George wouldn't like Rosa; she *was* rather ghastly; but then who had suggested inviting her? So Rosa came no more, and Bobby went out to meet her for a visit to the pictures, or for shopping. Meanwhile, George sat alone and thought uneasily about Bobby, or visited his old friends. A few months after they returned from Normandy, someone suggested to George that perhaps he was ill. This made George think about it, and he realized he was not far from being ill. It was because he could not sleep. Night after night he lay beside Bobby, after her cheerfully affectionate submission to him; and he saw the soft curve of her cheek on the pillow, the long dark lashes lying close and flat. Never had anything in his life moved him so deeply as that childish cheek, the shadow of those lashes. A small crease in one cheek seemed to him the signature of emotion; and the lock of black glossy hair falling across her forehead filled his throat with tears. His nights were long vigils of locked tenderness.

Then one night she woke and saw him watching her.

"What's the matter?" she asked, startled. "Can't you sleep?"

"I'm only watching you, dear," he said hopelessly.

She lay curled up beside him, her fist beside her on the pillow, between him and her. "Why aren't you happy?" she asked suddenly; and as George laughed with a sudden bitter irony, she sat up, arms around her knees, prepared to consider this problem practically.

"This isn't marriage; this isn't love," he announced. He sat up beside her. He did not know that he had never used that tone to her before. A portly man, his elderly face flushed with sorrow, he had forgotten her for the moment, and he was speaking across her from his past, resurrected in her, to his past. He was dignified with responsible experience and the warmth of a lifetime's responses. His eyes were heavy, satirical, and condemning. She rolled herself up against him and said with a small sad smile, "Then show me, George."

"Show you?" he said, almost stammering. "Show you?" But he held her, the obedient child, his cheek against hers, until she slept; then a too close pressure of his shoulder on hers caused her to shrink and recoil from him away to the edge of the bed.

In the morning she looked at him oddly, with an odd sad little respect, and said, "You know what, George? You've just got into the habit of loving."

"What do you mean, dear?"

She rolled out of bed and stood beside it, a waif in her white pajamas, her black hair ruffled. She slid her eyes at him and smiled. "You just want something in your arms, that's all. What do you do when you're alone? Wrap yourself around a pillow?"

He said nothing; he was cut to the heart.

"My husband was the same," she remarked gaily. "Funny thing is, he didn't care anything about me." She stood considering him, smiling mockingly. "Straingt, ain't it?" she commented and went off to the bathroom. That was the second time she had mentioned her husband.

That phrase, the habit of loving, made a revolution in George. It was true, he thought. He was shocked out of himself, out of the instinctive response to the movement of skin against his, the pressure of a breast. It seemed to him that was seeing Bobby quite newly. He had not really known her before. The delightful little girl had vanished, and he saw a young woman toughened and wary because of defeats and failures he had never stopped to think of. He saw that the sadness that lay behind the black eyes was not at all impersonal; he saw the first sheen of gray lying on her smooth hair; he saw that the full curve of her cheek was the beginning of the softening into middle-age. He was appalled at his egotism. Now, he thought, he would really know her, and she would begin to love him in response to it.

Suddenly, George discovered in himself a boy whose existence he had totally forgotten. He had been returned to his adolescence. The accidental touch of her hand delighted him; the swing of her skirt could make him shut his eyes with happiness. He looked at her through the jealous eyes of a boy and began questioning her about her past, feeling that he was slowly taking possession of her. He waited for a hint of emotion in the drop of her voice, or a confession in the wrinkling of the skin by the full, dark, comradely eyes. At night, a boy again, reverence shut him into ineptitude. The body of George's sensuality had been killed stone dead. A month ago he had been a man vigorous with the skilled harboring of memory; the long use of his body. Now he lay awake beside this woman, longing—not for the past, for that past had dropped away from him, but dreaming of the future. And when he questioned her, like a jealous boy, and she evaded him, he could see it only as the locked virginity of the girl who would wake in answer to the worshiping boy he had become.

But still she slept in a citadel, one fist before her face.

Then one night she woke again, roused by some movement of his. "What's the matter *now*, Gorge?" she asked, exasperated.

In the silence that followed, the resurrected boy in George died painfully.

"Nothing," he said. "Nothing at all." He turned away from her, defeated.

It was he who moved out of the big bed into the narrow bed in the study. She said with a sharp, sad smile, "Fed up with me, George? Well I can't help it, you know. I didn't ever like sleeping beside someone very much."

George, who had dropped out of his work lately, undertook to produce another play, and was very busy again; and he became drama critic for one of the big papers and was in the swim and at all the first nights. Sometimes Bobby was with him, in her startling, smart clothes, being amused with him at the whole business of being fashionable. Sometimes she stayed at home. She had the capacity for being by herself for hours, apparently doing nothing. George

25

would come home from some crowd of people, some party, and find her sitting cross-legged before the fire in her tight trousers, chin in hand, gone off by herself into some place where he was now afraid to try and follow. He could not bear it again, putting himself in a position where he might hear the cold, sharp words that showed she had never had an inkling of what he felt, because it was not in her nature to feel it. He would come in late, and she would make them both some tea; and they would sit hand in hand before the fire, his flesh and memories quiet. Dead, he thought. But his heart ached. He had become so used to the heavy load of loneliness in his chest that when, briefly, talking to an old friend, he became the George Talbot who had never known Bobby, and his heart lightened and his oppression went, he would look about him, startled, as if he had lost something. He felt almost lightheaded without the pain of loneliness.

He asked Bobby if she weren't bored, with so little to do, month after month after month, while he was so busy. She said no, she was quite happy doing nothing. She wouldn't like to take up her old work again?

"I wasn't ever much good, was I?" she said.

"If you'd enjoy it, dear, I could speak to someone for you."

She frowned at the fire but said nothing. Later he suggested it again, and she sparked up with a grin and: "Well, I don't maind if I dew. . . ."

So he spoke to an old friend, and Bobby returned to the theater, to a small act in a little intimate review. She had found somebody, she said, to be the other half of her act. George was very busy with a production of *Romeo and Juliet*, and did not have time to see her at rehearsal, but he was there on the night *The Offbeat Revue* opened. He was rather late and stood at the back of the gimcrack little theater, packed tight with fragile little chairs. Everything was so small that the well-dressed audience looked too big, like oversize people crammed in a box. The tiny stage was left bare, with a few black and white posters stuck here and there, and there was one piano. The pianist was good, a young man with black hair falling limp over his face, playing as if he were bored with the whole thing. But he played very well. George, the man of the theater, listened to the first number, so as to catch the mood, and thought, Oh Lord, not again. It was one of the songs from the First World War, and he could not stand the flood of easy emotion it aroused. He refused to feel. Then he realized that the emotion was, in any case, blocked; the piano was mocking the song; "There's a Long, Long Trail" was being played like a five-finger exercise; and "Keep the Home Fires Burning" and "Tipperary" followed, in the same style, as if the piano were bored. People were beginning to chuckle, they had caught the mood. A young blond man with a moustache and wearing the uniform of 1914 came in and sang fragments of the songs, like a corpse singing; and then George understood he was supposed to be one of the dead of that war singing. George felt all his responses blocked, first because he could not allow himself to feel any emotion from that time at all—it was too painful; and then because of the five-finger exercise style, which contradicted everything, all pain or protest, leaving nothing, an emptiness. The show went on; through the twenties, with bits of popular songs from that time, a number about the General Strike, which reduced the whole thing to the scale of marionettes without passion, and then on to the thirties. George saw it was a sort of potted history, as it were—Noel Coward's falsely heroic view of his time parodied. But it wasn't even that. There was no emotion, nothing. George did not know what he was supposed to feel. He looked curiously at the faces of the people around him and saw that the older people looked puzzled, affronted, as if the show were an insult to them. But the younger people were in the mood of the thing. But what mood? It was the parody of a parody. When the Second World War was evoked by "Run Rabbit Run," played like *Lohengrin*, while the soldiers in the uniforms of the time mocked their own understated heroism from the other side of death, then George could not stand it. He did not look at the stage at all. He was waiting for Bobby to come on, so he could say that he had seen her. Meanwhile he smoked and watched the face of a very young man near him; it was a pale, heavy, flaccid face, but it was responding, it seemed from a habit of rancour, to everything that went on on the stage. Suddenly, the young face lit into sarcastic delight, and George looked at the stage. On it were two urchins, identical it seemed, in tight black glossy trousers, tight crisp white shirts. Both had short black hair, neat little feet placed side by side. They were standing together, hands crossed loosely before them at the waist, waiting for the music to start. The man at the piano, who had a cigarette in the corner of his mouth, began playing something very sentimental. He broke off and looked with sardonic enquiry at the urchins. They had not moved. They shrugged and rolled their eyes at him. He played a marching song, very loud and pompous. The urchins twitched a little and stayed still. Then the piano broke fast and sudden into a rage of jazz. The two puppets on the stage began a furious movement, their limbs clashing with each other and with the music, until they fell into poses of helpless despair while the music grew louder and more desperate. They tried again, whirling themselves into a frenzied attempt to keep up with the music. Then, two waifs, they turned their two small white sad faces at each other, and, with a formal nod, each took a phrase of music from the fast flood of sound that had already swept by them, held it, and began to sing. Bobby sang her bad stage-cockney phrases, meaningless, jumbled up, flat, hopeless; the other urchin sang drawling languid phrases from the upperclass jargon of the moment. They looked at each other, offering the phrases as it were, to see if they would be accepted. Meanwhile, the hard, cruel, hurtful music went on. Again the two went limp and helpless, unwanted, unaccepted. George, outraged and hurt, asked himself again: What am I feeling? What am I supposed to be feeling? For that insane nihilistic music demanded some opposition, some statement of affirmation, but the two urchins, half-boy, half-girl, as alike as twins (George had to watch Bobby carefully so as not to confuse her with "the other half of her act") were not even trying to resist the music. Then, after a long, sad immobility, they changed roles. Bobby took the languid jaw-writhing part of a limp young man, and the other waif sang false-cockney phrases in a cruel copy of a woman's voice. It was the parody of a parody of a parody. George stood tense, waiting for a resolution. His nature demanded that now, and quickly, for the limp sadness of the turn was unbearable, the two false urchins should flash out in some sort of rebellion. But there was nothing. The jazz went on like hammers; the whole room shook— stage, walls, ceiling—and it seemed the people in the room jigged lightly and helplessly. The two children on the stage twisted their limbs into the willful mockery of a stage convention, and finally stood side by side, hands hanging limp, heads lowered meekly, twitching a little while the music rose into a final crashing discord and the lights went out. George could not applaud. He saw that the damp-faced young man next to him was clapping wildly, while his lank hair fell all over his face. George saw that the older people were all, like himself, bewildered and insulted.

When the show was over, George went backstage to fetch Bobby. She was with "the other half of the act," a rather good-looking boy of about twenty, who was being deferential to the impressive husband of Bobby. George said to her: "You were very good, dear, very good indeed." She looked smilingly at him, half-mocking, but he did not know what it was she was mocking now. And she had been good. But he never wanted to see it again.

The revue was a success and ran for some months before it was moved to a bigger theater. George finished his production of *Romeo and Juliet* which, so the critics said, was the best London had seen for many years, and refused other offers of work. He did not need the money for the time being, and besides, he had not seen very much of Bobby lately.

But of course now she was working. She was at rehearsals several times a week, and away from the flat every evening. But George never went to her theater. He did not want to see the sad, unresisting children twitching to the cruel music.

It seemed Bobby was happy. The various little parts she had played with him—the urchin, the cool hostess, the dear child—had all been absorbed into the hard-working female who cooked him his meals, looked after him, and went out to her theater giving him a friendly kiss on the cheek. Their relationship was most pleasant and amiable. George lived beside this good friend, his wife Bobby, who was doing him so much credit in every way, and ached permanently with loneliness.

One day he was walking down the Charing Cross Road, looking into the windows of bookshops, when he saw Bobby strolling up the other side with Jackie, the other half of her act. She looked as he had never seen her: her dark face was alive with animation, and Jackie was looking into her face and laughing. George thought the boy very handsome. He had a warm gloss of youth on his hair and in his eyes; he had the lithe, quick look of a young animal.

He was not jealous at all. When Bobby came in at night, gay and vivacious, he knew he owed this to Jackie and did not mind. He was even grateful to him. The warmth Bobby had for "the other half of the act" overflowed toward him; and for some months Myra and his wife were present in his mind, he saw and felt them, two loving presences, young women who loved George, brought into being by the feeling between Jackie and Bobby. Whatever that feeling was.

The Offbeat Revue ran for nearly a year, and then it was coming off, and Bobby and Jackie were working out another act. George did not know what it was. He thought Bobby needed a rest, but he did not like to say so. She had been tired recently, and when she came in at night there was strain beneath her gaiety. Once, at night, he woke to see her beside his bed. "Hold me for a little, George," she asked. He opened his arms and she came into them. He lay holding her, quite still. He had opened his arms to the sad waif, but it was an unhappy woman lying in his arms. He could feel the movement of her lashes on his shoulder, and the wetness of tears.

He had not lain beside her for a long time, years, it seemed. She did not come to him again.

"You don't think you're working too hard, dear?" he asked once, looking at her strained face; but she said briskly, "No, I've got to have something to do, can't stand doing nothing."

One night it was raining hard, and Bobby had been feeling sick that day, and she did not come home at her usual time. George became worried and took a taxi to the theater and asked the doorman if she was still there. It seemed she had left some time before. "She didn't look too well to me, sir," volunteered the doorman, and George sat for a time in the taxi, trying not to worry. Then he gave the driver Jackie's address; he meant to ask him if he knew where Bobby was. He sat limp in the back of the taxi, feeling the heaviness of his limbs, thinking of Bobby ill.

The place was in a mews, and he left the taxi and walked over rough cobbles to a door which had been the door of stables. He rang, and a young man he didn't know let him in, saying yes, Jackie Dickson was in. George climbed narrow, steep, wooden stairs slowly, feeling the weight of his body, while his heart pounded. He stood at the top of the stairs to get his breath, in a dark which smelled of canvas and oil and turpentine. There was a streak of light under a door; he went toward it, knocked, heard no answer, and opened it. The scene was a high, bare, studio sort of place, badly lighted, full of pictures, frames, junk of various kinds. Jackie, the dark, glistening youth, was seated cross-legged before the fire, grinning as he lifted his face to say something to Bobby, who sat in a chair, looking down at him. She was wearing a formal dark dress and jewelry, and her arms and neck were bare and white. She looked beautiful, George thought, glancing once, briefly, at her face, and then away; for he could see on it an emotion he did not want to recognize. The scene held for a moment before they realized he was there and turned their heads with the same lithe movement of disturbed animals, to see him standing there in the doorway. Both faces froze. Bobby looked quickly at the young man, and it was in some kind of fear. Jackie looked sulky and angry.

"I've come to look for you, dear," said George to his wife. "It was raining and the doorman said you seemed ill."

"It's very sweet of you," she said and rose from the chair, giving her hand formally to Jackie, who nodded with bad grace at George.

The taxi stood in the dark, gleaming rain, and George and Bobby got into it and sat side by side, while it splashed off into the street.

"Was that the wrong thing to do, dear?" asked George, when she said nothing.

"No," she said.

"I really did think you might be ill."

She laughed. "Perhaps I am."

"What's the matter, my darling? What is it? He was angry, wasn't he? Because I came?"

"He thinks you're jealous," she said shortly.

"Well, perhaps I am rather," said George.

She did not speak.

"I'm sorry, dear, I really am. I didn't mean to spoil anything for you."

"Well, that's certainly *that*," she remarked, and she sounded impersonally angry.

"Why? But why should it be?"

"He doesn't like—having things asked of him," she said, and he remained silent while they drove home.

Up in the warmed, comfortable old flat, she stood before the fire, while he brought her a drink. She smoked fast and angrily, looking into the fire.

"Please forgive me, dear," he said at last. "What is

33

it? Do you love him? Do you want to leave me? If you do, of course you must. Young people should be together."

She turned and stared at him, a black strange stare he knew well.

"George," she said, "I'm nearly forty."

"But darling, you're a child still. At least, to me."

"And he," she went on, "will be twenty-two next month. I'm old enough to be his mother." She laughed, painfully. "Very painful, maternal love . . . or so it seems . . . but then how should I know?" She held out her bare arm and looked at it. Then, with the fingers of one hand she creased down the skin of that bare arm toward the wrist, so that the aging skin lay in creases and folds. Then, setting down her glass, her cigarette held between tight, amused, angry lips, she wriggled her shoulders out of her dress, so that it slipped to her waist, and she looked down at her two small, limp, unused breasts. "Very painful, dear George," she said, and shrugged her dress up quickly, becoming again the formal woman dressed for the world. "He does not love me. He does not love me at all. Why should he?" She began singing:

> "He does not love me
> With a love that is trew. . . ."

Then she said in stage cockney, "Repeat; I could 'ave bin 'is muvver, see?" And with the old rolling derisive black flash of her eyes she smiled at George.

George was thinking only that this girl, his darling, was suffering now what he had suffered, and he could not stand it. She had been going through this for how long now? But she had been working with that boy for nearly two years. She had been living beside him, George, and he had had no idea at all of her unhappi-

34

ness. He went over to her, put his old arms around her, and she stood with her head on his shoulder and wept. For the first time, George thought, they were together. They sat by the fire a long time that night, drinking, smoking and her head was on his knee and he stroked it, and thought that now, at last, she had been admitted into the world of emotion and they would learn to be really together. He could feel his strength stirring along his limbs for her. He was still a man, after all.

Next day she said she would not go on with the new show. She would tell Jackie he must get another partner. And besides, the new act wasn't really any good. "I've had one little act all my life," she said, laughing. "And sometimes it's fitted in, and sometimes it hasn't."

"What was the new act? What's it about?" he asked her.

She did not look at him. "Oh, nothing very much. It was Jackie's idea, really. . . ." Then she laughed. "It's quite good really, I suppose. . . ."

"But what is it?"

"Well, you see. . . ." Again he had the impression she did not want to look at him. "It's a pair of lovers. We make fun . . . it's hard to explain, without doing it."

"You make fun of love?" he asked.

"Well, you know, all the attitudes . . . the things people say. It's a man and a woman—with music of course. All the music you'd expect, played offbeat. We wear the same costume as for the other act. And then we go through all the motions. . . . It's rather funny, really . . ." she trailed off, breathless, seeing George's face. "Well," she said, suddenly very savage, "if it isn't all bloody funny, what is it?" She turned away to take a cigarette.

"Perhaps you'd like to go on with it after all?" he asked ironically.

"No. I can't. I really can't. I can't stand it. I can't stand it any longer, George," she said, and from her voice he understood she had nothing to learn from him of pain.

He suggested they both needed a holiday, so they went to Italy. They traveled from place to place, never stopping anywhere longer than a day, for George knew she was running away from any place around which emotion could gather. At night he made love to her, but she closed her eyes and thought of the other half of the act; and George knew it and did not care. But what he was feeling was too powerful for his old body; he could feel a lifetime's emotions beating through his limbs, making his brain throb.

Again they curtailed their holiday, to return to the comfortable old flat in London.

On the first morning after their return, she said: "George, you know you're getting too old for this sort of thing—it's not good for you; you look ghastly."

"But, darling, why? What else am I still alive for?"

"People'll say I'm killing you," she said, with a sharp, half angry, half amused, black glance.

"But, my darling, believe me. . . ."

He could see them both in the mirror; he, an old pursy man, head lowered in sullen obstinacy; she . . . but he could not read her face.

"And perhaps *I'm* getting too old?" she remarked suddenly.

For a few days she was gay, mocking, then suddenly tender. She was provocative, teasing him with her eyes; then she would deliberately yawn and say, "I'm going to sleep. Good night George."

"Well of course, my darling, if you're tired."

One morning she announced she was going to have a birthday party; it would be her fortieth birthday soon. The way she said it made George feel uneasy.

On the morning of her birthday she came into his study where he had been sleeping, carrying his braekfast tray. He raised himself on his elbow and gazed at her, appalled. For a moment he had imagined it must be another woman. She had put on a severe navy blue suit, cut like a man's; heavy black-laced shoes; and she had taken the wisps of black hair back off her face and pinned them into a sort of clumsy knot. She was suddenly a middle-aged woman.

"But, my darling," he said, "my darling, what have you done to yourself?"

"I'm forty," she said. "Time to grow up."

"But, my darling, I do so love you in your nice clothes. I do so love you being beautiful in your lovely clothes."

She laughed, and left the breakfast tray beside his bed, and went clumping out on her heavy shoes.

That morning she stood in the kitchen beside a very large cake, on which she was carefully placing forty small pink candles. But it seemed only the sister had been asked to the party, for that afternoon the three of them sat around the cake and looked at one another. George looked at Rosa, the sister, in her ugly, straight, thick suit, and at his darling Bobby, all her grace and charm submerged into heavy tweed, her hair dragged back, without make-up. They were two middle-aged women, talking about food and buying.

George said nothing. His whole body throbbed with loss.

The dreadful Rosa was looking with her sharp eyes around the expensive flat, and then at George and then at her sister.

"You've let yourself go, haven't you, Bobby?" she commented at last. She sounded pleased about it.

Bobby glanced defiantly at George. "I haven't got time for all this nonsense any more," she said. "I simply haven't got time. We're all getting on now, aren't we?"

George saw the two women looking at him. He thought they had the same black, hard, inquisitive stare over sharp-bladed noses. He could not speak. His tongue was thick. The blood was beating through his body. His heart seemed to be swelling and filling his whole body, an enormous soft growth of pain. He could not hear for the tolling of the blood through his ears. The blood was beating up into his eyes, but he shut them so as not to see the two women.

2

The Words He Said

On the morning of the *braavleis*, Dad kept saying to Moira, as if he thought it was a joke, "Moy, it's going to rain." First she did not hear him, then she turned her head slowly and deliberately and looked at him so that he remembered what she had said the day before; and he got red in the face and went indoors, out of her way. The day before he had said to her, speaking to me, "What's Moy got into her head? Is the *braavleis* for her engagement or what?"

It was because Moira spent all morning cooking her lemon cake for the *braavleis*, and she went over to Sam the butcher's to order the best ribs of beef and best rump steak.

All the cold season she was not cooking, she was not helping Mom in the house at all, she was not taking an interest in life; and Dad was saying to Mom: "Oh, get the girl to town or something; don't let her moon about here. Who does she think she is?"

Mom just said, quiet and calm, the way she was with Dad when they did not agree: "Oh, let her alone, Dickson." When Mom and Dad were agreeing, they called each other Mom and Dad; when they were against each other, it was Marion and Dickson. And that is how it was for the whole of the dry season, and Moira was pale and moony and would not talk to me. It was no fun for me, I can tell you.

"What's this for?" Dad said once about halfway through the season, when Moira stayed in bed three days and Mom let her. "Has he said anything to her or hasn't he?"

Mom just said: "She's sick, Dickson."

But I could see what he said had gone into her, because I was in our bedroom when Mom came to Moira.

Mom sat down on the bed, but at the bottom of it, and she was worried. "Listen, girl," said Mom, "I don't want to interfere, I don't want to do that, but what did Greg say?" Moira was not properly in bed, but in her old pink dressing gown that used to be Mom's, and she was lying under the quilt. She lay there, not reading or anything, watching out of the window over at the big water tanks across the railway lines. Her face looked bad, and she said: "Oh, leave me alone, Mom."

Mom said: "Listen, dear, just let me say something. You don't have to follow what I say, do you?"

But Moira said nothing.

"Sometimes boys say a thing, and they don't mean it the way we think. They feel they have to say it. It's not they don't mean it, but they mean it different."

"He didn't say anything at all," said Moira. "Why should he?"

"Why don't you go into town and stay with Auntie Nora a while? You can come back for the holidays when Greg comes back."

"Oh, let me alone," said Moira, and she began to cry. That was the first time she cried. At least, in front of Mom. I used to hear her cry at night when she thought I was asleep.

Mom's face was tight and patient, and she put her hand on Moira's shoulder, and she was worried I could see. I was sitting on my bed pretending to do

40

my stamps, and she looked over at me and seemed to be thinking hard.

"He didn't say anything, Mom," I said. "But I know what happened."

Moira jerked her head up and she said: "Get that kid away from me."

They could not get me away from Moira because there were only two bedrooms, and I always slept with Moira. But she would not speak to me that night at all; and Mom said to me, "Little pitchers have big ears."

It was the last year's *braavleis* it happened. Moira was not keen on Greg then; I know for a fact because she was sweet on Jordan. Greg was mostly at the Cape in college; but he came back for the first time in a year, and I saw him looking at Moira. She was pretty then, because she had finished school and spent all her time making herself pretty. She was eighteen, and her hair was wavy because the rains had started. Greg was on the other side of the bonfire, and he came walking arund it through the sparks and the white smoke, and up to Moira. Moira smiled out of politeness, because she wanted Jordan to sit by her, and she was afraid he wouldn't if he saw her occupied by Greg.

"Moira Hughes?" he said. Moira smiled, and he said: "I wouldn't have known you."

"Go on," I said, "you've known us always."

They did not hear me. They were just looking. It was peculiar. I knew it was one of the peculiar moments of life because my skin was tingling all over, and that is how I always know.

Because of how she was looking at him, I looked at him too, but I did not think he was handsome. The holidays before, when I was sweet on Greg Jackson, I naturally thought he was handsome, but now he was just ordinary. He was very thin always, and his hair was ginger, and his freckles were thick, because naturally the sun is no good for people with white skin and freckles.

But he wasn't bad, particularly because he was in his sensible mood. Since he went to college he had two moods, one noisy and sarcastic; and then Moira used to say, all lofty and superior: "Medical students are always rowdy. It stands to reason because of the hard life they have afterward." His other mood was when he was quiet and grown-up; and some of the gang didn't like it, because he was better than us—he was the only one of the gang to go to university at the Cape.

After they had finished looking, he just sat down in the grass in the place Moira was keeping for Jordan, and Moira did not once look around for Jordan. They did not say anything else, just went on sitting, and when the big dance began, with everyone holding hands around the bonfire, they stood at one side watching.

That was all that happened at the *braavleis*, and that was all the words he said. Next day Greg went on a shooting trip with his father, who was the man at the garage. They went right up the Zambesi valley, and Greg did not come back to our station during those holidays or the holidays after.

I knew Moira was thinking of a letter, because she bought some of Croxley's best blue at the store, and she always went herself to the post office on mail days. But there was no letter. But after that she said to Jordan, "No thanks, I don't feel like it," when he asked her to go into town to the pictures.

She did not take any notice of any of the gang after that, though before she was leader of the gang, even over the boys.

That was when she stopped being pretty again; she looked as she did before she left school and was working hard at her studies. She was too thin; the curl went out of her hair and she didn't bother to curl it, either.

All that dry season she did nothing and hardly spoke and did not sing, and I knew it was because of that minute when Greg and she looked at each other —that was all; and when I thought of it, I could feel the cold-hot down my back.

Well, on the day before the *braavleis*, as I said, Moira was on the veranda, and she had on her the dress she wore last year to the *braavleis*. Greg had come back for the holidays the night before; we knew he had, because his mother said so when Mom met her at the store. But he did not come to our house. I did not like to see Moira's face, but I had to keep on looking at it—it was so sad and her eyes were sore. Mom kissed her, putting both her arms around her, but Moira gave a hitch of her shoulders like a horse with a fly bothering it.

Mom sighed, and then I saw Dad looking at her, and the look they gave each other was most peculiar; it made me feel very peculiar again. And then Moira started in on the lemon cake, and went to the butcher's, and that was when Dad said that about the *braavleis* being for the engagement. Moira looked at him, with her eyes all black and sad, and said: "Why have you got it in for me, Dad? What have *I* done?"

Dad said: "Greg's not going to marry you. Now he's got to college, and going to be a doctor, he won't be after you."

Moira was smiling, her lips small and angry.

Mom said: "Why, Dickson, Moira's got her diploma and she's educated. What's got into your head?"

Dad said: "I'm telling you, that's all."

Moira said, very grown-up and quiet: "Why are you

43

trying to spoil it for me, Dad? I haven't said anything about marrying, have I? And what have I done to *you*, anyway?"

Dad didn't like that. He went red and he laughed, but he didn't like it. And he was quiet, for a bit at least.

After lunch, when she'd finished with the cakes, she was sitting on the veranda when Jordan went past across to the store, and she called out: "Hi, Jordan, come and talk to me."

Now I know for a fact that Jordan wasn't sweet on Moira any more. He was sweet on Beth from the store, because I know for a fact he kissed her at the last station dance; I saw him. And he shouted out, "Thanks, Moy, but I'm on my way."

"Oh, please yourself then," said Moira, friendly and nice, but I knew she was cross, because she was set on it.

Anyway, he came in, and I've never seen Moira so nice to anyone, not even when she was sweet on him, and certainly never to Greg. Well, Jordan was embarrassed, because Moira was not pretty that season and all the station was saying she had gone off. She took Jordan into the kitchen to see the lemon cake and dough all folded, ready for the sausage rolls, and she said, slow and surprised, "But we haven't enough bread for the sandwiches, Mom. What are you thinking of?"

Mom said, quick and cross, because she was proud of her kitchen, "What do you mean? No one's going to eat sandwiches with all that meat you've ordered. And it'll be stale by tomorrow."

"I think we need more bread," said Moira. And she said to me in the same voice, slow and lazy, "Just run over to the Jacksons' and see if they can let us have some bread."

At this I didn't say anything, and Mom did not say anything either, and it was lucky Dad didn't hear. I looked at Mom, and she made no sign; so I went out across the railway lines to the garage. At the back of the garage was the Jacksons' house, and there was Greg Jackson reading a book about the body because he was going to be a doctor.

"Mom says," I said, "can you let us have some bread for the *braavleis?*"

He put down the book and said, "Oh, hullo, Betty."

"Hullo," I said.

"But the store will be open tomorrow," he said. "isn't the *braavleis* tomorrow?"

"It's Sunday tomorrow," I said.

"But the store's open now."

"We want some stale bread," I said. "Moy's making some stuffing for the chicken; our bread's all fresh."

"Mom's at the store," he said, "but help yourself."

So I went into the pantry and got half a stale loaf, and came out and said "Thanks," and walked past him.

He said, "Don't mention it." Then, when I was nearly gone, he said, "And how's Moy?" And I said, "Fine, thanks, but I haven't seen much of her this vacation because she's busy with Jordan." And I went away, and I could feel my back tingling; and sure enough there he was coming up behind me. And then he was beside me, and my side was tingling.

"I'll drop over and say hello," said Greg; and I felt peculiar, I can tell you, because what I was thinking was: *Well!* If *this* is *love*.

When we got near our house, Moira and Jordan were side by side on the veranda wall, and Moy was laughing; and I knew she had seen Greg coming because of the way she laughed.

45

Dad was not on the veranda, so I could see Mom had got him to stay indoors.

"I've got you the bread, Moy," I said, and with this I went into the kitchen, and there was Mom, and she was looking more peculiar than I've ever seen her. I could have bet she wanted to laugh; but she was sighing all the time. Because of the sighing I knew she had quarreled with Dad. "Well, I don't *know*," she said, and she threw the bread I'd fetched into the waste-bucket.

There sat Mom and I in the kitchen, smiling at each other off and on in a peculiar way, and Dad was rattling his paper in the bedroom where she had made him go. He was not at the station that day because the train had come at nine o'clock and there wasn't another one coming. When we looked out on the veranda in about half an hour Jordan was gone, and Greg and Moira were sitting on the veranda wall. And I can tell you she looked so pretty again—it was peculiar her getting pretty like that so suddenly.

That was about five, and Greg went back to supper at home. Moira did not eat anything; she was in our room curling her hair because she and Greg were going for a walk.

"Don't go too far; it's going to rain," Mom said, but Moira said, sweet and dainty, "Don't worry, Mom, I can look after myself."

Mom and Dad said nothing to each other all the evening.

I went to bed early for a change, so I'd be there when Moy got in, although I was thirteen that season and now my bedtime was up to ten o'clock.

Mom and Dad went to bed, although I could see Mom was worried because there was a storm blowing up; the dry season was due to end, and the lightning kept spurting all over the sky.

46

I lay awake saying to myself, Sleep sleep, go away, come again another day. But I went to sleep, and when I woke up, the room was full of the smell of rain, of the earth wet with rain, and the light was on and Moira was in the room.

"Have the rains come?" I said, and then I woke right up and saw of course they hadn't, because the air was as dry as sand, and Moira said, "Oh, shut up and go to sleep."

She did not look pretty as much as being different from how I'd seen her; her face was soft and smiling, and her eyes were different. She had blue eyes most of the time, but now they seemed quite black. And now that her hair was all curled and brushed, it looked pretty, like golden syrup. And she even looked a bit fatter. Usually when she wasn't too thin, she was rather fat, and when she was one of the gang we used to call her Pudding. That is, until she passed her J.C., and then she fought everyone, and the boys, too, so that she could be called Moy. So no one had called her Pudding for years now except Dad, to make her cross. He used to say, "You're going to make a fine figure of a woman like your mother." That always made Moy cross, I can tell you, because Mom was very fat, and she wore proper corsets these days, except just before the rains when it was so hot. I remember the first time the corsets came from the store, and she put them on. Moy had to lace her in, and Mom laughed so much Moy couldn't do the laces; and anyway she was cross because Mom laughed, and she said to me afterward, "It's disgusting, letting yourself go—I'm not going to let myself go."

So it would have been more than my life was worth to tell her she was looking a bit fatter already, or to tell her anything at all, because she sat smiling on the edge of her bed, and when I said, "What did he say,

Moy?" she just turned her head and made her eyes thin and black at me, and I saw I'd better go to sleep. But I knew something she didn't know I knew, because she had some dead jacaranda flowers in her hair; that meant she and Greg had been at the water tanks. There were only two jacaranda trees at our station, and they were at the big water tanks for the engines; and if they were at the water tanks, they must have been kissing, because it was romantic at the tanks. It was the end of October, and the jacarandas were shedding, and the tanks looked as if they were standing in pools of blue water.

Well, next morning Moy was already up when I woke, and she was singing, and even before breakfast she began ironing her muslin dress that she had made for last Christmas.

Mom said nothing; Dad kept rustling his newspaper; and I wouldn't have dared open my mouth. Besides, I wanted to find out what Greg had said. After breakfast, we sat around, because of its being Sunday; Dad didn't have to be at the station office because there weren't any trains on Sundays. And Dad kept grinning at Moira and saying: "I think it's going to rain," and she pretended she didn't know what he meant, until at last she jumped when he said it and turned herself and looked at him just the way she had the day before. That was when he got red in the face and said: "Can't you take a joke these days?" and Moira looked away from him with her eyebrows up, and Mom sighed, and then he said, very cross, "I'll leave you all to it, just tell me when you're in a better temper," and with this he took the newspaper inside to the bedroom.

Anybody could see it wasn't going to rain properly that day, because the clouds weren't thunderheads, but great big white ones, all silver and hardly any black in them.

Moy didn't eat any dinner, but went on sitting on the veranda, wearing her muslin dress, white with red spots and big puffed sleeves and a red sash around her waist.

After dinner, time went very slowly, and it was a long time before Greg came down off the Jacksons' veranda and came walking slowly along the gum-tree avenue. I was watching Moy's face, and she couldn't keep the smile off it. She got paler and paler until he got underneath our veranda, and she was looking at him so that I had gooseflesh all over.

Then he gave a jump up our steps to the veranda and said, "Hoy, Moy, how's it?" I thought she was going to fall right off the veranda wall, and her face had gone all different again.

"How are you, Gregory?" said Moira, all calm and proud.

"Oh, skidding along," he said; and I could see he felt awkward, because he hadn't looked at her once, and his skin was all red around the freckles. She didn't say anything, and she was looking at him as if she couldn't believe it was him.

"I hope the rain will keep off for the *braavleis*," said Mom, in her visiting voice; and she looked hard at me, and I had to get up and go inside with her. But I could see Greg didn't want us to go at all, and I could see Moy knew it; her eyes were blue again, a pale thin blue, and her mouth was small.

Well, Mom went into the kitchen to make the sausage rolls; and I went into our bedroom, because I could see what went on on the veranda from behind the curtains.

Greg sat on the veranda wall and whistled. He was

whistling "I Love You, Yes I Do"; and Moira was gazing at him as if he were a Christmas beetle she had just noticed. And then he began whistling "Three Little Words"; and suddenly Moira got down off the wall and stretched herself like a cat when it's going to walk off somewhere, and Greg said, "Skinny!"

At this she made her eyebrows go up, and I've never seen such a look.

And he was getting redder in the face, and he said: "You'd better not wear that dress to the *braavleis*; it's going to rain."

Moira didn't say a word for what seemed about half an hour, and then she said, in that lazy sort of voice, "Well, Greg Jackson, if you've changed your mind, it's O.K. with me."

"Changed my mind?" he said, very quickly, and he looked scared; and she looked scared, and she asked: "What did you say all those things for last night?"

"Say what?" he asked, more scared than ever; and I could see he was trying to remember what he'd said.

Moira was just looking at him, and I wouldn't have liked to be Greg Jackson just then, I can tell you. Then she walked off the veranda, letting her skirt swish slowly, and through the kitchen, and into our room, and then she sat on the bed.

"I'm not going to the *braavleis*, Mom," she said, in that sweet, slow voice like Mom uses when she's got visitors and she wishes they'd go.

Mom just sighed and slapped the dough about on the kitchen table. Dad made the springs of the bed creak and he said half aloud, "Oh, my God, preserve me!"

Mom left the pastry and glared through the door of their bedroom at Dad, and then came into our room. There was Moira sitting all lumped up on her bed as if she had a pain, and her face was like pastry dough.

Mom said nothing to Moira, but went on to the veranda. Greg was still sitting there, looking sick.

"Well, son," Mom said, in her easy voice, the voice she has when she was tired of everything, but keeping up, "well, son, I think Moy's got a bit of a headache from the heat."

As I've said, I wasn't sweet on Greg that vacation; but if I was Moy I would have been, the way he looked just then—all sad, but grown-up, like a man—when he said: "Mrs. Hughes, I don't know what I've done." Mom just smiled and sighed. "I can't marry, Mrs. Hughes. I've got five years training ahead of me."

Mom smiled and said, "Of course, son, of course."

I was lying on my bed with my stamps; and Moira was on her bed, listening, and the way *she* smiled gave me a bad shiver.

"Listen to him," she said, in a loud slow voice. "*Marry?* Why does everyone go on about marrying? They're nuts. I wouldn't marry Greg Jackson, anyway, if he were the last man on a desert island."

Outside, I could hear Mom sigh hard; then her voice, quick and low; and then the sound of Greg's feet crunching off over the cinders of the path.

Then Mom came back into our room, and Moira said, all despairing, "Mom, what made you say that about marrying?"

"He said it, my girl, I didn't."

"Marrying!" said Moira, laughing hard.

Mom said, "What did he *say* then—you talked about him saying something?"

"Oh, you all make me sick," said Moira, and she lay down on her bed, turned away from us. Mom hitched her head at me, and we went out. By then it was five in the afternoon and the cars would be leaving at six, so Mom finished the sausage rolls in the oven, and packed the food, and then she took off her apron and

51

went across to Jordan's house. Moira did not see her go, because she was still lost to the world in her pillow.

Soon Mom came back and put the food into the car. Then Jordan came over with Beth from the store and said to me, "Betty, my mom says, will you and Moy come in our car to the *braavleis*, because your car's full of food?"

"I will," I said, "but Moira's got a headache."

But at this moment Moira called out from our room, "Thanks, Jordan, I'd like to come."

So Mom called to Pop, and they went off in our car together, and I could see she was talking to him all the time, and he was just pulling the gears about and looking resigned to life.

Moira and I went with Jordan and Beth in their car. I could see Jordan was cross because he wanted to be with Beth; and Beth kept smiling at Moira with her eyebrows up, to tell her she knew what was going on; and Moira smiled back and talked a lot in her visiting voice.

The *braavleis* was at a high place at the end of a *vlei*, where it rose into a small hill full of big boulders. The grass had been cut that morning by natives of the farmer who always let us use his farm for the *braavleis*. It was pretty, with the hill behind and the moon coming up over it, and then the cleared space, and the *vlei* sweeping down to the river, and the trees on either side. The moon was just over the trees when we got there, so the trees looked black and big, and the boulders were big and looked as if they might topple over, and the grass was silvery; but the great bonfire was roaring up twenty feet, and in the space around the fire it was all hot and red. The trench of embers where the spits were for the meat was on one side, and as soon as she arrived Moira went there and helped with the cooking.

Greg was not there, and I thought he wouldn't come; but much later, when we were all eating the meat, and laughing because it burned our fingers it was so hot, I saw him on the other side of the fire talking to Mom. Moira saw him talking, and she didn't like it, but she pretended not to see.

By then we were seated in a half-circle on the side of the fire the wind was blowing, so that the red flames were sweeping off away from us. There were about fifty people from the station and some farmers from round about. Moira sat by me, quiet, eating grilled ribs and sausage rolls; and for once she was pleased I was there, so that she wouldn't seem to be by herself. She had changed her dress again, and it was the dress she had worn last year for the *braavleis;* it was blue with pleats, and it was the dress she had for best the last year at school, so it wasn't very modern any more. Across the fire, I could see Greg. He did not look at Moira, and she did not look at him. Except that this year Jordan did not want to sit by Moira but by Beth, I kept feeling peculiar, as if this year were really last year, and in a minute Greg would walk across past the fire, and say: "Moira Hughes? I wouldn't have known you."

But he stayed where he was. He was sitting on his legs, with his hands on his knees. I could see his legs and knees and his big hands all red from the fire and the yellow hair glinting in the firelight. His face was red, too, and wet with the heat.

Then everyone began singing. We were singing "Sarie Marais," and "Sugar Bush," and "Henrietta's Wedding" and "We don't want to go home." Moira and Greg were both singing as hard as they could.

53

It was getting late. The natives were damping down the cooking trench with earth and looking for scraps of meat and bits of sausage roll, and the big fire was sinking down. It would be time in a minute for the big dance in a circle around the fire.

Moira was just sitting. Her legs were tucked under her sideways, and they had got scratched from the grass—I could see the white dry scratches across the sunburn—and I can tell you it was a good thing she hadn't worn her best muslin because there wouldn't have been much left of it. Her hair, that she had curled yesterday, was tied back in a ribbon, so that her face looked small and thin.

I said, "Here, Moy, don't look like your own funeral"; and she said, "I will if I like." Then she gave me a bit of a grin, and she said: "Let me give you a word of warning for when you're grown-up: Don't believe a word men say, I'm telling you."

But I could see she was feeling better just then.

At that very moment the red light of the fire on the grass just in front of us went out and someone sat down. I hoped it was Greg, and it was. They were looking at each other again; but my skin didn't tingle at all, so I looked at his face and at her face, and they were both quiet and sensible.

Then Moira reached out for a piece of grass, pulled it clean and neat out of the socket, and began nibbling at the soft piece at the end; and it was just the way Mom reached out for her knitting when she was against Dad. But of course Greg did not know the resemblance.

"Moy," he said, "I want to talk to you."

"My name is Moira," said Moira, looking him in the eyes.

"Oh heck, Moira," he said, sounding exasperated, just like Dad.

54

I wriggled back away from the two of them into the crowd that was still singing softly "Sarie Marais" and looking at the way the fire was glowing low and soft, ebbing red and then dark as the wind came up from the river. The moon was half-covered with the big, soft, silvery clouds, and the red light was strong on our faces.

I could just hear what they said. I wasn't going to move too far off, I can tell you.

"I don't know what I've said," said Greg.

"It doesn't matter in the slightest," said Moira.

"Moira, for crying out aloud!"

"Why did you say that about marrying?" said Moira, and her voice was shaky. She was going to cry if she didn't watch out.

"I thought you thought I meant. . . ."

"You think too much," said Moira, tossing her head carefully so that her long tail of hair should come forward and lie on her shoulder. She put up her hand and stroked the curls smooth.

"Moira, I've got another five years at university. I couldn't ask you to be engaged for five years."

"I never said you should," said Moira, calm and lofty, examining the scratches on her legs.

The way she was sitting, curled up sideways, with her hair lying forward like syrup on her shoulder—it was pretty, it was as pretty as I've ever seen, and I could see his face, sad and almost sick.

"You're so pretty, Moy," he said, jerking it out.

Moira seemed not to be able to move. Then she turned her head slowly and looked at him. I could see the beginning of something terrible on her face. The shiver had begun under my hair at the back of my neck and was slowly moving down to the small of my back.

"You're so beautiful," he said, sounding angry, leaning forward with his face almost against hers.

And now she looked the way she had last night, when I was not awake and asked was it raining outside.

"When you look like that," he said, quite desperate about everything, "it makes me feel. . . ."

People were getting up now all around us. The fire had burned right down; it was a low wave of red heat coming out at us. The redness was on our shoulders and legs, but our faces were having a chance to cool off. The moon had come out again, full and bright, and the cloud had rolled on. It was funny the way the light was red to their shoulders, and the white of the moon on their faces, and their eyes glistening. I didn't like it; I was shivering; it was the most peculiar moment of all my life.

"Well," said Moira, and she sounded just too tired even to try to understand, "that's what you said last night, wasn't it?"

"Don't you see," he said, trying to explain, his tongue all mixed up, "I can't help—I love you, I don't know. . . ."

Now she smiled, and I knew the smile at once, it was the way Mom smiled at Dad when if he had any sense he'd shut up. It was sweet and loving, but it was sad and as if she were saying, Lord, you're a fool, Dickson Hughes!

Moira went on smiling like that at Greg, and he was sick and angry and not understanding a thing.

"I love you," he said again.

"Well, I love you—and what of it?" said Moira.

"But it will be five years."

"And what has that got to do with anything?" At this she began to laugh.

"But Moy. . . ."

"My name is Moira," she said, once and for all.

For a moment they were both white and angry, their eyes glimmering in the light of the big white moon over them.

There was a shout and a hustle; and suddenly all the people were in the big circle around the big low heap of fire; and they were whirling around and around, yelling and screaming. Greg and Moira stayed where they were, just outside the range of the feet, and they didn't hear a thing.

"You're so pretty," he was saying, in that rough, cross, helpless voice. "I love you, Moira. There couldn't ever be anyone but you."

She was smiling, and he went on saying: "I love you. I see your face all the time; I see your hair and your face and your eyes."

And I wished he'd go on, the poor sap, just saying it, for every minute it was more like last night when I woke up and I thought it had rained—the feeling of the dry earth with the rain just on it, that was how she was, and she looked as if she would sit there and listen and listen forever to the words he said, and she didn't want to hear him saying, "Why don't you say something, Moy? You don't say anything; you do understand, don't you?—It's not fair, it isn't right to bind you when we're so young." But he started saying it in just a minute, and then she smiled her visiting smile, and she said: "Gregory Jackson, you're a fool."

Then she got up off the grass and went across to Mom to help load the car, and she never once looked at Greg again, not for the rest of the holidays.

3

The Woman

The two elderly gentlemen emerged onto the hotel terrace at the same moment. They stopped, and checked movements that suggested they wished to retreat. Their first involuntary glances had been startled, even troubled. Now they allowed their eyes to exchange a long, formal glare of hate, before turning deliberately away from each other.

They surveyed the terrace. A problem! Only one of the tables still remained in sunlight. They stiffly marched toward it, pulled out chairs, seated themselves. At once they opened newspapers and lifted them up like screens.

A pretty waitress came sauntering across to take the orders. The two newspapers remained stationary. Around the edge of one Herr Scholtz ordered warmed wine; from the shelter of the other Captain Forster from England demanded tea—with milk.

When she returned with these fluids, neatly disposed on similar metal trays, both walls of print slightly lowered themselves. Captain Forster, with an aggressive flicker of uneasy blue eyes toward his opponent, suggested that it was a fine evening. Herr Scholtz remarked with warm freemasonry that it was a shame such a pretty girl should not be free to enjoy herself on such an evening. Herr Scholtz appeared to consider that he had triumphed, for his look toward the Englishman was boastful. To both remarks, however, Rosa responded with an amiable but equally perfunctory smile. She strolled away to the balustrade where she leaned indolently, her back to them.

Stirring sugar into tea, sipping wine, was difficult with those stiff papers in the way. First Herr Scholtz, then the Captain, folded his and placed it on the table. Avoiding each other's eyes, they looked away toward the mountains, which, however, were partly blocked by Rosa.

She wore a white blouse, low on the shoulders; a black skirt, with a tiny white apron; smart red shoes. It was at her shoulders that the gentlemen gazed. They coughed, tapped on the table with their fingers, narrowed their eyes in sentimental appreciation at the mountains, looked at Rosa again. From time to time their eyes almost met but quickly slid away. Since they could not fight, civilization demanded they should speak. Yes, conversation appeared imminent.

A week earlier they had arrived on the same morning and were given rooms at either end of a long corridor. The season was nearly over, the hotel half empty. Rosa therefore had plenty of time to devote to Herr Scholtz, who demanded it: he wanted bigger towels, different pillows, a glass of water. But soon the bell pealed from the other side of the corridor, and she excused herself and hastened over to Captain Forster who was also dissatisfied with the existing arrangements for his comfort. Before she had finished with him, Herr Scholtz's bell rang again. Between the two of them Rosa was kept busy until the midday meal, and not once did she suggest by her manner that she had any other desire in this world than to readjust Captain Forster's reading light or bring Herr Scholtz cigarettes and newspapers.

That afternoon Captain Forster happened to open

his door; and he found he had a clear view into the room opposite, where Rosa stood at the window smiling, in what seemed to him charming surrender, at Herr Scholtz, who was reaching out a hand toward her elbow. The hand dropped. Herr Scholtz scowled, walked across, indignantly closed his door as if it were the Captain's fault it had been left open. . . . Almost at once the Captain's painful jealousy was eased, for Rosa emerged from that door, smiling with perfect indifference, and wished him good day.

That night, very late, quick footsteps sounded on the floor of the corridor. The two doors gently opened at the same moment; and Rosa, midway between them, smiled placidly at first Herr Scholtz, then the Captain, who gave each other contemptuous looks after she had passed. They both slammed their doors.

Next day Herr Scholtz asked her if she would care to come with him up the funicular on her afternoon off, but unfortunately she was engaged. The day after Captain Forster made the same suggestion.

Finally, there was a repetition of that earlier incident. Rosa was passing along the corridor late at night on her way to her own bed, when those two doors cautiously opened and the two urgent faces appeared. This time she stopped, smiled politely, wished them a very good night. Then she yawned. It was a slight gesture, but perfectly timed. Both gentlemen solaced themselves with the thought that it must have been earned by his rival; for Herr Scholtz considered the Captain ridiculously gauche, while the Captain thought Herr Scholtz's attitude toward Rosa disgustingly self-assured and complacent. They were therefore able to retire to their beds with philosophy.

Since then Herr Scholtz had been observed in conversation with a well-preserved widow of fifty who unfortunately was obliged to retire to her own room every evening at nine o'clock for reasons of health and was, therefore, unable to go dancing with him, as he longed to do. Captain Forster took his tea every afternoon in a café where there was a charming waitress who might have been Rosa's sister.

The two gentlemen looked through each other in the dining room, and each crossed the street if he saw the other approaching. There was a look about them which suggested that they might be thinking Switzerland—at any rate, so late in the season—was not all that it had been.

Gallant, however, they both continued to be; and they might continually be observed observing the social scene of flirtations and failures and successes with the calm authority of those well-qualified by long familiarity with it to assess and make judgments. Men of weight, they were; men of substance; men who expected deference.

And yet . . . here they were seated on opposite sides of that table in the last sunlight, the mountains rising about them, all mottled white and brown and green with melting spring, the warm sun folding delicious but uncertain arms around them—and surely they were entitled to feel aggrieved? Captain Forster —a lean, tall, military man, carefully suntanned, spruced, brushed—was handsome still, no doubt of it. And Herr Scholtz—large, rotund, genial, with infinite resources of experience—was certainly worth more than the teatime confidences of a widow of fifty?

Unjust to be sixty on such a spring evening; particularly hard with Rosa not ten paces away, shrugging her shoulders in a low-cut embroidered blouse.

And almost as if she were taking a pleasure in the cruelty, she suddenly stopped humming and leaned forward over the balustrade. With what animation did she wave and call down the street, while a very handsome young man below waved and called back. Rosa watched him stride away, and then she sighed and turned, smiling dreamily.

There sat Herr Scholtz and Captain Forster gazing at her with hungry resentful appreciation.

Rosa narrowed her blue eyes with anger and her mouth went thin and cold, in disastrous contrast with her tenderness of a moment before. She shot bitter looks from one gentleman to the other, and then she yawned again. This time it was a large, contemptuous, prolonged yawn; and she tapped the back of her hand against her mouth for emphasis and let out her breath in a long descending note, which, however, was cut off short as if to say that she really had no time to waste even on this small demonstration. She then swung past them in a crackle of starched print, her heels tapping. She went inside.

The terrace was empty. Gay painted tables, striped chairs, flowery sun umbrellas—all were in cold shadow, save for the small corner where the gentlemen sat. At the same moment, from the same impulse, they rose and pushed the table forward into the last well of golden sunlight. And now they looked at each other straight and frankly laughed.

"Will you have a drink?" inquired Herr Scholtz in English, and his jolly smile was tightened by a consciously regretful stoicism. After a moment's uncertainty, during which Captain Forster appeared to be thinking that the stoicism was too early an admission of defeat, he said, "Yes—Yes. Thanks, I will."

Herr Scholtz raised his voice sharply, and Rosa appeared from indoors, ready to be partly defensive. But now Herr Scholtz was no longer a suppliant. Master to servant, a man who habitually employed labor, he ordered wine without looking at her once. And Captain Forster was the picture of a silky gentleman.

When she reappeared with the wine they were so deep in good fellowship they might have been saying aloud how foolish it was to allow the sound companionship of men to be spoiled, even for a week, on account of the silly charm of women. They were roaring with laughter at some joke. Or rather, Herr Scholtz was roaring, a good stomach laugh from depths of lusty enjoyment. Captain Forster's laugh was slightly nervous, emitted from the back of his throat, and suggested that Herr Scholtz's warm Bavarian geniality was all very well, but that there were always reservations in any relationship.

It soon transpired that during the war—the First War, be it understood—they had been enemies on the same sector of the front at the same time. Herr Scholtz had been wounded in his arm. He bared it now, holding it forward under the Captain's nose to show the long white scar. Who knew but that it was the Captain who had dealt that blow—indirectly, of course—thirty-five years before? Nor was this all. During the Second War Captain Forster had very nearly been sent to North Africa, where he would certainly have had the pleasure of fighting Herr, then Oberst-leutnant, Scholtz. As it happened, the fortunes of war had sent him to India instead. While these happy coincidences were being established, it was with the greatest amity on both sides; and if the Captain's laugh tended to follow Herr Scholtz's just a moment late, it could easily be accounted for by those unavoidable differences of temperament. Before half an hour was out, Rosa was despatched for a second flask of the deep crimson wine.

When she returned with it, she placed the glasses so,

the flasks so, and was about to turn away when she glanced at the Captain and was arrested. The look on his face certainly invited comment. Herr Scholtz was just remarking, with that familiar smiling geniality, how much he regretted that the "accidents of history" —a phrase that caused the Captain's face to tighten very slightly—had made it necessary for them to be enemies in the past. In the future, he hoped, they would fight side by side, comrades in arms against the only possible foe for either. . . . But now Herr Scholtz stopped, glanced swiftly at the Captain, and after the briefest possible pause, and without a change of tone, went on to say that as for himself he was a man of peace, a man of creation: he caused innumerable tubes of toothpaste to reach the bathrooms of his country, and he demanded nothing more of life than to be allowed to continue to do so. Besides, had he not dropped his war title, the Oberst-leutnant, in proof of his fundamentally civilian character?

Here, as Rosa still remained before them, contemplating them with a look that can only be described as ambiguous, Herr Scholtz blandly inquired what she wanted. But Rosa wanted nothing. Having inquired if that was all she could do for the gentlemen, she passed to the end of the terrace and leaned against the balustrade there, looking down into the street where the handsome young man might pass.

Now there was a pause. The eyes of both men were drawn painfully toward her. Equally painful was the effort to withdraw them. Then, as if reminded that any personal differences were far more dangerous than the national ones, they plunged determinedly into gallant reminiscences. How pleasant, said that hearty masculine laughter—how pleasant to sit here in snug happy little Switzerland, comfortable in easy friendship, and after such fighting, such obviously meaningless hostilities! Citizens of the world they were, no less, human beings enjoying civilized friendship on equal terms. And each time Herr Scholtz or the Captain succumbed to that fatal attraction and glanced toward the end of the terrace, he as quickly withdrew his eyes and, as it were, set his teeth to offer another gauge of friendship across the table.

But fate did not intend this harmony to continue.

Cruelly, the knife was turned again. The young man appeared at the bottom of the street and, smiling, waved toward Rosa. Rosa leaned forward, arms on the balustrade, the picture of bashful coquetry, rocking one heel up and down behind her and shaking her hair forward to conceal the frankness of her response.

There she stood, even after he had gone, humming lightly to herself, looking after him. The crisp white napkin over her arm shone in the sunlight; her bright white apron shone; her mass of rough fair curls glowed. She stood there in the last sunlight and looked away into her own thoughts, singing softly as if she were quite alone.

Certainly she had completely forgotten the existence of Herr Scholtz and Captain Forster.

The Captain and the ex-Oberst-leutnant had apparently come to the end of their sharable memories. One cleared his throat; the other, Herr Scholtz, tapped his signet ring irritatingly on the table.

The Captain shivered. "It's getting cold," he said, for now they were in the blue evening shadow. He made a movement, as if ready to rise.

"Yes," said Herr Scholtz. But he did not move. For a while he tapped his ring on the table, and the Captain set his teeth against the noise. Herr Scholtz was smiling. It was a smile that announced a new trend in the drama. Obviously. And obviously the Captain disapproved of it in advance. A blatant fellow, he was thinking, altogether too noisy and vulgar. He glanced impatiently toward the inside room, which would be warm and quiet.

Herr Scholtz remarked, "I always enjoy coming to this place. I always come here."

"Indeed?" asked the Captain, taking his cue in spite of himself. He wondered why Herr Scholtz was suddenly speaking German. Herr Scholtz spoke excellent English, learned while he was interned in England during the latter part of the Second World War. Captain Forster had already complimented him on it. His German was not nearly so fluent, no.

But Herr Scholtz, for reasons of his own, was speaking his own language, and rather too loudly, one might have thought. Captain Forster looked at him, wondering, and was attentive.

"It is particularly pleasant for me to come to this resort," remarked Herr Scholtz in that loud voice, as if to an inner listener who was rather deaf, "because of the happy memories I have of it."

"Really?" inquired Captain Forster, listening with nervous attention. Herr Scholtz, however, was speaking very slowly, as if out of consideration for him.

"Yes," said Herr Scholtz. "Of course during the war it was out of bounds for both of us, but now. . . ."

The Captain suddenly interrupted: "Actually I'm very fond of it myself. I come here every year it is possible."

Herr Scholtz inclined his head, admitting that Captain Forster's equal right to it was incontestable, and continued, "I associate with it the most charming of my memories—perhaps you would care to. . . ."

"But certainly," agreed Captain Forster hastily. He glanced involuntarily toward Rosa—Herr Scholtz was speaking with his eyes on Rosa's back. Rosa was no longer humming. Captain Forster took in the situation and immediately colored. He glanced protestingly toward Herr Scholtz. But it was too late.

"I was eighteen," said Herr Scholtz very loudly. "Eighteen." He paused, and for a moment it was possible to resurrect, in the light of his rueful reminiscent smile, the delightful, ingenuous bouncing youth he had certainly been at eighteen. "My parents allowed me, for the first time, to go alone for a vacation. It was against my mother's wishes; but my father on the other hand. . . ."

Here Captain Forster necessarily smiled, in acknowledgment of that international phenomenon, the sweet jealousy of mothers.

"And here I was, for a ten days' vacation, all by myself—imagine it!"

Captain Forster obligingly imagined it, but almost at once interrupted: "Odd, but I had the same experience. Only I was twenty-five."

Herr Scholtz exclaimed: "Twenty-five!" He cut himself short, covered his surprise, and shrugged as if to say: Well, one must make allowances. He at once continued to Rosa's listening back. "I was in this very hotel. Winter. A winter vacation. There was a woman. . . ." He paused, smiling, "How can I describe her?"

But the Captain, it seemed, was not prepared to assist. He was frowning uncomfortably toward Rosa. His expression said quite clearly: Really, *must* you?

Herr Scholtz appeared not to notice it. "I was, even in those days, not backward—you understand?" The Captain made a movement of his shoulders which suggested that to be forward at eighteen was not a matter for congratulation, whereas at twenty-five. . . .

"She was beautiful—beautiful," continued Herr

Scholtz with enthusiasm. "And she was obviously rich, a woman of the world; and her clothes. . . ."

"Quite," said the Captain.

"She was alone. She told me she was here for her health. Her husband unfortunately could not get away, for reasons of business. And I, too, was alone."

"Quite," said the Captain.

"Even at that age I was not too surprised at the turn of events. A woman of thirty . . . a husband so much older than herself . . . and she was beautiful . . . and intelligent. . . . Ah, but she was magnificent!" He almost shouted this, and drained his glass reminiscently toward Rosa's back. "Ah . . ." he breathed gustily. "And now I must tell you. All that was good enough, but now there is even better. Listen. A week passed. And what a week! I loved her as I never loved anyone. . . ."

"Quite," said the Captain, fidgeting.

But Herr Scholtz swept on. "And then one morning I wake, and I am alone." Herr Scholtz shrugged and groaned.

The Captain observed that Herr Scholtz was being carried away by the spirit of his own enjoyment. This tale was by now only half for the benefit of Rosa. That rich dramatic groan—Herr Scholtz might as well be in the theater, thought the Captain uncomfortably.

"But there was a letter, and when I read it. . . ."

"A letter?" interrupted the Captain suddenly.

"Yes, a letter. She thanked me so that the tears came into my eyes. I wept."

One could have sworn that the sentimental German eyes swam with tears, and Captain Forster looked away. With eyes averted he asked nervously, "What was in the letter?"

"She said how she hated her husband. She had married him against her will—to please her parents. In those days, this thing happened. And she had sworn a vow to herself never to have his child. But she wanted a child. . . ."

"*What?*" exclaimed the Captain. He was leaning forward over the table now, intent on every syllable.

This emotion seemed unwelcome to Herr Scholtz, who said blandly, "Yes, that was how it was. That was my good fortune, my friend."

"*When* was that?" inquired the Captain hungrily.

"I beg your pardon?"

"When was it? What year?"

"What year? Does it matter? She told me she had arranged this little holiday on grounds of her bad health, so that she might come by herself to find the man she wanted as the father of her child. She had chosen me. I was her choice. And now she thanked me and was returning to her husband." Herr Scholtz stopped, in triumph, and looked at Rosa. Rosa did not move. She could not possibly have failed to hear every word. Then he looked at the Captain. But the Captain's face was scarlet, and very agitated.

"What was her name?" barked the Captain.

"Her name?" Herr Scholtz paused. "Well, she would clearly have used a false name?" he inquired. As the Captain did not respond, he said firmly: "That is surely obvious, my friend. And I did not know her address." Herr Scholtz took a slow sip of his wine, then another. He regarded the Captain for a moment thoughtfully, as if wondering whether he could be trusted to behave according to the rules, and then continued: "I ran to the hotel manager—no, there was no information. The lady had left unexpectedly, early that morning. No address. I was frantic. You can imagine. I wanted to rush after her, find her, kill her husband, marry her!" Herr Scholtz laughed in amused, regretful indulgence at the follies of youth.

"You *must* remember the year," urged the Captain.

"But my friend . . ." began Herr Scholtz after a pause, very annoyed. "What can it matter, after all?"

Captain Forster glanced stiffly at Rosa and spoke in English, "As it happened, the same thing happened to me."

"Here?" inquired Herr Scholtz politely.

"Here."

"In this valley?"

"In this hotel."

"Well," shrugged Herr Scholtz, raising his voice even more, "well, women—women you know. At eighteen, of course—and perhaps even at twenty-five —" Here he nodded indulgently toward his opponent —"Even at twenty-five perhaps one takes such things as miracles that happen only to oneself. But at our age . . . ?"

He paused, as if hoping against hope that the Captain might recover his composure.

But the Captain was speechless.

"I tell you, my friend," continued Herr Scholtz, good-humoredly relishing the tale, "I tell you, I was crazy; I thought I would go mad. I wanted to shoot myself; I rushed around the streets of every city I happened to be in, looking into every face. I looked at photographs in the papers—actresses, society women; I used to follow a woman I had glimpsed in the street, thinking that perhaps this was she at last. But no," said Herr Scholtz dramatically, bringing down his hand on the table, so that his ring clicked again, "no, never, never was I successful!"

"What did she look like?" asked the Captain agitatedly in English, his anxious eyes searching the by now very irritated eyes of Herr Scholtz.

71

Herr Scholtz moved his chair back slightly, looked toward Rosa, and said loudly in German: "Well, she was beautiful, as I have told you." He paused, for thought. "And she was an aristocrat."

"Yes, yes," said the Captain impatiently.

"She was tall, very slim, with a beautiful body—beautiful! She had that black hair, you know, black, black! And black eyes, and beautiful teeth." He added loudly and spitefully toward Rosa: "She was not the country bumpkin type, not at all. One has some taste."

With extreme discomfort the Captain glanced toward the plump village Rosa. He said, pointedly using English even at this late stage, "Mine was fair. Tall and fair. A lovely girl. Lovely!" he insisted with a glare. "Might have been an English girl."

"Which was entirely to her credit," suggested Herr Scholtz, with a smile.

"That was in 1913," said the Captain insistently, and then: "You say she had *black* hair?"

"Certainly, black hair. On that occasion—but that was not the last time it happened to me." He laughed. "I had three children by my wife, a fine woman—she is now dead, unfortunately." Again, there was no doubt tears filled his eyes. At the sight, the Captain's indignation soared. But Herr Scholtz had recovered and was speaking: "But I ask myself, how many children in addition to the three? Sometimes I look at a young man in the streets who has a certain resemblance, and I ask myself: Perhaps he is my son? Yes, yes, my friend, this is a question that every man must ask himself, sometimes, is it not?" He put back his head and laughed wholeheartedly, though with an undertone of rich regret.

The Captain did not speak for a moment. Then he said in English, "It's all very well, but it did happen to

72

me—it *did*." He sounded like a defiant schoolboy, and Herr Scholtz shrugged.

"It happened to me, here. In this hotel."

Herr Scholtz controlled his irritation, glanced at Rosa, and, for the first time since the beginning of this regrettable incident, he lowered his voice to a reasonable tone and spoke English. "Well," he said, in frank irony, smiling gently, with a quiet shrug, "well, perhaps if we are honest we must say that this is a thing that has happened to every man? Or rather, if it did not exist, it was necessary to invent it?"

And now—said his look toward the Captain, and now, for heaven's sake!—for the sake of decency, masculine solidarity, for the sake of our dignity in the eyes of that girl over there, who has so wounded us both—pull yourself together, my friend, and consider what you are saying!

But the Captain was oblivious in memories. "No," he insisted. "No. Speak for yourself. It *did* happen. Here." He paused, and then brought out, with difficulty, "I never married."

Herr Scholtz shrugged, at last, and was silent. Then he called out, "Fräulein, Fräulein—may I pay?" It was time to put an end to it.

Rosa did not immediately turn around. She patted her hair at the back. She straightened her apron. She took her napkin from one forearm and arranged it prettily on the other. Then she turned and came, smiling, toward them. It could at once be seen that she intended her smile to be noticed.

"You wish to pay?" she asked Herr Scholtz. She spoke calmly and deliberately in English, and the Captain started and looked extremely uncomfortable. But Herr Scholtz immediately adjusted himself and said in English, "Yes, I am paying."

She took the note he held out and counted out the

change from the small satchel under her apron. Having laid the last necessary coin on the table, she stood squarely in front of them, smiling down equally at both, her hands folded in front of her. At last, when they had had the full benefit of her amused, maternal smile, she suggested in English: "Perhaps the lady changed the color of her hair to suit what you both like best?" Then she laughed. She put back her head and laughed a full, wholehearted laugh.

Herr Scholtz, accepting the defeat with equanimity, smiled a rueful, appreciative smile.

The Captain sat stiffly in his chair, regarding them both with hot hostility, clinging tight to his own, authentic, memories.

But Rosa laughed at him, until with a final swish of her dress she clicked past them both and away off the terrace.

4

Through the Tunnel

Going to the shore on the first morning of the vacation, the young English boy stopped at a turning of the path and looked down at a wild and rocky bay, and then over to the crowded beach he knew so well from other years. His mother walked on in front of him, carrying a bright striped bag in one hand. Her other arm, swinging loose, was very white in the sun. The boy watched that white, naked arm, and turned his eyes, which had a frown behind them, toward the bay and back again to his mother. When she felt he was not with her, she swung around. "Oh, there you are, Jerry!" she said. She looked impatient, then smiled. "Why, darling, would you rather not come with me? Would you rather—" She frowned, conscientiously worrying over what amusements he might secretly be longing for, which she had been too busy or too careless to imagine. He was very familiar with that anxious, apologetic smile. Contrition sent him running after her. And yet, as he ran, he looked back over his shoulder at the wild bay; and all morning, as he played on the safe beach, he was thinking of it.

Next morning, when it was time for the routine of swimming and sunbathing, his mother said, "Are you tired of the usual beach, Jerry? Would you like to go somewhere else?"

"Oh, no!" he said quickly, smiling at her out of that unfailing impulse of contrition—a sort of chivalry. Yet, walking down the path with her, he blurted out, "I'd like to go and have a look at those rocks down there."

She gave the idea her attention. It was a wild-looking place, and there was no one there; but she said, "Of course, Jerry. When you've had enough, come to the big beach. Or just go straight back to the villa, if you like." She walked away, that bare arm, now slightly reddened from yesterday's sun, swinging. And he almost ran after her again, feeling it unbearable that she should go by herself, but he did not.

She was thinking, Of course he's old enough to be safe without me. Have I been keeping him too close? He mustn't feel he ought to be with me. I must be careful.

He was an only child, eleven years old. She was a widow. She was determined to be neither possessive nor lacking in devotion. She went worrying off to her beach.

As for Jerry, once he saw that his mother had gained her beach, he began the steep descent to the bay. From where he was, high up among red-brown rocks, it was a scoop of moving bluish green fringed with white. As he went lower, he saw that it spread among small promontories and inlets of rough, sharp rock, and the crisping, lapping surface showed stains of purple and darker blue. Finally, as he ran sliding and scraping down the last few yards, he saw an edge of white surf and the shallow, luminous movement of water over white sand, and, beyond that, a solid, heavy blue.

He ran straight into the water and began swimming. He was a good swimmer. He went out fast over the gleaming sand, over a middle region where rocks lay like discolored monsters under the surface, and then he was in the real sea—a warm sea where irregular cold currents from the deep water shocked his limbs.

When he was so far out that he could look back not only on the little bay but past the promontory that was between it and the big beach, he floated on the buoyant surface and looked for his mother. There she was, a speck of yellow under an umbrella that looked like a slice of orange peel. He swam back to shore, relieved at being sure she was there, but all at once very lonely.

On the edge of a small cape that marked the side of the bay away from the promontory was a loose scatter of rocks. Above them, some boys were stripping off their clothes. They came running, naked, down to the rocks. The English boy swam toward them, but kept his distance at a stone's throw. They were of that coast; all of them were burned smooth dark brown and speaking a language he did not understand. To be with them, of them, was a craving that filled his whole body. He swam a little closer; they turned and watched him with narrowed, alert dark eyes. Then one smiled and waved. It was enough. In a minute, he had swum in and was on the rocks beside them, smiling with a desperate, nervous supplication. They shouted cheerful greetings at him; and then, as he preserved his nervous, uncomprehending smile, they understood that he was a foreigner strayed from his own beach, and they proceeded to forget him. But he was happy. He was with them.

They began diving again and again from a high point into a well of blue sea between rough, pointed rocks. After they had dived and come up, they swam around, hauled themselves up, and waited their turn to dive again. They were big boys—men, to Jerry. He dived, and they watched him; and when he swam around to take his place, they made way for him. He felt he was accepted and he dived again, carefully, proud of himself.

Soon the biggest of the boys poised himself, shot down into the water, and did not come up. The others stood about, watching. Jerry, after waiting for the sleek brown head to appear, let out a yell of warning; they looked at him idly and turned their eyes back toward the water. After a long time, the boy came up on the other side of a big dark rock, letting the air out of his lungs in a sputtering gasp and a shout of triumph. Immediately the rest of them dived in. One moment, the morning seemed full of chattering boys; the next, the air and the surface of the water were empty. But through the heavy blue, dark shapes could be seen moving and groping.

Jerry dived, shot past the school of underwater swimmers, saw a black wall of rock looming at him, touched it, and bobbed up at once to the surface, where the wall was a low barrier he could see across. There was no one visible; under him, in the water, the dim shapes of the swimmers had disappeared. Then one, and then another of the boys came up on the far side of the barrier of rock, and he understood that they had swum through some gap or hole in it. He plunged down again. He could see nothing through the stinging salt water but the blank rock. When he came up the boys were all on the diving rock, preparing to attempt the feat again. And now, in a panic of failure, he yelled up, in English, "Look at me! Look!" and he began splashing and kicking in the water like a foolish dog.

They looked down gravely, frowning. He knew the frown. At moments of failure, when he clowned to claim his mother's attention, it was with just this grave, embarrassed inspection that she rewarded him. Through his hot shame, feeling the pleading grin on his face like a scar that he could never remove, he looked up at the group of big brown boys on the rock and shouted, *"Bonjour! MERCI! Au revoir! Monsieur, monsieur!"* while he hooked his fingers round his ears and waggled them.

Water surged into his mouth; he choked, sank, came up. The rock, lately weighted with boys, seemed to rear up out of the water as their weight was removed. They were flying down past him, now, into the water; the air was full of falling bodies. Then the rock was empty in the hot sunlight. He counted one, two, three. . . .

At fifty, he was terrified. They must all be drowning beneath him, in the watery caves of the rock! At a hundred, he stared around him at the empty hillside, wondering if he should yell for help. He counted faster, faster, to hurry them up, to bring them to the surface quickly, to drown them quickly—anything rather than the terror of counting on and on into the blue emptiness of the morning. And then, at a hundred and sixty, the water beyond the rock was full of boys blowing like brown whales. They swam back to the shore without a look at him.

He climbed back to the diving rock and sat down, feeling the hot roughness of it under his thighs. The boys were gathering up their bits of clothing and running off along the shore to another promontory. They were leaving to get away from him. He cried openly, fists in his eyes. There was no one to see him, and he cried himself out.

It seemed to him that a long time had passed, and he swam out to where he could see his mother. Yes, she was still there, a yellow spot under an orange umbrella. He swam back to the big rock, climbed up, and dived into the blue pool among the fanged and angry boulders. Down he went, until he touched the wall of rock again. But the salt was so painful in his eyes that he could not see.

He came to the surface, swam to shore and went back to the villa to wait for his mother. Soon she walked slowly up the path, swinging her striped bag, the flushed, naked arm dangling beside her. "I want some swimming goggles," he panted, defiant and beseeching.

She gave him a patient, inquisitive look as she said casually, "Well, of course, darling."

But now, now, now! He must have them this minute, and no other time. He nagged and pestered until she went with him to a shop. As soon as she had bought the goggles, he grabbed them from her hand as if she were going to claim them for herself, and was off, running down the steep path to the bay.

Jerry swam out to the big barrier rock, adjusted the goggles, and dived. The impact of the water broke the rubber-enclosed vacuum, and the goggles came loose. He understood that he must swim down to the base of the rock from the surface of the water. He fixed the goggles tight and firm, filled his lungs, and floated, face down, on the water. Now, he could see. It was as if he had eyes of a different kind—fish eyes that showed everything clear and delicate and wavering in the bright water.

Under him, six or seven feet down, was a floor of perfectly clean, shining white sand, rippled firm and hard by the tides. Two grayish shapes steered there, like long, rounded pieces of wood or slate. They were fish. He saw them nose toward each other, poise motionless, make a dart forward, swerve off, and come around again. It was like a water dance. A few inches above them the water sparkled as if sequins were dropping through it. Fish again—myriads of minute fish, the length of his fingernail, were drifting through the water, and in a moment he could feel the innumerable tiny touches of them against his limbs. It was like swimming in flaked silver. The great rock the big boys had swum through rose sheer out of the white sand—black, tufted lightly with greenish weed. He could see no gap in it. He swam down to its base.

Again and again he rose, took a big chestful of air, and went down. Again and again he groped over the surface of the rock, feeling it, almost hugging it in the desperate need to find the entrance. And then, once, while he was clinging to the black wall, his knees came up and he shot his feet out forward and they met no obstacle. He had found the hole.

He gained the surface, clambered about the stones that littered the barrier rock until he found a big one, and, with this in his arms, let himself down over the side of the rock. He dropped, with the weight, straight to the sandy floor. Clinging tight to the anchor of stone, he lay on his side and looked in under the dark shelf at the place where his feet had gone. He could see the hole. It was an irregular, dark gap; but he could not see deep into it. He let go of his anchor, clung with his hands to the edges of the hole, and tried to push himself in.

He got his head in, found his shoulders jammed, moved them in sidewise, and was inside as far as his waist. He could see nothing ahead. Something soft and clammy touched his mouth; he saw a dark frond moving against the grayish rock, and panic filled him. He thought of octopuses, of clinging weed. He pushed himself out backward and caught a glimpse, as he retreated, of a harmless tentacle of seaweed drifting in the mouth of the tunnel. But it was enough. He reached the sunlight, swam to shore, and lay on the diving rock. He looked down into the blue well of water. He knew he must find his way through that cave, or hole, or tunnel, and out the other side.

First, he thought, he must learn to control his breathing. He let himself down into the water with another big stone in his arms, so that he could lie effortlessly on the bottom of the sea. He counted. One, two, three. He counted steadily. He could hear the movement of blood in his chest. Fifty-one, fifty-two. . . . His chest was hurting. He let go of the rock and went up into the air. He saw that the sun was low. He rushed to the villa and found his mother at her supper. She said only "Did you enjoy yourself?" and he said "Yes."

All night the boy dreamed of the water-filled cave in the rock, and as soon as breakfast was over he went to the bay.

That night, his nose bled badly. For hours he had been underwater, learning to hold his breath, and now he felt weak and dizzy. His mother said, "I shouldn't overdo things, darling, if I were you."

That day and the next, Jerry exercised his lungs as if everything, the whole of his life, all that he would become, depended upon it. Again his nose bled at night, and his mother insisted on his coming with her the next day. It was a torment to him to waste a day of his careful self-training, but he stayed with her on that other beach, which now seemed a place for small children, a place where his mother might lie safe in the sun. It was not his beach.

He did not ask for permission, on the following day, to go to his beach. He went, before his mother could consider the complicated rights and wrongs of the matter. A day's rest, he discovered, had improved his count by ten. The big boys had made the passage while he counted a hundred and sixty. He had been counting fast, in his fright. Probably now, if he tried, he could get through that long tunnel, but he was not going to try yet. A curious, most unchildlike persistence, a controlled impatience, made him wait. In the meantime, he lay underwater on the white sand, littered now by stones he had brought down from the upper air, and studied the entrance to the tunnel. He knew every jut and corner of it, as far as it was possible to see. It was as if he already felt its sharpness about his shoulders.

He sat by the clock in the villa, when his mother was not near, and checked his time. He was incredulous and then proud to find he could hold his breath without strain for two minutes. The words "two minutes," authorized by the clock, brought close the adventure that was so necessary to him.

In another four days, his mother said casually one morning, they must go home. On the day before they left, he would do it. He would do it if it killed him, he said defiantly to himself. But two days before they were to leave—a day of triumph when he increased his count by fifteen—his nose bled so badly that he turned dizzy and had to lie limply over the big rock like a bit of seaweed, watching the thick red blood flow on to the rock and trickle slowly down to the sea. He was frightened. Supposing he turned dizzy in the tunnel? Supposing he died there, trapped? Supposing—his head went around, in the hot sun, and he almost gave up. He thought he would return to the house and lie down, and next summer, perhaps, when he had another year's growth in him—*then* he would go through the hole.

But even after he had made the decision, or thought he had, he found himself sitting up on the rock and looking down into the water; and he knew that now, this moment, when his nose had only just stopped

83

bleeding, when his head was still sore and throbbing—
this was the moment when he would try. If he did not
do it now, he never would. He was trembling with
fear that he would not go; and he was trembling with
horror at that long, long tunnel under the rock, under
the sea. Even in the open sunlight, the barrier rock
seemed very wide and very heavy; tons of rock
pressed down on where he would go. If he died there,
he would lie until one day—perhaps not before next
year—those big boys would swim into it and find it
blocked.

He put on his goggles, fitted them tight, tested the
vacuum. His hands were shaking. Then he chose the
biggest stone he could carry and slipped over the edge
of the rock until half of him was in the cool, enclosing
water and half in the hot sun. He looked up once at
the empty sky, filled his lungs once, twice, and then
sank fast to the bottom with the stone. He let it go
and began to count. He took the edges of the hole in
his hands and drew himself into it, wriggling his
shoulders in sidewise as he remembered he must, kicking himself along with his feet.

Soon he was clear inside. He was in a small rock-
bound hole filled with yellowish-gray water. The
water was pushing him up against the roof. The roof
was sharp and pained his back. He pulled himself
along with his hands—fast, fast—and used his legs as
levers. His head knocked against something; a sharp
pain dizzied him. Fifty, fifty-one, fifty-two. . . . He
was without light, and the water seemed to press upon
him with the weight of rock. Seventy-one, seventy-
two. . . . There was no strain on his lungs. He felt
like an inflated balloon, his lungs were so light and
easy, but his head was pulsing.

He was being continually pressed against the sharp
roof, which felt slimy as well as sharp. Again he

thought of octopuses, and wondered if the tunnel might be filled with weed that could tangle him. He gave himself a panicky, convulsive kick forward, ducked his head, and swam. His feet and hands moved freely, as if in open water. The hole must have widened out. He thought he must be swimming fast, and he was frightened of banging his head if the tunnel narrowed.

A hundred, a hundred and one. . . . The water paled. Victory filled him. His lungs were beginning to hurt. A few more strokes and he would be out. He was counting wildly; he said a hundred and fifteen, and then, a long time later, a hundred and fifteen again. The water was a clear jewel-green all around him. Then he saw, above his head, a crack running up through the rock. Sunlight was falling through it, showing the clean, dark rock of the tunnel, a single mussel shell, and darkness ahead.

He was at the end of what he could do. He looked up at the crack as if it were filled with air and not water, as if he could put his mouth to it to draw in air. A hundred and fifteen, he heard himself say inside his head—but he had said that long ago. He must go on into the blackness ahead, or he would drown. His head was swelling, his lungs cracking. A hundred and fifteen, a hundred and fifteen pounded through his head, and he feebly clutched at rocks in the dark, pulling himself forward, leaving the brief space of sunlit water behind. He felt he was dying. He was no longer quite conscious. He struggled on in the darkness between lapses into unconsciousness. An immense, swelling pain filled his head, and then the darkness cracked with an explosion of green light. His hands, groping forward, met nothing; and his feet, kicking back, propelled him out into the open sea.

He drifted to the surface, his face turned up to the

air. He was gasping like a fish. He felt he would sink now and drown; he could not swim the few feet back to the rock. Then he was clutching it and pulling himself up on to it. He lay face down, gasping. He could see nothing but a red-veined, clotted dark. His eyes must have burst, he thought; they were full of blood. He tore off his goggles and a gout of blood went into the sea. His nose was bleeding, and the blood had filled the goggles.

He scooped up handfuls of water from the cool, salty sea, to splash on his face, and did not know whether it was blood or salt water he tasted. After a time, his heart quieted, his eyes cleared, and he sat up. He could see the local boys diving and playing half a mile away. He did not want them. He wanted nothing but to get back home and lie down.

In a short while, Jerry swam to shore and climbed slowly up the path to the villa. He flung himself on his bed and slept, waking at the sound of feet on the path outside. His mother was coming back. He rushed to the bathroom, thinking she must not see his face with bloodstains, or tearstains, on it. He came out of the bathroom and met her as she walked into the villa, smiling, her eyes lighting up.

"Have a nice morning?" she asked, laying her hand on his warm brown shoulder a moment.

"Oh, yes, thank you," he said.

"You look a bit pale." And then, sharp and anxious, "How did you bang your head?"

"Oh, just banged it," he told her.

She looked at him closely. He was strained; his eyes were glazed-looking. She was worried. And then she said to herself, Oh, don't fuss! Nothing can happen. He can swim like a fish.

They sat down to lunch together.

"Mummy," he said, "I can stay under water for

two minutes—three minutes, at least." It came bursting out of him.

"Can you, darling?" she said. "Well, I shouldn't overdo it. I don't think you ought to swim any more today."

She was ready for a battle of wills, but he gave in at once. It was no longer of the least importance to go to the bay.

5

Lucy Grange

The farm was fifty miles from the nearest town, in a maize-growing district. The mealie lands began at a stone's throw from the front door of the farmhouse. At the back were several acres of energetic and colorful domestic growth: chicken runs, vegetables, pumpkins. Even on the veranda there were sacks of grain and bundles of hoes. The life of the farm, her husband's life, washed around the house, leaving old scraps of iron on the front step where the children played wagon-and-driver, or a bottle of medicine for a sick animal on her dressing table among the bottles of Elizabeth Arden.

One walked straight from the veranda of this gaunt, iron-roofed, brick barracks of a house into a wide drawing room that was shaded in green and orange Liberty linens.

"Stylish?" said the farmers' wives when they came on formal calls, asking the question of themselves while they discussed with Lucy Grange the price of butter and servants' aprons and their husbands discussed the farm with George Grange. They never "dropped over" to see Lucy Grange; they never rang her up with invitations to "spend the day." They would finger the books on child psychology, politics, art; gaze guiltily at the pictures on her walls, which they felt they ought to be able to recognize; and say: "I can see you are a great reader, Mrs. Grange."

There were years of discussing her among themselves before their voices held the good-natured amusement of acceptance: "I found Lucy in the vegetable patch wearing gloves full of cold cream." "Lucy has ordered another dress pattern from town." And later still, with self-consciously straightened shoulders, eyes directly primly before them, discreet noncommittal voices: "Lucy is very attractive to men."

One can imagine her, when they left at the end of those mercifully short visits, standing on the veranda and smiling bitterly after the satisfactory solid women with their straight tailored dresses, made by the Dutch-woman at the store at seven-and-six a time, buttoned loosely across their well-used breasts; with their untidy hair permanent waved every six months in town; with their femininity which was asserted once and for all by a clumsy scrawl of red across the mouth. One can imagine her clenching her fists and saying fiercely to the mealie fields that rippled greenly all around her, cream-topped like the sea: "I won't. I simply won't. He needn't imagine that I will!"

"Do you like my new dress, George?"

"You're the best-looking woman in the district, Lucy." So it seemed, on the face of it, that he didn't expect, or even want, that she should. . . .

Meanwhile she continued to order cookbooks from town, to make new recipes of pumpkin and green mealies and chicken, to put skin food on her face at night; she constructed attractive nursery furniture out of packing cases enameled white—the farm wasn't doing too well; and discussed with George how little Betty's cough was probably psychological.

"I'm sure you're right, my dear."

Then the rich, overcontrolled voice: "Yes, darling.

No, my sweetheart. Yes, of course, I'll play bricks with you, but you must have your lunch first." Then it broke, hard and shrill: "*Don't* make all that noise, darling. I can't stand it. Go on, go and play in the garden and leave me in peace."

Sometimes, storms of tears. Afterward: "Really, George, didn't your mother ever tell you that all women cry sometimes? It's as good as a tonic. Or a holiday." And a lot of high laughter and gay explanations at which George hastened to guffaw. He liked her gay. She usually was. For instance, she was a good mimic. She would "take off," deliberately trying to relieve his mind of farm worries, the visiting policemen, who toured the district once a month to see if the natives were behaving themselves, or the government agricultural officials.

"Do you want to see my husband?"

That was what they had come for, but they seldom pressed the point. They sat far longer than they had intended, drinking tea, talking about themselves. They would go away and say at the bar in the village: "Mrs. Grange is a smart woman, isn't she?"

And Lucy would be acting, for George's benefit, how a khaki-clad, sun-raw youth had bent into her room, looking around him with comical surprise; had taken a cup of tea, thanking her three times; had knocked over an ashtray, stayed for lunch and afternoon tea, and left saying with awkward gallantry: "It's a real treat to meet a lady like you who is interested in things."

"You shouldn't be so hard on us poor colonials, Lucy."

Finally one can imagine how one day, when the houseboy came to her in the chicken runs to say that there was a *baas* waiting to see her at the house, it was no sweating policeman, thirsty after fifteen dusty miles on a motorcycle, to whom she must be gracious.

He was a city man, of perhaps forty or forty-five, dressed in city clothes. At first glance she felt a shudder of repulsion. It was a coarse face, and sensual; and he looked like a patient vulture as the keen, heavy-lidded eyes traveled up and down her body.

"Are you looking for my husband, perhaps? He's in the cowsheds this morning."

"No, I don't think I am. I was."

She laughed. It was as if he had started playing a record she had not heard for a long time, and which started her feet tapping. It was years since she had played this game. "I'll get you some tea," she said hurriedly and left him in her pretty drawing room.

Collecting the cups, her hands were clumsy. Why, Lucy! she said to herself, archly. She came back, very serious and responsible, to find him standing in front of the picture that filled half the wall at one end of the room. "I should have thought you had sunflowers enough here," he said, in his heavy, overemphasized voice, which made her listen for meanings behind his words. And when he turned away from the wall and came to sit down, leaning forward, examining her, she suppressed an impulse to apologize for the picture: Van Gogh *is* obvious, but he's rather effective, she might have said; and she felt that the whole room was that: effective but obvious. But she was pleasantly conscious of how she looked: graceful and cool in her green linen dress, with her corn-colored hair knotted demurely on her neck. She lifted wide, serious eyes to his face and asked, "Milk? Sugar?" and knew that the corners of her mouth were tight with self-consciousness.

When he left, three hours later, he turned her hand over and lightly kissed the palm. She looked down at the greasy dark head, the red folded neck, and stood rigid, thinking of the raw, creased necks of vultures.

Then he straightened up and said with simple kindliness, "You must be lonely here, my dear"; and she was astounded to find her eyes full of tears.

"One does what one can to make a show of it." She kept her lids lowered and her voice light. Inside she was weeping with gratitude. Embarrassed, she said quickly, "You know, you haven't said what you came for."

"I sell insurance. And besides, I've heard people talk of you."

She imagined the talk and smiled stiffly. "You don't seem to take your work very seriously."

"If I may, I'll come back another time and try again?"

She did not reply. He said, "My dear, I'll tell you a secret: one of the reasons I chose this district was because of you. Surely there aren't so many people in this country one can really talk to that we can afford not to take each other seriously?"

He touched her cheek with his hand, smiled, and went.

She heard the last thing he had said like a parody of the things she often said and felt a violent revulsion.

She went to her bedroom, where she found herself in front of the mirror. Her hands went to her cheeks and she drew in her breath with the shock. "Why, Lucy, whatever is the matter with you?" Her eyes were dancing, her mouth smiled irresistibly. Yet she heard the archness of her "Why, Lucy," and thought: I'm going to pieces. I must have gone to pieces without knowing it.

Later she found herself singing in the pantry as she made a cake, stopped herself; made herself look at the insurance salesman's face against her closed eyelids; and instinctively wiped the palms of her hands against her skirt.

He came three days later. Again, in the first shock of seeing him stand at the door, smiling familiarly, she thought, It's the face of an old animal. He probably chose this kind of work because of the opportunities it gives him.

He talked of London, where he had lately been on leave; about the art galleries and the theaters.

She could not help warming, because of her hunger for this kind of talk. She could not help an apologetic note in her voice, because she knew that after so many years in this exile she must seem provincial. She liked him because he associated himself with her abdication from her standards by saying: "Yes, yes, my dear, in a country like this we all learn to accept the second-rate."

While he talked his eyes were roving. He was listening. Outside the window the turkeys were scraping in the dust and gobbling. In the next room the house-boy was moving; then there was silence because he had gone to get his midday meal. The children had had their lunch and gone off to the garden with the nurse.

No, she said to herself. No, no, no.

"Does your husband come back for lunch?"

"He takes it on the lands at this time of the year, he's so busy."

He came over and sat beside her. "Well, shall we console each other?" She was crying in his arms. She could feel their impatient and irritable tightening.

In the bedroom she kept her eyes shut. His hand traveled up and down her back. "What's the matter, little one? What's the matter?"

His voice was a sedative. She could have fallen

asleep and lain there for a week inside the anonymous, comforting arms. But he was looking at his watch over her shoulder. "We'd better get dressed, hadn't we?"

"Of course."

She sat naked in the bed, covering herself with her arms, looking at his white hairy body in loathing, and then at the creased red neck. She became extremely gay; and in the living room they sat side by side on the big sofa, being ironical. Then he put his arm around her, and she curled up inside it and cried again. She clung to him and felt him going away from her; and in a few minutes he stood up, saying, "Wouldn't do for your old man to come in and find us like this, would it?" Even while she was hating him for the "old man," she put her arms around him and said, "You'll come back soon."

"I couldn't keep away." The voice purred caressingly over her head, and she said: "You know, I'm very lonely."

"Darling, I'll come as soon as I can. I've a living to make, you know."

She let her arms drop, and smiled, and watched him drive away down the rutted red-rust farm road, between the rippling sea-colored mealies.

She knew he would come again, and next time she would not cry; she would stand again like this, watching him go, hating him, thinking of how he had said: In this country we learn to accept the second-rate. And he would come again and again and again; and she would stand here, watching him go and hating him.

6

Pleasure

There were two great feasts, or turning points, in Mary Rogers' year. She began preparing for the second as soon as the Christmas decorations were down. This year, she was leafing through a fashion magazine when her husband said, "Dreaming of the sun, old girl?"

"I don't see why not," she said, rather injured. "After all, it's been four years."

"I really don't see how we can afford it."

On her face he saw a look that he recognized.

Her friend Mrs. Baxter, the manager's wife, also saw the magazine, and said, "You'll be off to the south of France again, this year, I suppose, now that your daughter won't be needing you." She added those words which in themselves were justification for everything: "We'll stay faithful to Brighton, I expect."

And Mary Rogers said, as she always did: "I can't imagine why anyone takes a holiday in Britain when the same money'd take them to the continent."

For four years she had gone with her daughter and the grandchildren to Cornwall. It sounded a sacrifice on the altar of the family, the way she put it to her friends. But this year the daughter was going to the other grandmother in Scotland, and everyone knew it. Everyone. That is, Mrs. Baxter, Mrs. Justin-Smith, and Mrs. Jones.

Mary Rogers bought gay cottons and spread them over the living room. Outside, a particularly grim February held the little Midlands town in a steady shiver. Rain swept the windowpanes. Tommy Rogers saw the cottons and said not a word. But a week later she was fitting a white linen sunsuit before the mirror when he said, "I say, old girl, that shows quite a bit of leg, you know. . . ."

At that moment it was acknowledged that they should go. Also, that the four years had made a difference in various ways. Mary Rogers secretly examined her thighs and shoulders before the glass, and thought they might very well be exposed. But the clothes she made were of the sensible but smart variety. She sewed at them steadily through the evenings of March, April, May, June. She was a good needlewoman. Also, for a few happy months before she married, she had studied fashion designing in London. That had been a different world. In speaking of it now, to the women of her circle—Mrs. Baxter, Mrs. Justin-Smith, and Mrs. Jones, her voice conveyed the degree of difference. And Mrs. Baxter would say, kindly as always, "Ah well, we none of us know what's in store for us when we're young."

They were to leave toward the end of July. A week before, Tommy Rogers produced a piece of paper on which were set out certain figures. They were much lower figures than ever before. "Oh, we'll manage," said Mary vaguely. Her mind was already moving among scenes of blue sea, blue sky.

"Perhaps we'd better book at the Plaza."

"Oh, surely no need. They know us there."

The evening before they left there was a bridge party in the Baxters' house for the jaunting couple. Tommy Rogers was seen to give his wife an uneasy glance as she said, "With air travel as cheap as it is now, I really can't understand why. . . ."

For they had booked by train, of course, as usual.

They successfully negotiated the Channel, a night in a Paris hotel, and the catching of the correct train.

In a few hours they would see the little village on the sea where they had first come twenty-five years ago on their honeymoon. They had chosen it because Mary Hill had met, in those artistic circles which she had enjoyed for, alas, so short a time, a certain well-known stage decorator who had a villa there. During that month of honeymoon, they had spent a happy afternoon at the villa.

As the train approached, she was looking to see the villa, alone on its hill above the sea. But the hill was now thick with little white villas, green-shuttered, red-roofed in the warm southern green.

"The place seems to have grown quite a bit," said Tommy. The station had grown, too. There was a long platform now, and a proper station building. And gazing down toward the sea, they saw a cluster of shops and casinos and cafés. Even four years before, there had been only a single shop, a restaurant, and a couple of hotels.

"Well," said Mary bitterly, "if the place is full of tourists now, it won't be the same at all."

But the sun was shining, the sea tossed and sparkled, and the palm trees stood along the white beach. They carried their suitcases down the slope of the road to the Plaza, feeling at home.

Outside the Plaza, they looked at each other. What had been a modest building was now an imposing one, surrounded by gay awnings and striped umbrellas. "Old Jaques is spreading himself," said Tommy, and they walked up the neat gravel path to the foyer, looking for Jaques, who had welcomed them so often.

At the office, Mary inquired in her stiff, correct French for Monsieur Jaques. The clerk smiled and regretted that Monsieur Jaques had left them three years before. "He knew us well," said Mary, her voice coming aggrieved and shrill. "He always had room for us here."

But certainly there was a room for Madame. Most certainly. At once attendants came hurrying for the suitcases.

"Hold your horses a minute," said Tommy. "Wait. Ask what it costs now."

Mary inquired, casually enough, what the rates now were. She received the information with a lengthening of her heavy jaw, and rapidly transmitted it to Tommy. He glanced, embarrassed, at the clerk, who, recognizing a situation, turned tactfully to a ledger and prepared to occupy himself so that the elderly English couple could confer.

They did, in rapid, angry undertones.

"We can't, Mary. It's no good. We'd have to go back at the end of a week."

"But we've always stayed here. . . ."

At last she turned toward the clerk, who was immediately attentive, and said with a stiff smile: "I'm afraid the currency regulations make things difficult for us." She had spoken in English, such was her upset; and it was in English that he replied pleasantly, "I understand perfectly, Madame. Perhaps you would care to try the Belle Vue across the street. There are many English people there."

The Rogerses left, carrying their two suitcases ignominiously down the neat graveled path, among the gay tables where people already sat at dinner. The sun had gone down. Opposite, the Belle Vue was a glow of lights. Tommy Rogers was not surprised when

Mary walked past it without a look. For years, staying at the Plaza, they had felt superior to the Belle Vue. Also, had that clerk not said it was full of English people?

Since this was France, and the season, the Agency was of course open. An attractive mademoiselle deplored that they had not booked rooms earlier.

"We've been here every year for twenty-five years," said Mary, pardonably overlooking the last four, and another stretch of five when the child had been small. "We've never had to look before."

Alas, alas, suggested the mademoiselle with her shoulders and her pretty eyes, what a pity that St. Nichole had become so popular, so attractive. There was no fact she regretted more. She suggested the Belle Vue.

The Rogerses walked the hundred yards back to the Belle Vue, feeling they were making a final concession to fate, only to find it fully booked up. Returning to the Agency, they were informed that there was, happily, one room vacant in a villa on the hillside. They were escorted to it. And now it was the turn of the pretty mademoiselle to occupy herself, not with a ledger, but in examining the view of brilliant stars and the riding lights of ships across the bay, while the Rogerses conferred. Their voices were now not only angry, but high with exasperation. For this room—an extremely small one, at the bottom of a big villa, stone-floored, uncarpeted; with a single large bed of the sort Mary always thought of as French; a wardrobe that was no wardrobe, since it had been filled with shelves; a sink and a small gas stove—they were asked to pay a sum which filled them with disbelief. If they desired hot water, as the English so often do, they would have to heat it in a saucepan on the stove.

But, as the mademoiselle pointed out, turning from her appreciative examination of the exotic night scene, it would be such an advantage to do one's own cooking.

"I suggest we go back to the Plaza. Better one week of comfort than three of this," said Mary. They returned to the Plaza to find that the room had been taken, and none were available.

It was now nearly ten in the evening, and the infinitely obliging mademoiselle returned them to the little room in the villa, for which they agreed to pay more than they had done four years before for comfort, good food, and hot water in the Plaza. Also, they had to pay a deposit of over ten pounds in case they might escape in the night with the bed, the wardrobe, or the tin spoons, or in case they refused to pay the bills for electricity, gas, and water.

The Rogerses went to bed immediately, worn out with traveling and disappointment.

In the morning Mary announced that she had no intention of cooking on a holiday, and they took *petit-déjeuner* at a café, paid the equivalent of twelve shillings for two small cups of coffee and two rolls, and changed their minds. They would have to cook in the room.

Preserving their good humor with an effort, they bought cold food for lunch, left it in the room, and prepared themselves for enjoyment. For the sea was blue, blue and sparkling. And the sunshine was hot and golden. And after all, this was the south of France, the prettiest place in Europe, as they had always agreed. And in England now, said the *Daily Telegraph*, it was pouring rain.

On the beach they had another bad moment. Umbrellas stretched six deep, edge to edge, for half a mile along the silvery beach. Bodies lay stretched out, baking in the sun, hundreds to the acre, a perfect bed of heated brown flesh.

"They've ruined the place, ruined it," cried Mary, as she surveyed the untidy scene. But she stepped heavily down into the sand and unbuttoned her dress. She was revealed to be wearing a heavy black bathing suit; and she did not miss the relieved glance her husband gave her. She felt it to be unfair. There he stood, a tall, very thin, fair man, quite presentable in an absurd bathing slip that consisted of six inches of material held on by a string round his hips. And there *she* was, a heavy firm woman, with clear white flesh—but middle-aged, and in a black bathing suit.

She looked about. Two feet away was a mess of tangled brown limbs belonging to half a dozen boys and girls, the girls wearing nothing but colored cotton brassieres and panties. She saw Tommy looking at them, too. Then she noticed, eighteen inches to the other side, a vast, gray-haired lady, bulging weary pallid flesh out of a white cotton playsuit. Mary gave her a look of happy superiority and lay down flat on the sand, congratulating herself.

All the morning the English couple lay there, turning over and over on the sand like a pair of grilling herrings, for they felt their pale skins to be a shame and a disgrace. When they returned to their room for lunch, it was to find that swarms of small black ants had infested their cold meats. They were unable to mind very much, as it had become evident they had overdone the sunbathing. Both were bright scarlet, and their eyes ached. They lay down in the cool of the darkened room, feeling foolish to be such amateurs—they, who should know better! They kept to their beds that afternoon, and the next day . . . several days passed. Sometimes, when hunger overcame them, Mary winced down to the village to buy cold

103

food—impossible to keep supplies in the room because of the ants. After eating, she hastily washed up in the sink where they also washed. Twice a day, Tommy went reluctantly outside, while she washed herself inch by inch in water heated in the saucepan. Then she went outside while he did the same. After these indispensable measures of hygiene, they retired to the much-too-narrow bed, shrinking away from any chance of contact with each other.

At last the discomfort of the room, as much as their healing flesh, drove them forth again, more cautiously clothed, to the beach. Skin was ripping off them both in long shreds. At the end of a week, however, they had become brown and shining, able to take their places without shame among the other brown and glistening bodies that littered the beach like so many stranded fish.

Day after day the Rogerses descended the steep path to the beach, after having eaten a hearty English breakfast of ham and eggs, and stayed there all morning. All morning they lay, and then all afternoon, but at a good distance from a colony of English, which kept itself to itself some hundreds of yards away.

They watched the children screaming and laughing in the unvarying blue waves. They watched the groups of French adolescents flirt and roll each other over on the sand in a way that Mary, at least, thought appallingly free. Thank heavens her daughter had married young and was safely out of harm's way! Nothing could have persuaded Mary Rogers of the extreme respectability of these youngsters. She suspected them all of shocking and complicated vices. Incredible that, in so few a number of years, they would be sorted by some powerful and comforting social process into these decent, well-fed French couples, each so anxiously absorbed in the welfare of one, or perhaps two small children.

They watched also, with admiration, the more hardened swimmers cleave out through the small waves into the sea beyond the breakwater with their masks, their airtubes, their frog's feet.

They were content.

This is what they had come for. This is what all these hundreds of thousands of people along the coast had come for—to lie on the sand and receive the sun on their heating bodies; to receive, too, in small doses, the hot blue water which dried so stickily on them. The sea was very salty and warm-smelling—smelling of a little more than salt and weed, for beyond the breakwater the town's sewers spilled into the sea, washing back into the inner bay rich deposits which dried on the perfumed oiled bodies of the happy bathers.

This is what they had come for.

Yet, there was no doubt that in the Plaza things had been quite different. There, one rose late; lingered over coffee and rolls; descended, or did not descend, to the beach for a couple of hours' sun worship; returned to a lengthy lunch; slept, bathed again, enjoyed an even more lengthy dinner. That, too, was called a seaside vacation. Now, the beach was really the only place to go. From nine until one, from two until seven, the Rogerses were on it. It was a seaside vacation with a vengeance.

About the tenth day, they realized that half of their time had gone; and Tommy showed his restlessness, his feeling that there should be more to it than this, by diving into one of the new and so terribly expensive shops and emerging with a mask, frog's feet, and airtube. With an apology to Mary for leaving her, he

105

plunged out into the bay, looking like—or so she rather tartly remarked—a spaceman in a children's comic. He did not return for some hours.

"This is better than anything, old girl, you should try it," he said, wading out of the sea with an absorbed excited look. That afternoon she spent on the beach alone, straining her eyes to make out which of the bobbing periscopes in the water was his.

Thus engaged, she heard herself addressed in English: "I always say I am an undersea widow, too." She turned to see a slight girl, clearly English, with pretty fair curls, a neat blue bathing suit, pretty blue eyes, good legs stretched out in the warm sand. An English girl. But her voice was, so Mary decided, passable, in spite of a rather irritating giggle. She relented and, though it was her principle that one did not go to France to consort with the English, said: "Is your husband out there?"

"Oh, I never see him between meals," said the girl cheerfully and lay back on the sand.

Mary thought that this girl was very similar to herself at that age—only, of course, *she* had known how to make the best of herself. They talked, in voices drugged by sea and sun, until first Tommy Rogers, and then the girl's husband, rose out of the sea. The young man was carrying a large fish speared through the back by a sort of trident. The excitement of this led the four of them to share a square yard of sand for a few minutes, making cautious overtures.

The next day, Tommy Rogers insisted that his wife should don mask and flippers and try the new sport. She was taken out into the bay, like a ship under escort, by the two men and young Betty Clarke. Mary Rogers did not like the suffocating feeling of the mask pressing against her nose. The speed the frog feet lent her made her nervous, for she was not a strong swimmer. But she was not going to appear a coward with that young girl sporting along so easily just in front.

Out in the bay a small island, a mere cluster of warm, red-brown rock, rose from a surf of frisking white. Around the island, a couple of feet below the surface, submerged rocks lay; and all over them floated the new race of frog-people, face down, tridents poised, observing the fish that darted there. As Mary looked back through her goggles to the shore, it seemed very far, and rather commonplace, with the striped umbrellas, the lolling browned bodies, the paddling children. That was the other sea. This was something different indeed. Here were the adventurers and explorers of the sea, who disdained the safe beaches.

Mary lay loose on the surface of the water and looked down. Enormous, this undersea world, with great valleys and boulders, all wavering green in the sun-dappled water. On a dazzling patch of white sand —twenty feet down, it seemed—sprouted green grass as fresh and bright as if it grew on the shore in sunlight. By reaching down her hand she could almost touch it. Farther away, long fronds of weed rocked and swayed, a forest of them. Mary floated over them, feeling with repugnance how they reached up to touch her knees and shoulders with their soft, dragging touch. Underneath her, now, a floor of rock, covered with thick growth. Pale gray-green shapes, swelling like balloons, or waving like streamers; delicate whitey-brown flowers and stars, bubbled silver with air; soft swelling udders or bladders of fine white film, all rocking and drifting in the slow undersea movement. Mary was fascinated—a new world, this was. But also repelled. In her ears there was nothing but a splash and crash of surf, and, through it, voices that sounded a long way off. The rocks were now

107

very close below. Suddenly, immediately below her, a thin brown arm reached down, groped in a dark gulf of rock, and pulled out a writhing tangle of gray-dappled flesh. Mary floundered up, slipping painfully on the rocks. She had drifted unknowingly close to the islet; and on the rocks above her stood a group of half-naked bronzed boys, yelling and screaming with excitement as they killed the octopus they had caught by smashing it repeatedly against a great boulder. They would eat it—so Mary heard—for supper. No, it was too much. She was in a panic. The loathsome thing must have been six inches below her—she might have touched it! She climbed onto a rock and looked for Tommy, who was lying on a rock fifty feet off, pointing down at something under it, while Francis Clarke dived for it, and then again. She saw him emerge with a small striped fish, while Tommy and Betty Clarke yelled their excitement.

But she looked at the octopus, which was now lying draped over a rock like a limp, fringed, gray rag; she called her husband, handed over the goggles, the flippers and the tube, and swam slowly back to shore.

There she stayed. Nothing would tempt her out again.

That day Tommy bought an underwater fish gun. Mary found herself thinking, first, that it was all very well to spend over five pounds on this bizarre equipment; and then, that they weren't going to have much fun at Christmas if they went on like this.

A couple of days passed. Mary was alone all day. Betty Clarke, apparently, was only a beach widow when it suited her, for she much preferred the red-rock island to staying with Mary. Nevertheless, she did sometimes spend half an hour making conversation, and then, with a flurry of apology, darted off through the blue waves to rejoin the men.

Quite soon, Mary was able to say casually to Tommy, "Only three days to go."

"If only I'd tried this equipment earlier," he said. "Next year I'll know better."

But for some reason the thought of next year did not enchant Mary. "I don't think we ought to come here again," she said. "It's quite spoiled now it's so fashionable."

"Oh, well—anywhere, provided there's rocks and fish."

On that next day, the two men and Betty Clarke were on the rock island from seven in the morning until lunchtime, to which meal they grudgingly allowed ten minutes, because it was dangerous to swim on a full stomach. Then they departed again until the darkness fell across the sea. All this time Mary Rogers lay on her towel on the beach, turning over and over in the sun. She was now a warm red-gold all over. She imagined how Mrs. Baxter would say: "You've got yourself a fine tan!" And then, inevitably, "You won't keep it long here, will you?" Mary found herself unaccountably close to tears. What did Tommy see in these people? she asked herself. As for that young man, Francis—she had never heard him make any remark that was not connected with the weights, the varieties, or the vagaries of fish!

That night, Tommy said he had asked the young couple to dinner at the Plaza.

"A bit rash, aren't you?"

"Oh, well, let's have a proper meal, for once. Only another two days."

Mary let that "proper meal" pass. But she said, "I shouldn't have thought they were the sort of people to make friends of."

A cloud of irritation dulled his face. "What's the matter with them?"

"In England, I don't think. . . ."

"Oh come off it, Mary!"

In the big garden of the Plaza, where four years ago they had eaten three times a day by right, they found themselves around a small table just over the sea. There was an orchestra and more waiters than guests, or so it seemed. Betty Clarke, seen for the first time out of a bathing suit, was revealed to be a remarkably pretty girl. Her thin brown shoulders emerged from a full white frock, which Mary Rogers conceded to be not bad at all; and her wide blue eyes were bright in her brown face. Again Mary thought: If I were twenty—well, twenty-five, years younger, they'd take us for sisters.

As for Tommy, he looked as young as the young couple—it simply wasn't fair, thought Mary. She sat and listened while they talked of judging distances underwater and the advantages of various types of equipment.

They tried to draw her in; but there she sat, silent and dignified. Francis Clarke, she had decided, looked stiff and commonplace in his suit, not at all the handsome young sea god of the beaches. As for the girl, her giggle was irritating Mary.

They began to feel uncomfortable. Betty mentioned London, and the three conscientiously talked about London, while Mary said yes and no.

The young couple lived in Clapham, apparently; and they went into town for a show once a month.

"There's ever such a nice show running now," said Betty. The one at the Princess."

"We never get to a show these days," said Tommy. "It's five hours by train. Anyway, it's not in my line."

"Speak for yourself," said Mary.

"Oh I know you work in a matinee when you can."

At the irritation in the look she gave him, the

Clarkes involuntarily exchanged a glance; and Betty said tactfully, "I like going to the theater; it gives you something to talk about."

Mary remained silent.

"My wife," said Tommy, "knows a lot about the theater. She used to be in a theater set—all that sort of thing."

"Oh, how interesting!" said Betty eagerly.

Mary struggled with temptation, then fell. "The man who did the décor for the show at the Princess used to have a villa here. We visited him quite a bit."

Tommy gave his wife an alarmed and warning look, and said, "I wish to God they wouldn't use so much garlic."

"It's not much use coming to France," said Mary, "if you're going to be insular about food."

"You never cook French at home," said Tommy suddenly. "Why not, if you like it so much?"

"How can I? If I do, you say you don't like your food messed up."

"I don't like garlic either," said Betty, with the air of one confessing a crime. "I must say I'm pleased to be back home where you can get a bit of good plain food."

Tommy now looked in anxious appeal at his wife, but she inquired, "Why don't you go to Brighton or somewhere like that?"

"Give me Brighton anytime," said Francis Clarke. "Or Cornwall. You can get damned good fishing off Cornwall. But Betty drags me here. France is over-rated, that's what I say."

"It would really seem to be better if you stayed at home."

But he was not going to be snubbed by Mary Rogers. "As for the French," he said aggressively, "they think of nothing but their stomachs. If they're not eating, they're talking about it. If they spent half the time they spend on eating on something worthwhile, they would make something of themselves, that's what I say."

"Such as—catching fish?"

"Well, what's wrong with that? Or . . . for instance. . . ." Here he gave the matter his earnest consideration. "Well, there's that government of theirs for instance. They could do something about that."

Betty, who was now flushed under her tan, rolled her blue eyes, and let out a high, confused laugh. "Oh well, you've got to consider what people say. France is so much the rage."

A silence. It was to be hoped the awkward moment was over. But no; for Francis Clarke seemed to think matters needed clarifying. He said, with a sort of rallying gallantry toward his wife: "She's got a bee in her bonnet about getting on."

"Well," cried Betty, "it makes a good impression, you must admit that. And when Mr. Beaker—Mr. Beaker is his boss," she explained to Mary, "when you said to Mr. Beaker at the whist drive you were going to the south of France, he was impressed, you can say what you like."

Tommy offered his wife an entirely disloyal, sarcastic grin.

"A woman should think of her husband's career," said Betty. "It's true, isn't it? And I know I've helped Francie a lot. I'm sure he wouldn't have got that raise if it weren't for making a good impression. Besides you meet such nice people. Last year, we made friends well, acquaintance, if you like—with some people who live at Ealing. We wouldn't have, otherwise. He's in the films."

"He's a cameraman," said Francis, being accurate.

112

"Well, that's films, isn't it? And they asked us to a party. And who do you think was there?"

"Mr. Beaker?" inquired Mary finely.

"How did you guess? Well, they could see, couldn't they? And I wouldn't be surprised if Francis couldn't be buyer, now they know he's used to foreigners. He should learn French, I tell him."

"Can't speak a word," said Francis. "Can't stand it anyway—gabble, gabble, gabble."

"Oh, but Mrs. Rogers speaks it so beautifully," cried Betty.

"She's cracked," said Francis, good-humoredly, nodding to indicate his wife. "She spends half the year making clothes for three weeks' holiday at the sea. Then the other half making Christmas presents out of bits and pieces. That's all she ever does."

"Oh, but it's so nice to give people presents with that individual touch," said Betty.

"If you want to waste your time I'm not stopping you," said Francis. "I'm not stopping you. It's your funeral."

"They're not grateful for what we do for them," said Betty, wrestling with tears, trying to claim the older woman as an ally. "If I didn't work hard, we couldn't afford the friends we got. . . ."

But Mary Rogers had risen from her place. "I think I'm ready for bed," she said. "Good night, Mrs. Clarke. Good night, Mr. Clarke." Without looking at her husband, she walked away.

Tommy Rogers hastily got up, paid the bill, bade the young couple an embarrassed good night, and hurried after his wife. He caught her up at the turning of the steep road up to the villa. The stars were brilliant overhead; the palms waved seductively in the soft breeze. "I say," he said angrily, "that wasn't very nice of you."

113

"I haven't any patience with that sort of thing," said Mary. Her voice was high and full of tears. He looked at her in astonishment and held his peace.

But next day he went off fishing. For Mary, the holiday was over. She was packing and did not go to the beach.

That evening he said, "They've asked us back to dinner."

"You go. I'm tired."

"I shall go," he said defiantly, and went. He did not return until very late.

They had to catch the train early next morning. At the little station, they stood with their suitcases in a crowd of people who regretted the holiday was over. But Mary was regretting nothing. As soon as the train came, she got in and left Tommy shaking hands with crowds of English people whom, apparently, he had met the night before. At the last minute, the young Clarkes came running up in bathing suits to say good-bye. She nodded stiffly out of the train window and went on arranging the baggage. Then the train started and her husband came in.

The compartment was full and there was an excuse not to talk. The silence persisted, however. Soon Tommy was watching her anxiously and making remarks about the weather, which worsened steadily as they went north.

In Paris there were five hours to fill in.

They were walking beside the river, by the open-air market, when she stopped before a stall selling earthenware.

"That big bowl," she exclaimed, her voice newly alive, "that big red one, there—it would be just right for the Christmas tree."

"So it would. Go ahead and buy it, old girl," he agreed at once, with infinite relief.

7

A Mild Attack of Locusts

The rains that year were good; they were coming nicely just as the crops needed them—or so Margaret gathered when the men said they were not too bad. She never had an opinion of her *own* on matters like the weather, because even to know about what seems a simple thing like the weather needs experience. Which Margaret had not got. The men were Richard her husband, and old Stephen, Richard's father, a farmer from way back; and these two might argue for hours whether the rains were ruinous or just ordinarily exasperating. Margaret had been on the farm three years. She still did not understand how they did not go bankrupt altogether, when the men never had a good word for the weather, or the soil, or the government. But she was getting to learn the language. Farmers' language. And they neither went bankrupt nor got very rich. They jogged along doing comfortably.

Their crop was maize. Their farm was three thousand acres on the ridges that rise up toward the Zambesi escarpment—high, dry windswept country, cold and dusty in winter, but now, in the wet season, steamy with the heat rising in wet soft waves off miles of green foliage. Beautiful it was, with the sky blue and brilliant halls of air, and the bright green folds and hollows of country beneath, and the mountains lying sharp and bare twenty miles off across the rivers. The sky made her eyes ache; she was not used to it. One does not look so much at the sky in the city she came from. So that evening when Richard said: "The government is sending out warnings that locusts are expected, coming down from the breeding grounds up North," her instinct was to look about her at the trees. Insects—swarms of them—horrible! But Richard and the old man had raised their eyes and were looking up over the mountain. "We haven't had locusts in seven years," they said. "They go in cycles, locusts do." And then: "There goes our crop for this season!"

But they went on with the work of the farm just as usual until one day they were coming up the road to the homestead for the midday break, when old Stephen stopped, raised his finger and pointed: "Look, look, there they are!"

Out ran Margaret to join them, looking at the hills. Out came the servants from the kitchen. They all stood and gazed. Over the rocky levels of the mountain was a streak of rust-colored air. Locusts. There they came.

At once Richard shouted at the cookboy. Old Stephen yelled at the houseboy. The cookboy ran to beat the old ploughshare hanging from a tree branch, which was used to summon the laborers at moments of crisis. The houseboy ran off to the store to collect tin cans, any old bit of metal. The farm was ringing with the clamor of the gong; and they could see the laborers come pouring out of the compound, pointing at the hills and shouting excitedly. Soon they had all come up to the house, and Richard and old Stephen were giving them orders—Hurry, hurry, hurry.

And off they ran again, the two white men with

them, and in a few minutes Margaret could see the smoke of fires rising from all round the farmlands. Piles of wood and grass had been prepared there. There were seven patches of bared soil, yellow and oxblood color and pink, where the new mealies were just showing, making a film of bright green; and around each drifted up thick clouds of smoke. They were throwing wet leaves on to the fires now, to make it acrid and black. Margaret was watching the hills. Now there was a long, low cloud advancing, rust-color still, swelling forward and out as she looked. The telephone was ringing. Neighbors—quick, quick, there come the locusts. Old Smith had had his crop eaten to the ground. Quick, get your fires started. For of course, while every farmer hoped the locusts would overlook his farm and go on to the next, it was only fair to warn each other; one must play fair. Everywhere, fifty miles over the countryside, the smoke was rising from myriads of fires. Margaret answered the telephone calls, and between calls she stood watching the locusts. The air was darkening. A strange darkness, for the sun was blazing—it was like the darkness of a veldt fire, when the air gets thick with smoke. The sunlight comes down distorted, a thick, hot orange. Oppressive it was, too, with the heaviness of a storm. The locusts were coming fast. Now half the sky was darkened. Behind the reddish veils in front, which were the advance guards of the swarm, the main swarm showed in dense black cloud, reaching almost to the sun itself.

Margaret was wondering what she could do to help. She did not know. Then up came old Stephen from the lands. "We're finished, Margaret, finished! Those beggars can eat every leaf and blade off the farm in half an hour! And it is only early afternoon—

117

if we can make enough smoke, make enough noise till the sun goes down, they'll settle somewhere else perhaps. . . ." And then: "Get the kettle going. It's thirsty work, this."

So Margaret went to the kitchen, and stoked up the fire, and boiled the water. Now, on the tin roof of the kitchen she could hear the thuds and bangs of falling locusts, or a scratching slither as one skidded down. Here were the first of them. From down on the lands came the beating and banging and clanging of a hundred gasoline cans and bits of metal. Stephen impatiently waited while one gasoline can was filled with tea, hot, sweet and orange-colored, and the other with water. In the meantime, he told Margaret about how twenty years back he was eaten out, made bankrupt, by the locust armies. And then, still talking, he hoisted up the gasoline cans, one in each hand, by the wood pieces set cornerwise across each, and jogged off down to the road to the thirsty laborers. By now the locusts were falling like hail on to the roof of the kitchen. It sounded like a heavy storm. Margaret looked out and saw the air dark with a crisscross of the insects, and she set her teeth and ran out into it—what the men could do, she could. Overhead the air was thick, locusts everywhere. The locusts were flopping against her, and she brushed them off, heavy red-brown creatures, looking at her with their beady old-men's eyes while they clung with hard, serrated legs. She held her breath with disgust and ran through into the house. There it was even more like being in a heavy storm. The iron roof was reverberating, and the clamor of iron from the lands was like thunder. Looking out, all the trees were queer and still, clotted with insects, their boughs weighed to the ground. The earth seemed to be moving, locusts crawling every-

118

where, she could not see the lands at all, so thick was the swarm. Toward the mountains it was like looking into driving rain—even as she watched, the sun was blotted out with a fresh onrush of them. It was a half-night, a perverted blackness. Then came a sharp crack from the bush—a branch had snapped off. Then another. A tree down the slope leaned over and settled heavily to the ground. Through the hail of insects a man came running. More tea, more water was needed. She supplied them. She kept the fires stoked and filled cans with liquid, and then it was four in the afternoon, and the locusts had been pouring across overhead for a couple of hours. Up came old Stephen again, crunching locusts underfoot with every step, locusts clinging all over him; he was cursing and swearing, banging with his old hat at the air. At the doorway he stopped briefly, hastily pulling at the clinging insects and throwing them off, then he plunged into the locust-free living room.

"All the crops finished. Nothing left," he said.

But the gongs were still beating, the men still shouting, and Margaret asked: "Why do you go on with it, then?"

"The main swarm isn't settling. They are heavy with eggs. They are looking for a place to settle and lay. If we can stop the main body settling on our farm, that's everything. If they get a chance to lay their eggs, we are going to have everything eaten flat with hoppers later on." He picked a stray locust off his shirt and split it down with his thumbnail—it was clotted inside with eggs. "Imagine that multiplied by millions. You ever seen a hopper swarm on the march? Well, you're lucky."

Margaret thought an adult swarm was bad enough. Outside now the light on the earth was a pale, thin

119

yellow, clotted with moving shadows; the clouds of moving insects thickened and lightened like driving rain. Old Stephen said, "They've got the wind behind them, that's something."

"Is it very bad?" asked Margaret fearfully, and the old man said emphatically: "We're finished. This swarm may pass over, but once they've started, they'll be coming down from the North now one after another. And then there are the hoppers—it might go on for two or three years."

Margaret sat down helplessly, and thought: Well, if it's the end, it's the end. What now? We'll all three have to go back to town. . . . But at this, she took a quick look at Stephen, the old man who had farmed forty years in this country, been bankrupt twice, and she knew nothing would make him go and become a clerk in the city. Yet her heart ached for him, he looked so tired, the worry lines deep from nose to mouth. Poor old man. . . . He had lifted up a locust that had got itself somehow into his pocket, holding it in the air by one leg. "You've got the strength of a steel-spring in those legs of yours," he was telling the locust, good-humoredly. Then, although he had been fighting locusts, squashing locusts, yelling at locusts, sweeping them in great mounds into the fires to burn for the last three hours, nevertheless he took this one to the door and carefully threw it out to join its fellows, as if he would rather not harm a hair of its head. This comforted Margaret; all at once she felt irrationally cheered. She remembered it was not the first time in the last three years the man had announced their final and irremediable ruin.

"Get me a drink, lass," he then said, and she set the bottle of whisky by him.

In the meantime, out in the pelting storm of insects,

her husband was banging the gong, feeding the fires with leaves, the insects clinging to him all over—she shuddered. "How can you bear to let them touch you?" she asked. He looked at her, disapproving. She felt suitably humble—just as she had when he had first taken a good look at her city self, hair waved and golden, nails red and pointed. Now she was a proper farmer's wife, in sensible shoes and a solid skirt. She might even get to letting locusts settle on her—in time.

Having tossed back a whisky or two, old Stephen went back into the battle, wading now through glistening brown waves of locusts.

Five o'clock. The sun would set in an hour. Then the swarm would settle. It was as thick overhead as ever. The trees were ragged mounds of glistening brown.

Margaret began to cry. It was all so hopeless—if it wasn't a bad season, it was locusts; if it wasn't locusts, it was army-worm or veldt fires. Always something. The rustling of the locust armies was like a big forest in the storm; their settling on the roof was like the beating of the rain; the ground was invisible in a sleek, brown, surging tide—it was like being drowned in locusts, submerged by the loathsome brown flood. It seemed as if the roof might sink in under the weight of them, as if the door might give in under their pressure and these rooms fill with them—and it was getting so dark . . . she looked up. The air was thinner; gaps of blue showed in the dark, moving clouds. The blue spaces were cold and thin—the sun must be setting. Through the fog of insects she saw figures approaching. First old Stephen, marching bravely along, then her husband, drawn and haggard with weariness. Behind them the servants. All were crawling all over

121

with insects. The sound of the gongs had stopped. She could hear nothing but the ceaseless rustle of a myriad wings.

The two men slapped off the insects and came in.

"Well," said Richard, kissing her on the cheek, "the main swarm has gone over."

"For the Lord's sake," said Margaret angrily, still half-crying, "what's here is bad enough, isn't it?" For although the evening air was no longer black and thick, but a clear blue, with a pattern of insects whizzing this way and that across it, everything else—trees, buildings, bushes, earth, was gone under the moving brown masses.

"If it doesn't rain in the night and keep them here—if it doesn't rain and weight them down with water, they'll be off in the morning at sunrise."

"We're bound to have some hoppers. But not the main swarm—that's something."

Margaret roused herself, wiped her eyes, pretended she had not been crying, and fetched them some supper, for the servants were too exhausted to move. She sent them down to the compound to rest.

She served the supper and sat listening. There is not one maize plant left, she heard. Not one. The men would get the planters out the moment the locusts had gone. They must start all over again.

But what's the use of that, Margaret wondered, if the whole farm was going to be crawling with hoppers? But she listened while they discussed the new government pamphlet that said how to defeat the hoppers. You must have men out all the time, moving over the farm to watch for movement in the grass. When you find a patch of hoppers, small lively black things, like crickets, then you dig trenches around the patch or spray them with poison from pumps supplied by the government. The government wanted them to cooperate in a world plan for eliminating this plague forever. You should attack locusts at the source. Hoppers, in short. The men were talking as if they were planning a war, and Margaret listened, amazed.

In the night it was quiet; no sign of the settled armies outside, except sometimes a branch snapped, or a tree could be heard crashing down.

Margaret slept badly in the bed beside Richard, who was sleeping like the dead, exhausted with the afternoon's fight. In the morning she woke to yellow sunshine lying across the bed—clear sunshine, with an occasional blotch of shadow moving over it. She went to the window. Old Stephen was ahead of her. There he stood outside, gazing down over the bush. And she gazed, astounded—and entranced, much against her will. For it looked as if every tree, every bush, all the earth, were lit with pale flames. The locusts were fanning their wings to free them of the night dews. There was a shimmer of red-tinged gold light everywhere.

She went out to join the old man, stepping carefully among the insects. They stood and watched. Overhead the sky was blue, blue and clear.

"Pretty," said old Stephen, with satisfaction.

Well, thought Margaret, we may be ruined, we may be bankrupt, but not everyone has seen an army of locusts fanning their wings at dawn.

Over the slopes in the distance, a faint red smear showed in the sky, thickened and spread. "There they go," said old Stephen. "There goes the main army, off south."

And now from the trees, from the earth all round them, the locusts were taking wing. They were like small aircraft, maneuvering for the take-off, trying their wings to see if they were dry enough. Off they went. A reddish brown steam was rising off the miles of bush, off the lands, the earth. Again the sunlight darkened.

And as the clotted branches lifted, the weight on them lightening, there was nothing but the black spines of branches, trees. No green left, nothing. All morning they watched, the three of them, as the brown crust thinned and broke and dissolved, flying up to mass with the main army, now a brownish-red smear in the southern sky. The lands which had been filmed with green, the new tender mealie plants, were stark and bare. All the trees stripped. A devastated landscape. No green, no green anywhere.

By midday the reddish cloud had gone. Only an occasional locust flopped down. On the ground were the corpses and the wounded. The African laborers were sweeping these up with branches and collecting them in tins.

"Ever eaten sun-dried locust?" asked old Stephen. "That time twenty years ago, when I went broke, I lived on mealie meal and dried locusts for three months. They aren't bad at all—rather like smoked fish, if you come to think of it."

But Margaret preferred not even to think of it.

After the midday meal the men went off to the lands. Everything was to be replanted. With a bit of luck another swarm would not come traveling down just this way. But they hoped it would rain very soon, to spring some new grass, because the cattle would die otherwise—there was not a blade of grass left on the farm. As for Margaret, she was trying to get used to the idea of three or four years of locusts. Locusts were going to be like bad weather, from now on, always imminent. She felt like a survivor after war—if this devastated and mangled countryside was not ruin, well, what then was ruin?

But the men ate their supper with good appetites.

"It could have been worse," was what they said. "It could be much worse."

8

The Witness

In the mornings, when Mr. Brooke had hung his hat carefully on the nail over his desk and arranged his pipe and tobacco at his elbow, he used to turn to the others and say hopefully: "You should have just seen Twister today. He brought my newspaper from the doorstep without dropping it once." Then he looked at the polite, hostile faces; laughed a short, spluttering, nervous laugh; and bent his head to his papers.

Miss Jenkins, the private secretary, kept a peke called Darling; and she had only to mention him for everyone to listen and laugh. As for Richards, he was engaged, and they pulled his leg about it. Every time he went purple and writhed delightedly under his desk. The accountant, Miss Ives, a tart old maid who lived some proud, defiant life of her own, had a garden. When she talked about trees the office grew silent with respect. She won prizes at flower shows. There was no getting past her.

At eight, as they settled down for the day; at eleven when cups of tea came round, slopped into saucers; at three in the afternoon when they ate cream cakes—they all had something.

Mr. Brooke had bought his terrier Twister simply so that he could make them notice him sometimes. First it was a canary, but he decided at last canaries couldn't be interesting. Although Miss Jenkins' peke did nothing but eat, she could talk about it every day and get an audience, but then she was a very attractive girl. She wouldn't have been the boss's private secretary if she weren't. Mr. Brooke's dog did everything. He taught it at night, in his room, to beg and balance and wait for sugar. He used to rub its ears gratefully, thinking: It will make them sit up when I tell them he can keep perfectly still for ten minutes by the watch the office gave me when I had worked for them twenty years. He used to say things like that to himself long after he had given up trying to attract their notice.

And, after all, he had not been alone, had not added up figures from eight to four for thirty years, without making something of his own he could live from. He decided to keep the canary, because it took no room and he had come to enjoy its noise. He kept the dog, too, because it was company, of a kind. The real reason why he got rid of neither was because they annoyed his landlady, with whom he bickered continually. After office hours he used to walk home thinking that after supper he would make the dog bark so that she would come in and make a scene. These scenes usually ended in her crying; and then he could say: "I am alone in the world, too, my dear." Sometimes she made him a cup of tea before going to bed, saying bitterly, "If you won't look after yourself I suppose someone must. But don't let that damned dog spill it all over the floor."

After she had gone to bed, and there was no chance of meeting her in the passage, he cut out pictures from magazines, sent off postal orders to addresses he was careful to keep hidden from her inquisitive eyes, and was not in the least ashamed of himself. He was proud of it; it was a gesture of defiance, like getting drunk every Friday. He chose Fridays because on Saturday mornings, when he was really not fit for work, he could annoy Miss Ives by saying: "I went on the loose last night." Then he got through the hours somehow. A man was entitled to something, and he did not care for gardens.

The rest of the week he used to sit quietly at his desk, watching them talk together as if he were simply not there, and wish that Miss Jenkins' dog would get ill, and she would ask him for advice; or that Miss Ives would say: "Do help me with my ledger; I have never seen anyone who could calculate as fast as you"; or that Richards would quarrel with his girl and confide in him. He imagined himself saying: "Women! Of course! You can't tell me anything."

Other times he stood looking out of the window, listening to the talk behind him, pretending not to, pretending he was indifferent. Two stories down in the street life rushed past. Always, he felt, he had been looking out of windows. He dreamed, often, that two of the cars down below would crash into each other, and that he was the only witness. Police would come stamping up the stairs with notebooks; the typists would ask avidly "What actually happened, Mr. Brooke?"; the boss would slap him on the shoulder and say: "How lucky you saw it. I don't know what I would do without you." He imagined himself in court, giving evidence. "Yes, your worship, I always look out of the window at that time every day. I make a habit of it. I saw everything. . . ."

But there never was an accident. The police only came once, and that was to talk to Miss Jenkins when her peke got lost; and he hardly saw Mr. Jones except to nod to. It was Miss Ives who was his real boss.

He used to peep through the door of the typists'

room, where six girls worked, when the boss went through each morning, and go sick with envious admiration.

Mr. Jones was a large, red-faced man with hair grown white over the ears; and after lunch every day he smelled of beer. Nevertheless, the girls would do anything for him. He would say breezily, "Well, and how's life today?" Sometimes he put his arm round the prettiest and said, "You're too cute to keep long. You'll be getting married. . . ." He said it as if he were handing out medals, something one had to do, part of his job. It's only to make them work harder, thought Mr. Brooke bitterly, surreptitiously shutting the door and listening to how the typewriters started clattering furiously the moment Mr. Jones left. Then he used to go to the washroom and look at his own face in the glass. He had no white hair himself; he was quite a goodlooking man, he thought. But if he put his arm round a girl's shoulder he would get his face slapped, he knew that.

It was the year he was fifty-five, retiring age, that Marnie de Kok came into the office as a junior, straight from school. Mr. Brooke did not want to leave off working. He couldn't live on what he had saved; and in any case the office was all he had. For some weeks he looked crumpled up with apprehension; but Mr. Jones said nothing, and after a while he took heart again. He did not want to think about it; and besides, with Marnie there everything was changed. After one morning there was a different feeling in the office.

She was a girl of eighteen from some little dorp miles away, the youngest of ten children. She had a small plump, fresh face that always had a look of delighted expectation, and a shrill, expressive voice, and was as slim and as quick as a fish. She darted about the place, talking to the staff as if it had never entered her head anyone in the world could not be pleased to waste his time on her account. She shattered the sacred silence of the main office with her gossip about her family; sat on the desks and swung her legs; put vases of flowers among the telephones. And even Miss Ives took off her glasses and watched her. They all watched her; and particularly Mr. Jones, who made plenty of excuses to leave his desk, with the indulgent, amused, faintly ironic smile with which one looks at children, remembering what all that fearlessness and charm is going to come to. As for Mr. Brooke, he couldn't keep his eyes off her. For a while he was afraid to speak, for Marnie, like the others, seemed not to know he was there; and when he did, she looked at him with startled distaste, a look he was used to, though it in no way corresponded with what he felt about himself. She might be my daughter, he said to himself defensively; and he used to ask her with whom she ate lunch, what picture she had seen the night before, as a jealous lover can't resist talking about his mistress, feeling that even to speak about what she has been doing robs it of its danger, makes the extraordinary and wonderful life she leads apart from him, in some way his. But Marnie answered shortly, or not at all, wrinkling up her nose.

Even that he found attractive. What was so charming about her was her directness, the simplicity of her responses. She knew nothing of the secret sycophancy of the office that made the typists speak to Mr. Jones in one voice and Miss Ives in another. She treated everyone as if she had known them always. She was as confiding as a child, read her letters out loud, jumped with joy when parcels came from home, and wept when someone suggested gently that there were better ways of doing her work.

131

For she was catastrophically inefficient. She was supposed to learn filing; but in actual fact she made the tea, slipped over to the teashop across the road ten times a day for cream cakes, and gave people advice about their colds or how to make their dresses.

The other typists, who were after all her natural enemies, were taken by surprise and treated her with the tenderest indulgence. It was because it occurred to no one that she could last out the first month. But Miss Ives made out her second paycheck, which was very generous, with a grim face, and snubbed her until she cried.

It was Miss Ives, who was afraid of nothing, who at last walked into Mr. Jones's office and said that the child was impossible and most leave at once. As it was the files would take months to get straight. No one could find anything.

She came back to her desk looking grimmer than ever, her lips twitching.

She said angrily, "I've kept myself for twenty-seven years this March. I've never had anything. How many women have the qualifications I have? I should have had a pretty face." And then she burst into tears. It was mild hysterics. Mr. Brooke was the first to fuss around with water and handkerchiefs. No one had ever seen Miss Ives cry.

And what about? All Mr. Jones had said was that Marnie was the daughter of an old school friend and he had promised to look after her. If she was no good at filing, then she must be given odd jobs.

"Is this an office or a charitable institution?" demanded Miss Ives. "I've never seen anything like this, never." And then she turned to Mr. Brooke, who was leaning ineffectually over her, and said, "There are other people who should go too. I suppose he was a friend of your father? Getting drunk and making a

132

pig of yourself. Pictures of girls in your desk, and putting grease on your hair in the washrooms. . . ."

Mr. Brooke went white, tried to find words, looked helplessly round for support to Miss Jenkins and Richards. They did not meet his eyes. He felt as if they were dealing him invisible blows on the face; but after a few moments Miss Ives put away her handkerchief, picked up her pen with a gesture of endurance, and went back to her ledger. No one looked at Mr. Brooke.

He made himself forget it. She was hysterical, he said. Women would say anything. He knew from what men had told him that there were times you should take no notice of them. An old maid, too, he said spitefully, wishing he could say it aloud, forgetting that she, too, had made of her weakness a strength, and that she could not be hurt long by him, any more than he could by her.

But that was not the only case of hysteria. It seemed extraordinary that for years these people had worked together, making the same jokes, asking after each other's health, borrowing each other's things, and then everything went wrong from one day to the next.

For instance, one of the typists wept with rage all of one morning because Mr. Jones sent back a letter to be retyped. Such a thing had never been known. Such was his manner, as a rule, that a reprimand was almost as warming as praise.

As for Marnie herself, she was like a small child who does not know why it had been slapped. She wandered about the office miserably, sniffing a little, until by chance Mr. Jones saw her and asked what was wrong. She began to cry, and he took her into his room. The door was shut for over an hour while clients waited. When she came out, subdued but cheerful, the typists cold-shouldered her. Then she rushed into Miss Ives and asked if she could move her desk in to the main office, because the other girls were "nasty" to her. Very naturally Miss Ives was unsympathetic, and she cried again, with her head among the papers on Mr. Brooke's desk. It happened to be the nearest.

It was lunch hour. Everyone left but Marnie and Mr. Brooke. The repugnance she felt for this elderly man with the greasy faded hair, the creased white hands, the intimate unpleasant eyes, melted in the violence of her misery. She allowed him to stroke her hair. She cried on his shoulder as she had cried on Mr. Jones's shoulder that morning.

"No one likes me," she sobbed.

"Of course everyone like you."

"Only Mr. Jones likes me."

"But Mr. Jones is the boss . . ." stammered Mr. Brooke, appalled at her incredible ingenuousness. His heart ached for her. He caressed the damp bundle huddled over his desk gently, paternally, wanting only to console her. "If you could just remember this is an office, Marnie."

"I don't want to work in an office. I want to go home. I want my mother. I want Mr. Jones to send me home. He says I can't. He says he will look after me. . . ."

When they heard steps on the stairs Mr. Brooke guiltily slipped back to his corner; and Marnie stood up, sullen and defiant, to face Miss Ives, who ignored her. Marnie dragged her feet across the floor to the typists' room.

"I suppose you have been encouraging her," said Miss Ives. "She needs a good spanking. I'll give it to her myself soon."

"She's homesick," he said.

134

"What about her stepfather in there?" snapped Miss Ives, jerking her head at Mr. Jones's door.

"He's sorry for her," said Mr. Brooke, defending his own new feeling of protectiveness for the girl.

"Some people have no eyes in their heads," she said unpleasantly. "Taking her to the pictures. Taking her to dinner every night. I suppose that is being sorry for her, too?"

"Yes, it is," said Mr. Brooke hotly. But he was sick with dismay and anger. He wanted to hit Miss Ives, wanted to run into Mr. Jones's room and hit him, wanted to do something desperate. But he sat himself down at his desk and began adding figures. He was behindhand as usual. "Slow but sure, that's what I am," he said to himself, as always, when he saw how the work piled up and he never was level with it. But that afternoon Miss Ives returned him three sheets of calculations and said "Try to be more accurate, Mr. Brooke, *if* you please."

At four, when Mr. Jones came through the front office on his way home, Marnie was waiting to catch his eyes. He stopped, smiling; then realized the entire staff were watching, and went on, reddening.

Marnie's lips quivered again.

"More rain coming," said Miss Ives acidly.

"Can I take you to your bus stop?" asked Mr. Brooke, defying Miss Ives. There was laughter from the open door of the typists' room. Mr. Brooke had heard that kind of laugh too often, after he had left a room, to care about it now. Marnie tossed her head at Miss Ives. "I should be pleased," she said daintily.

They walked down the stairs, she racing in front, he trying to keep up. She seemed to dance down the street; the sun was shining; it dazzled in her bright hair. Mr. Brooke was panting, smiling, trying to find breath to talk. He knew that above their heads Miss Ives and the others were leaning over the sill and watching them with scornful disgusted faces. He did not care; but when he saw Mr. Jones come out of a shop, as if he had been waiting for Marnie, he stopped guiltily and said "Good night, sir."

Mr. Jones nodded, not looking at him. To Marnie he said, smiling gently, "Feeling happier? Don't worry, you won't be in an office for long. Some lucky man will marry you soon." It was the sort of thing he said to his typists. But not as he said it now.

Marnie laughed, ran up to him, kissed his cheek.

"Well!" said Mr. Jones, looking fatuously pleased. He glared over Marnie's head at Mr. Brooke, who hurried off down the street as if he had been given an order, without looking around. Soon he heard Marnie pattering up behind him.

"You shouldn't have done that," he said reproachfully.

Her face was happy, guileless. "He's like my dad," she said.

At the bus stop Mr. Brooke suddenly could not bear to see her go. He caught her arm and said, "Come to my place and see my dog Twister. You would like him."

She said, "You know, I didn't like you at first. I do now."

"My dog can fetch the newspaper in the morning," he said. "He never tears it."

"I like dogs," she said confidingly, as if it were the most surprising news in the world.

When they reached his room he was so proud, so flustered, that he could only look at her and smile. He unlocked it with shaking hands and dropped the key when he saw the landlady peeping through her

136

window. Marnie picked it up and went before him into his room as if taking possession of it.

"What a nice room," she said. "But it's too small. If you moved your bed. . . ."

She darted over to the divan he slept on and pushed it across a corner. Then she patted cushions, moved a chair, and turned to him. "That's much better," she said. "I'm good at this sort of thing. I'm a home girl. That's what my mum says. She didn't want me to come to an office. Dad and Mr. Jones fixed it up."

"Your mother is quite right," said Mr. Brooke devotedly.

It was then she paused to look about her, and it was then her face changed and Mr. Brooke slowly went cold. He saw the room with her eyes, and saw himself, too, as she would see him henceforward.

It was a small room, with patterned wallpaper, all roses and ribbons. The canary hung in the window, the dog's basket was under the bed. There was nothing else of Mr. Brooke in the room that had been inhabited by so many people before him. Except the pictures, which covered most of the wallpaper.

Marnie moved forward slowly, with a queer hunching of her shoulders, as if a draught blew on them, and Mr. Brooke went after her, unconsciously holding out his hands behind her back in appeal.

"I must buy some pictures," he said, trying to sound casual.

There were film stars, bathing beauties, half-nude women all over his walls, dozens of them.

He knew, instinctively, that he should ask for her pity, as she had asked for his. He said "I can't afford to buy pictures."

But when she turned toward him at last, he knew his expression must be wrong, for she searched his

137

face, and looked as if she had trodden on something unpleasant.

"I had forgotten about them," he cried, truthfully and desperately. Then: "I'm not like that, Marnie, not really."

Her hand swung out and stung his cheek. "You dirty old man," she said. "You dirty, dirty old man."

She ran out of his room, and as she went the landlady came in.

"Baby-snatching?" she said. "You can't have women here, I told you."

"She's my daughter," said Mr. Brooke.

The door slammed. He sat on his bed and looked at the walls, and felt, for just a few moments, old and mean and small. Then he recovered himself and said aloud: "Well, and what do you expect, making me live alone?" He was addressing, not only Marnie and the landlady, but all the women he had seen in the street, or on the screen, or eating at the next table.

"You wouldn't have stayed, anyway," he muttered at last. He began tearing the pictures off the walls. Then he slowly put them back again. He even cut out a new one from a paper called *Parisian Fancies*, which he had sent for because of an advertisement, and hung it immediately over his bed. "That will give you something to think about," he said to the landlady, whom he could hear stomping about in the next room. Then he went out and got very drunk indeed.

Next morning the landlady saw the picture while he was in his bath, and told him he must go or she would fetch the police. "Indecent exposure, that's what it is," she said.

"Do you think I care?" said Mr. Brooke.

He was still a little drunk when he reached the office. He walked in aggressively, and at once Miss

Ives sniffed and stared at him. She got up immediately and went in to Mr. Jones's room. Mr. Jones came out with her and said "If you do this again, Brooke, you must go. There's a limit to everything."

Through the open door, Mr. Brooke could see Marnie swinging herself round and round in Mr. Jones's big chair, eating sweets.

Toward the middle of the morning Miss Jenkins started to cry and said, "Either she goes or I do."

"Don't worry," said Miss Ives. She nodded her head up and down significantly. "It won't last. Something will happen, one way or the other. Things can't go on like this." Miss Jenkins went home, saying she had a headache. Richards went in to Mr. Jones's office for something and came out, too angry to speak. The typewriters were silent next door. No one did any work except Miss Ives. It seemed everyone was waiting.

At lunchtime they all left early. Mr. Brooke stayed in the office. His head ached, his limbs were stiff, and he couldn't face the two flights of stairs. He ate sandwiches and then went to sleep with his head on his desk. When he woke he was still alone. He could not think clearly and wondered for a moment where he was. Then he saw flies gathering over the crumbs on his papers and got up stiffly to fetch a duster. The door into the typists' room was closed. He opened it a few inches and peered cautiously through. He thought for a moment he was still asleep, for there were Marnie and Mr. Jones. His face was buried in her hair, and he was saying "Please Marnie, please, please, please . . ." as if he were drunk.

Mr. Brooke stared, his eyes focusing with difficulty. Then Marnie gave a little scream and Mr. Jones jumped up. "Spying!" he said angrily.

Mr. Brooke had lost his breath. His mouth fell open; his hands spread out helplessly. Finally, he said to Marnie "Why didn't you slap *his* face?"

She ran across the room shouting, "You dirty old man, you dirty old man!"

"He's older than I am."

"You shut up, Brooke," said Mr. Jones.

"He has grown-up children. He has grandchildren, Marnie."

Mr. Jones lifted his fist; but at that moment Marnie said triumphantly, "I'm going to marry him. I'm going to get married. So there!" Mr. Jones dropped his arm; and his angry red face became slowly complacent, grateful, adoring.

Mr. Brooke saw that she had said that for the first time; that if he had not entered perhaps she would never have said it.

He looked at Mr. Jones, and out of his knowledge of himself hated him, but with a small feeling of envious admiration. The confused thought in his mind was: If he had pictures he would be careful to keep them hidden.

After a while, he said, half-pityingly, half-spitefully, to Marnie, "You are a silly little girl. You'll be sorry." Then he turned and groped his way out, holding on to the walls.

Later in the afternoon Miss Ives brought him a check. He was dismissed with a bonus of ten pounds. Ten pounds for thirty years' work! He was too numbed to notice it.

"Did you know she was marrying him?" he asked Miss Ives, wanting to see her made angry.

But she sounded pleased. "He told us just now."

"He's older than I am. . . ."

"Serves her right," snapped Miss Ives. "Little fool like that. It's all she's good for. Getting married.

That's all these girls think of. She'll learn what men are."

And then she handed him his hat and began gently pushing him to the door. "You'd better go," she said, but not unkindly. "He doesn't want to see you again. He said so. And you look after yourself. You can't go drinking like that, at your age."

Then she shut the door behind him. When he saw he was quite alone in the passage he began to laugh. He laughed hysterically for some time. Then he went slowly and carefully down the stairs, holding his hat in one hand and his fountain pen in the other. He began to walk down the street, but at the corner he came back, and waited at the foot of the stairs. He wanted to say goodbye to the people he had worked with so long. He could imagine them saying in the typists' room: "What! old Brooke has gone, has he? I am sorry I didn't have a chance to see him before he left."

9

Flavors of Exile

At the foot of the hill, near the well, was the vegetable garden, an acre fenced off from the Big Field where the earth was so rich that mealies grew there, year after year, ten feet tall. Nursed from that fabulous soil, carrots, lettuces, beets, tasting as I have never found vegetables taste since, loaded our table and the tables of our neighbors. Sometimes, if the garden boy was late with the supply for lunch, I would run down the steep pebbly path through the trees at the back of the hill and along the red dust of the wagon road until I could see the windlass under its shed of thatch. There I stopped. The smell of manure, of sun on foliage, of evaporating water, rose to my head; two steps farther, and I could look down into the vegetable garden enclosed within its tall pale of reeds—rich chocolate earth studded emerald green, frothed with the white of cauliflowers, jeweled with the purple globes of eggplant and the scarlet wealth of tomatoes. Around the fence grew lemons, pawpaws, bananas—shapes of gold and yellow in their patterns of green.

In another five minutes I would be dragging from the earth carrots ten inches long, so succulent they snapped between two fingers. I ate my allowance of these before the cook could boil them and drown them in the white flour sauce without which—and unless they were served in the large china vegetable dishes brought from that old house in London—they were not carrots to my mother.

For her, that garden represented a defeat.

When the family first came to the farm, she built vegetable beds on the *kopje* near the house. She had in her mind, perhaps, a vision of the farmhouse surrounded by outbuildings and gardens like a hen sheltering its chicks.

The *kopje* was all stone. As soon as the grass was cleared off its crown where the house stood, the fierce rain beat the soil away. Those first vegetable beds were thin sifted earth walled by pebbles. The water was brought up from the well in the water cart.

"Water is gold," grumbled my father, eating peas which, he reckoned, must cost a shilling a mouthful. "Water is gold!" he came to shout at last, as my mother toiled and bent over those reluctant beds. But she got more pleasure from them than she ever did from the exhaustless plenty of the garden under the hill.

At last, the spaces in the bush where the old beds had been were seeded by wild or vagrant plants, and we children played there. Someone must have thrown away gooseberries, for soon the low-spreading bushes covered the earth. We used to creep under them, William MacGregor and I, lie flat on our backs, and look through the leaves at the brilliant sky, reaching around us for the tiny sharp-sweet yellow fruits in their jackets of papery white. The smell of the leaves was spicy. It intoxicated us. We would laugh and shout, then quarrel; and William, to make up, shelled a double handful of the fruit and poured it into my skirt, and we ate together, pressing the biggest berries on each other. When we could eat no more, we filled baskets and took them to the kitchen to be made into that rich jam, which, if allowed to burn just the right amount on the pan, is the best jam in the world—clear sweet amber, with lumps of sticky sharpness in it, as if the stings of bees were preserved in honey.

But my mother did not like it. "Cape gooseberries!" she said bitterly. "They aren't gooseberries at all. Oh, if I could let you taste a pie made of real English gooseberries."

In due course, the marvels of civilization made this possible; she found a tin of gooseberries in the Greek store at the station and made us a pie.

My parents and William's ate the pie with a truly religious emotion.

It was this experience with the gooseberries that made me cautious when it came to Brussels sprouts. Year after year my mother yearned for Brussels sprouts, whose name came to represent to me something exotic and forever unattainable. When at last she managed to grow half a dozen spikes of this plant in one cold winter that offered us sufficient frost, she of course sent a note to the MacGregors, so that they might share the treat. They came from Glasgow, they came from Home, and they could share the language of nostalgia. At the table the four grownups ate the bitter little cabbages and agreed that the soil of Africa was unable to grow food that had any taste at all. I said scornfully that I couldn't see what all the fuss was about. But William, three years older than myself, passed his plate up and said he found them delicious. It was like a betrayal; and afterward I demanded how he could like such flavorless stuff. He smiled at me and said it cost us nothing to pretend, did it?

That smile, so gentle, a little whimsical, was a lesson to me; and I remembered it when it came to the affair of the cherries. She found a tin of cherries at the store, we ate them with cream; and while she sighed over

145

memories of barrows loaded with cherries in the streets of London, I sighed with her, ate fervently, and was careful not to meet her eyes.

And when she said: "The pomegranates will be fruiting soon," I offered to run down and see how they progressed. I returned from the examination saying: "It won't be long now, really it won't—perhaps next year."

The truth was, my emotion over the pomegranates was not entirely due to the beautiful lesson in courtesy given me by William. Brussels sprouts, cherries, English gooseberries—they were my mother's; they recurred in her talk as often as "a real London peasouper," or "chestnuts by the fire," or "cherry blossom at Kew." I no longer grudged these to her; I listened and was careful not to show that my thoughts were on my own inheritance of veldt and sun. But pomegranates were an exotic for my mother; and therefore more easily shared with her. She had been in Persia, where, one understood, pomegranate juice ran in rivers. The wife of a minor official, she had lived in a vast stone house cooled by water trickling down a thousand stone channels from the mountains; she had lived among roses and jasmine, walnut trees and pomegranates. But, unfortunately, for too short a time.

Why not pomegranates here, in Africa? Why not?

The four trees had been planted at the same time as the first vegetable beds; and almost at once two of them died. A third lingered on for a couple of seasons and then succumbed to the white ants. The fourth stood lonely among the Cape gooseberry bushes, bore no fruit, and at last was forgotten.

Then one day my mother was showing Mrs. MacGregor her chickens; and as they returned through tangles of grass and weed, their skirts lifted

146

high in both hands, my mother exclaimed: "Why, I do believe the pomegranate is fruiting at last. Look, look, it is!" She called to us, the children, and we went running, and stood around a small thorny tree, and looked at a rusty-red fruit the size of a child's fist. "It's ripe," said my mother, and pulled it off.

Inside the house we were each given a dozen small seeds on saucers. They were bitter, but we did not like to ask for sugar. Mrs. MacGregor said gently: "It's wonderful. How you must miss all that!"

"The roses!" said my mother. "And sacks of walnuts . . . and we used to drink pomegranate juice with the melted snow water . . . nothing here tastes like that. The soil is no good."

I looked at William, sitting opposite to me. He turned his head and smiled. I fell in love.

He was then fifteen, home for the holidays. He was a silent boy, thoughtful; and the quietness in his deep gray eyes seemed to me like a promise of warmth and understanding I had never known. There was a tightness in my chest, because it hurt to be shut out from the world of simple kindness he lived in. I sat there, opposite to him, and said to myself that I had known him all my life and yet until this moment had never understood what he was. I looked at those extraordinarily clear eyes, that were like water over gray pebbles; I gazed and gazed, until he gave me a slow, direct look tht showed he knew I had been staring. It was like a warning, as if a door had been shut.

After the MacGregors had gone, I went through the bushes to the pomegranate tree. It was about my height, a tough, obstinate-looking thing; and there was a round yellow ball the size of a walnut hanging from a twig.

I looked at the ugly little tree and thought, Pomegranates! Breasts like pomegranates and a belly like a heap of wheat! The golden pomegranates of the sun, I thought . . . pomegranates like the red of blood.

I was in a fever, more than a little mad. The space of thick grass and gooseberry bushes between the trees was haunted by William; and his deep, calm, gray eyes looked at me across the pomegranate tree.

Next day I sat under the tree. It gave no shade, but the acrid sunlight was barred and splotched under it. There was hard, cracked, red earth beneath a covering of silvery dead grass. Under the grass I saw grains of red and half a hard brown shell. It seemed that a fruit had ripened and burst without our knowing—yes, everywhere in the soft old grass lay the tiny crimson seeds. I tasted one; warm sweet juice flooded my tongue. I gathered them up and ate them until my mouth was full of dry seeds. I spat them out and thought that a score of pomegranate trees would grow from that mouthful.

As I watched, tiny black ants came scurrying along the roots of the grass, scrambling over the fissures in the earth, to snatch away the seeds. I lay on my elbow and watched. A dozen of them were levering at a still unbroken seed. Suddenly the frail tissue split as they bumped it over a splinter, and they were caught in a sticky red ooze.

The ants would carry these seeds for hundreds of yards; there would be an orchard of pomegranates. William MacGregor would come visiting with his parents and find me among the pomegranate trees; I could hear the sound of his grave voice mingled with the tinkle of camel bells and the splashing of falling water.

I went to the tree every day and lay under it, watching the single yellow fruit ripening on its twig. There would come a moment when it must burst and scatter crimson seeds; I must be there when it did; it

148

seemed as if my whole life was concentrated and ripening with that single fruit.

It was very hot under the tree. My head ached. My flesh was painful with the sun. Yet there I sat all day, watching the tiny ants at their work, letting them run over my legs, waiting for the pomegranate fruit to ripen. It swelled slowly; it seemed set on reaching perfection, for when it was the size that the other had been picked, it was still a bronzing yellow, and the rind was soft. It was going to be a big fruit, the size of both my fists.

Then something terrifying happened. One day I saw that the twig it hung from was splitting off the branch. The wizened, dry little tree could not sustain the weight of the fruit it had produced. I went to the house, brought down bandages from the medicine chest, and strapped the twig firm and tight to the branch, in such a way that the weight was supported. Then I wet the bandage, tenderly, and thought of William, William, William. I wet the bandage daily, and thought of him.

What I thought of William had become a world, stronger than anything around me. Yet, since I was mad, so weak, it vanished at a touch. Once, for instance, I saw him, driving with his father on the wagon along the road to the station. I remember I was ashamed that that marvelous feverish world should depend on a half-grown boy in dusty khaki, gripping a piece of grass between his teeth as he stared ahead of him. It came to this—that in order to preserve the dream, I must not see William. And it seemed he felt something of the sort himself, for in all those weeks he never came near me, whereas once he used to come every day. And yet I was convinced it must happen that William and the moment when the pomegranate split open would coincide.

I imagined it in a thousand ways, as the fruit continued to grow. Now, it was a clear bronze yellow with faint rust-colored streaks. The rind was thin, so soft that the swelling seeds within were shaping it. The fruit looked lumpy and veined, like a nursing breast. The small crown where the stem fastened on it, which had been the sheath of the flower, was still green. It began to harden and turn back into iron-gray thorns.

Soon, soon, it would be ripe. Very swiftly, the skin lost its smooth thinness. It took on a tough, pored look, like the skin of an old weatherbeaten countryman. It was a ruddy scarlet now, and hot to the touch. A small crack appeared, which in a day had widened so that the packed red seeds within were visible, almost bursting out. I did not dare leave the tree. I was there from six in the morning until the sun went down. I even crept down with the candle at night, although I argued it could not burst at night, not in the cool of the night; it must be the final unbearable thrust of the hot sun that would break it.

For three days nothing happened. The crack remained the same. Ants swarmed up the trunk, along the branches, and into the fruit. The scar oozed red juice in which black ants swam and struggled. At any moment it might happen. And William did not come. I was sure he would; I watched the empty road helplessly, waiting for him to come striding along, a piece of grass between his teeth, to me and the pomegranate tree. Yet he did not. In one night, the crack split another half inch. I saw a red seed push itself out of the crack and fall. Instantly it was borne off by the ants into the grass.

I went up to the house and asked my mother when the MacGregors were coming to tea.

"I don't know, dear. Why?"

"Because. I just thought. . . ."

She looked at me. Her eyes were critical. In one moment, she would say the name "William." I struck first. To have William and the moment together, I must pay fee to the family gods. "There's a pomegranate nearly ripe, and you know how interested Mrs. MacGregor is. . . ."

She looked sharply at me. "Pick it, and we'll make a drink of it."

"Oh, no, it's not quite ready. Not altogether. . . ."

"Silly child," she said at last. She went to the telephone and said: "Mrs. MacGregor, this daughter of mine, she's got it into her head—you know how children are."

I did not care. At four that afternoon I was waiting by the pomegranate tree. Their car came thrusting up the steep road to the crown of the hill. There was Mr. MacGregor in his khaki, Mrs. MacGregor in her best afternoon dress—and William. The adults shook hands, kissed. William did not turn round and look at me. It was not possible, it was monstrous, that the force of my dream should not have had the power to touch him at all, that he knew nothing of what he must do.

Then he slowly turned his head and looked down the slope to where I stood. He did not smile. It seemed he had not seen me, for his eyes traveled past me, and back to the grownups. He stood to one side while they exchanged their news and greetings; and then all four laughed, and turned to look at me and my tree. It seemed for a moment they were all coming. At once, however, they went into the house, William trailing after them, frowning.

In a moment he would have gone in; the space in

front of the old house would be empty. I called "William!" I had not known I would call. My voice sounded small in the wide afternoon sunlight.

He went on as if he had not heard. Then he stopped, seemed to think, and came down the hill toward me while I anxiously examined his face. The low tangle of the gooseberry bushes was around his legs, and he swore sharply.

"Look at the pomegranate," I said. He came to a halt beside the tree, and looked. I was searching those clear gray eyes now for a trace of that indulgence they had shown my mother over the Brussels sprouts, over that first unripe pomegranate. Now all I wanted was indulgence; I abandoned everything else.

"It's full of ants," he said at last.

"Only a little, only where it's cracked."

He stood, frowning, chewing at his piece of grass. His lips were full and thin-skinned; and I could see the blood, dull and dark around the pale groove where the grass stem pressed.

The pomegranate hung there, swarming with ants.

"Now," I thought wildly, "now—crack now."

There was not a sound. The sun came pouring down, hot and yellow, drawing up the smell of the grasses. There was, too, a faint sour smell from the fermenting juice of the pomegranate.

"It's bad," said William, in that uncomfortable, angry voice. "And what's that bit of dirty rag for?"

"It was breaking, the twig was breaking off—I tied it up."

"Mad," he remarked, aside, to the afternoon. "Quite mad." He was looking about him in the grass. He reached down and picked up a stick.

"No," I cried out, as he hit at the tree. The pomegranate flew into the air and exploded in a scatter of crimson seeds, fermenting juice, and black ants.

The cracked empty skin, with its white, clean-looking inner skin faintly stained with juice, lay in two fragments at my feet.

He was poking sulkily with the stick at the little scarlet seeds that lay everywhere on the earth.

Then he did look at me. Those clear eyes were grave again, thoughtful, and judging. They held that warning I had seen in them before.

"That's your pomegranate," he said at last.

"Yes," I said.

He smiled, "We'd better go up, if we want any tea."

We went together up the hill to the house, and as we entered the room where the grownups sat over the teacups, I spoke quickly, before he could. In a bright, careless voice I said: "It was bad, after all; the ants had got at it. It should have been picked before."

10

Getting Off the Altitude

That night of the dance, years later, when I saw Mrs. Slatter come into the bedroom at midnight, not seeing me because the circle of lamplight was focused low, with a cold and terrible face I never would have believed could be hers after knowing her so long during the daytimes and the visits—that night, when she had dragged herself out of the room again, still not knowing I was there, I went to the mirror to see my own face. I held the lamp as close as I could and looked into my face. For I had not known before that a person's face could be smooth and comfortable, though often sorrowful, like Molly Slatter's had been all those years, and then hard-set, in the solitude away from the dance and the people (that night they had drunk a great deal and the voices of the singing reminded me of when dogs howl at the full moon), into an old and patient stone. Yes, her face looked like white stone that the rain has trickled over and worn through the wet seasons.

My face, that night in the mirror, dusted yellow from the lamplight, with the dark watery spaces of the glass behind, was smooth and enquiring, with the pert, flattered look of a girl in her first long dress and dancing with the young people for the first time. There was nothing in it, a girl's face, empty. Yet I had been crying just before, and I wished then I could go away into the dark and stay there forever. Yet Molly Slatter's terrible face was familiar to me, as if it were her own face, her real one. I seemed to know it. And that meant that the years I had known her, comfortable and warm in spite of all her troubles, had been saying something else to me about her. But only now I was prepared to listen.

I left the mirror, set the lamp down on the dressing table, went out into the passage, and looked for her among the people; and there she was in her red satin dress, looking just as usual, talking to my father, her hand on the back of his chair, smiling down at him.

"It hasn't been a bad season, Mr. Farquar," she was saying. "The rains haven't done us badly at all."

Driving home in the car that night, my mother asked, "What was Molly saying to you?"

And my father said, "Oh I don't know, I really don't know." His voice was sad and angry.

She said, "That dress of hers. Her evening dresses look like a cheap night club."

He said, troubled and sorrowful, "Yes. Actually I said something to her."

"Somebody should."

"No," he said, quick against the cold criticizing voice. "No. It's a—pretty color. But I said to her, 'There's not much *to* that dress, is there?' "

"What did she say?"

"She was hurt. I was sorry I said anything."

"H'mm," said my mother, with a little laugh.

He turned his head from his driving, so that the car lights swung wild over the rutted track for a moment, and said direct at her: "She's a good woman. She's a nice woman."

But she gave another offended gulp of laughter. As a woman insists in an argument because she won't give in, even when she knows she is wrong.

As for me, I saw that dress again, with its crisscross of narrow, sweat-darkened straps over the aging white back; and I saw Mrs. Slatter's face when my father criticized her. I might have been there, I saw it so clearly. She colored, lifted her head, lowered her lids so that the tears would not show, and she said, "I'm sorry you feel like that, Mr. Farquar." It was with dignity. Yes. She had put on that dress in order to say something. But my father did not approve. He had said so.

She cared what my father said. They cared very much for each other. She called him Mr. Farquar always, and he called her Molly; and when the Slatters came over to tea, and Mr. Slatter was being brutal, there was a gentleness and a respect for her in my father's manner that made even Mr. Slatter feel it and even, sometimes, repeat something he had said to his wife in a lower voice, although it was still impatient.

The first time I knew my father felt for Molly Slatter and that my mother grudged it to her was when I was perhaps seven or eight. Their house was six miles away over the veldt, but ten by the road. Their house, like ours, was on a ridge. At the end of the dry season, when the trees were low and the leaves thinning, we could see their lights flash out at sundown, low and yellow across the miles of country. My father, after coming back from seeing Mr. Slatter about some farm matter, stood by our window looking at their lights, and my mother watched him. Then he said, "Perhaps she should stand up to him? No, that's *not* it. She does, in her way. But Lord, he's a tough customer—Slatter."

My mother said, her head low over her sewing: "She married him."

He let his eyes swing around at her, startled. Then he laughed. "That's right, she married him."

157

"Well?"

"Oh, come off it, old girl," he said, almost gay, laughing and hard. Then, still laughing angrily, he went over and kissed her on the cheek.

"I like Molly," she said, defensive. "I like her. She hasn't got what you might call conversation, but I like her."

"Living with Slatter, I daresay she's got used to keeping her mouth shut."

When Molly Slatter came over to spend the day with my mother the two women talked eagerly for hours about household things. Then, when my father came in for tea or dinner, there was a lock of sympathies and my mother looked ironical while he went to sit by Mrs. Slatter, even if only for a minute, saying: "Well, Molly? Everything all right with you?"

"I'm very well, thank you, Mr. Farquar, and so are the children."

Most people were frightened of Mr. Slatter. There were four Slatter boys, and when the old man was in a temper and waving the whip he always had with him, they ran off into the bush and stayed there until he had cooled down. All the natives on their farm were afraid of him. Once when he knew their house-boy had stolen some soap he tied him to a tree in the garden without food and water all of one day, and then through the night, and beat him with his whip every time he went past, until the boy confessed. And once, when he had hit a farm boy, and the boy complained to the police, Mr. Slatter tied the boy to his horse and rode it at a gallop to the police station twelve miles off and made the boy run beside, and told him if he complained to the police again he would kill him. Then he paid the ten-shilling fine and made the boy run beside the horse all the way back again.

I was so frightened of him that I could feel myself begin trembling when I saw his car turning to come up the drive from the farmlands.

He was a square, fair man, with small sandy-lashed blue eyes and small puffed cracked lips and red ugly hands. He used to come up the wide red shining steps of the veranda, grinning slightly, looking at us. Then he would take a handful of towhair from the heads of whichever of his sons were nearest, one in each fist, and tighten his fists slowly, not saying a word, while they stood grinning back and their eyes filled slowly. He would grin over their heads at Molly Slatter, while she sat silent, saying nothing. Then, one or other of the boys would let out a sound of pain, and Mr. Slatter showed his small discolored teeth in a grin of triumphant good humor and let them both go. Then he stamped off in his big farm boots into the house.

Mrs. Slatter would say to her sons, "Don't cry. Your father doesn't know his own strength. Don't cry." And she went on sewing, composed and pale.

Once, at the station, the Slatter car and ours were drawn up side by side outside the store. Mrs. Slatter was sitting in the front seat, beside the driver's seat. In our car my father drove and my mother was beside him. We children were in the back seats. Mr. Slatter came out of the bar with Mrs. Pritt and stood on the store veranda talking to her. He stood before her legs apart, in his way of standing, head back on his shoulders, eyes narrowed, grinning, red fists loose at his sides, and talked on for something like half an hour. Meanwhile Mrs. Pritt let her weight slump on to one hip and lolled in front of him. She wore a tight, shrill green dress, so short it showed the balls of her thin knees.

And my father leaned out of our car window,

159

though we had all our stores in and might very well leave for home now, and talked steadily and gently to Mrs. Slatter, who was quiet, not looking at her husband, but making conversation with my father and across him to my mother. And so they went on talking until Mr. Slatter left Mrs. Pritt and slammed himself into the driver's seat and started the car.

I did not like Mrs. Pritt and I knew neither of my parents did. She was a thin, wiry, tall woman with black, short, jumpy hair. She had a sharp, knowing face and a sudden laugh like the scream of a hen caught by the leg. Her voice was always loud, and she laughed a great deal.

But seeing Mr. Slatter with her was enough to know that they fitted. She was not gentle and kindly like Mrs. Slatter. She was as tough in her own way as Mr. Slatter. And long before I ever heard it said I knew well enough that, as my mother said primly, they liked each other. I asked her, meaning her to tell the truth, "Why does Mr. Slatter always go over when Mr. Pritt is away?" And she said, "I expect Mr. Slatter likes her."

In our district, with thirty or forty families on the farms spread over a hundred square miles or so, nothing happened privately. That day at the station I must have been ten years old, or eleven; but it was not the first or the last time I heard the talk between my parents:

My father: "I daresay it could make things easier for Molly."

She, then: "Do you?"

"But if he's got to have an affair, he might at least not push it down our throats, for Molly's sake."

And she: "Does he have to have an affair?"

She said the word "affair" with difficulty. It was not her language. Nor, and that was what she was protesting against, my father's. For they were both conventional and religious people. Yet at moments of crisis, at moments of scandal and irregularity, my father spoke this other language, cool and detached, as if he were born to it.

"A man like Slatter," he said thoughtfully, as if talking to another man, "it's obvious. And Emmy Pritt. Yes. Obviously, obviously! But it depends on how Molly takes it. Because if she doesn't take it the right way, she could make it hell for herself."

"*Take it the right way,*" said my mother, with bright protesting eyes, and my father did not answer.

I used to stay with Mrs. Slatter sometimes during the holidays. I went across country over the *kaffir* paths, walking or on my bicycle, with some clothes in a small suitcase.

The boys were, from having to stand up to Mr. Slatter, tough and indifferent boys, and went about the farm in a closed gang. They did man's work, driving tractors and superintending the gangs of boys before they were in their teens. I stayed with Mrs. Slatter. She cooked a good deal and sewed and gardened. Most of the day she sat on the veranda, sewing. We did not talk much. She used to make her own dresses, cotton prints and pastel linens, like all the women of the district wore. She made Mr. Slatter's khaki farm shirts and the boys' shirts. Once she made herself a petticoat that was too small for her to get into, and Mr. Slatter saw her struggling with it in front of the mirror, and he said, "What size do you think you are, Bluebell?" in the same way he would say, as we sat down to table, "What have you been doing with your lily-white hands today, Primrose?" To which she would reply, pleasantly, as if he had really asked a question, "I've made some cakes." Or, "I got some salt meat from the butcher at the station today, fresh out of the pickle." About the petticoat she said, "Yes, I must have been putting on more weight than I knew."

When I was twelve or thereabouts, I noticed that the boys had turned against their mother, not in the way of being brutal to her, but they spoke to her as their father did, calling her Bluebell, or the Fat Woman at the Fair. It was odd to hear them, because it was as if they said, simply, Mum, or Mother. Not once did I hear her lose her temper with them. I could see she had determined to herself not to make them any part of what she had against Mr. Slatter. I knew she was pleased to have me there, during that time, with the five men coming in only for meals.

One evening during a long stay, the boys as usual had gone off to their rooms to play when supper was done, and Mr. Slatter said to his wife: "I'm off. I'll be back tomorrow for breakfast." He went out into the dark and the wet. It was raining hard that night. The window panes were streaked with rain and shaking with the wind. Mrs. Slatter looked across at me and said—and this was the first time it had been mentioned how often he went off after dinner, coming back as the sun rose, or sometimes not for two or three days: "You must remember something. There are some men, like Mr. Slatter, who've got more energy than they know what to do with. Do you know how he started? When I met him and we were courting he was a butcher's boy at the corner. And now he's worth as much as any man in the district."

"Yes," I said, understanding for the first time that she was very proud of him.

She waited for me to say something more, and then said: "Yes, we have all kinds of ideas when we're young. But Mr. Slatter's a man that does not know his own strength. There are some things he doesn't

162

understand, and it all comes from that. He never understands that other people aren't as strong as he is."

We were sitting in the big living room. It had a stone floor with rugs and skins on it. A boot clattered on the stone and we looked up and there was Mr. Slatter. His teeth were showing. He wore his big black boots, shining now from the wet, and his black oilskin glistened. "The bossboy says the river's up," he said. "I won't get across tonight." He took off his oilskin there, scattering wet on Mrs. Slatter's polished stone floor; tugged off his boots; and reached out through the door to hang his oilskin in the passage and set his boots under it; and came back.

There were two rivers between the Slatters' farm and the Pritts's farm, twelve miles off; and when the water came down they could be impassable for hours.

"So I don't know my own strength?" he said to her, direct, and it was a soft voice, more frightening than I had ever heard from him, for he bared grinning teeth as usual, and his big fists hung at his sides.

"No," she said steadily, "I don't think you do." She did not lift her eyes, but stayed quiet in the corner of the sofa under the lamp. "We aren't alone," she added quickly, and now she did look warningly at him.

He turned his head and looked toward me. I made fast for the door. I heard her say, "Please. I'm sorry about the river. But leave me alone, please."

"So you're sorry about the river."

"Yes."

"And I don't know my own strength?"

I shut the door. But it was a door that was never shut, and it swung open again and I ran down the passage away from it, as he said: "So that's why you keep your bedroom door locked, Lady Godiva, is that it?"

And she screamed out: "Ah, leave me alone. I don't

163

care what you do. I don't care now. But you aren't going to make use of me. *I won't let you make use of me.*"

It was a big house, rooms sprawling everywhere. The boys had two rooms and a playroom off at one end of a long stone passage. Dairies and larders and kitchen opened off the passage. Then a dining room and some offices and a study. Then the living room. And another passage off at an angle, with the room where I slept and beside it Mrs. Slatter's big bedroom with the double bed and after that a room they called the work-room, but it was an ordinary room and Mr. Slatter's things were in it, with a bed.

I had not thought before that they did not share a bedroom. I knew no married people in the district who had separate rooms, and that is why I had not thought about the small room where Mr. Slatter slept.

Soon after I had shut the door on myself, I heard them come along the passage outside, I heard voices in the room next door. Her voice was pleading, his loud; and he was laughing a lot.

In the morning at breakfast I looked at Mrs. Slatter, but she was not taking any notice of us children. She was pale. She was helping Mr. Slatter to his breakfast. He always had three or four eggs on thick slabs of bacon, and then slice after slice of toast, and half a dozen cups of tea as black as it would come from the pot. She had some toast and a cup of tea and watched him eat. When he went out to the farm work he kissed her, and she blushed.

When we were on the veranda after breakfast, sewing, she said to me, apologetically and pink-cheeked: "I hope you won't think anything about last night. Married people often quarrel. It doesn't mean anything."

My parents did not quarrel. At least, I had not

164

thought of them as quarreling. But because of what she said I tried to remember times when they disagreed and perhaps raised their voices and then afterward laughed and kissed each other. Yes, I thought, it is true that married people quarrel, but that doesn't mean they aren't happy together.

That night after supper, when the boys had gone to their room, Mr. Slatter said, "The rivers are down; I'm off." Mrs. Slatter, sitting quiet under the lamp, kept her eyes down and said nothing. He stood there staring at her, and she said: "Well, you know what that means, don't you?"

He simply went out, and we heard the lorry start up; and the headlights swung up against the window panes a minute, so that they dazzled up gold and hard and went black again.

Mrs. Slatter said nothing, so that my feeling that something awful had happened slowly faded. Then she began talking about her childhood in London. She was a shop assistant before she met Mr. Slatter. She often spoke of her family, and the street she lived in, so I wondered if she were homesick, but she never went back to London so perhaps she was not homesick at all.

Soon after that Emmy Pritt got ill. She was not the sort of woman one thought of as being ill. She had some kind of operation; and they all said she needed a holiday, she needed to get off the altitude. Our part of Central Africa was high, nearly four thousand feet; and we all knew that when a person got run down they needed a rest from the altitude in the air at sea level. Mrs. Pritt went down to the Cape; and soon after Mr. and Mrs. Slatter went, too, with the four children, and they all had a holiday together at the same hotel.

When they came back, the Slatters brought a farm

assistant with them. Mr. Slatter could not manage the farm work, he said. I heard my father say that Slatter was taking things a bit far; he was over at the Pritts's every weekend from Friday night to Monday morning and nearly every night from after supper until morning. Slatter, he said, might be as strong as a herd of bulls, but no one could go on like that; and in any case, one should have a sense of proportion. Mr. Pritt was never mentioned, though it was not for years that I thought to consider what this might mean. We used to see him about the station, or at gymkhanas. He was an ordinary man, not like a farmer, as we knew farmers—men who could do anything; he might have been anybody, or an office person. He was ordinary in height, thinnish, with his pale hair leaving his narrow forehead high and bony. He was an accountant as well. People used to say that Charlie Slatter helped Emmy Pritt run their farm, and most of the time Mr. Pritt was off staying at neighboring farms doing their accounts.

The new assistant was Mr. Andrews; and, as Mrs. Slatter said to my mother when she came over for tea, he was a gentleman. He had been educated at Cambridge in England. He came of a hard-up family, though, for he had only a few hundred pounds of capital of his own. He would be an assistant for two years and then start his own farm.

For a time I did not go to stay with Mrs. Slatter. Once or twice I asked if she had said anything to my mother about my coming, and she said in a dry voice, meaning to discourage me, "No, she hasn't said anything." I understood when I heard my father say: "Well, it might not be such a bad thing. For one thing, he's a nice lad; and for another, it might make Slatter see things differently." And another time: "Perhaps Slatter would give Molly a divorce? After all, he

166

practically lives at the Pritts's! And then Molly could have some sort of a life at last."

"But the boy's not twenty-five," said my mother. And she was really shocked, as distinct from her obstinate little voice when she felt him to be wrongheaded or loose in his talk—a threat of some kind. "And what about the children? Four children!"

My father said nothing to his, but after some minutes he came off some track of thought with: "I hope Molly's taking it sensibly. I do hope she is. Because she could be laying up merry hell for herself if she's not."

I saw George Andrews at a gymkhana, standing at the rail with Mrs. Slatter. Although he was an Englishman he was already brown; and his clothes were loosened up and easy, as our men's clothes were. So there was nothing to dislike about him on that score. He was rather short, not fat, but broad, and you could see he would be fat. He was healthy-looking above all, with a clear, reddish face the sun had laid a brown glisten over; and very clear blue eyes; and his hair was thick and short, glistening like fur. I wanted to like him and so I did. I saw the way he leaned beside Mrs. Slatter, with her dust coat over his arm, holding out his program for her to mark. I could understand that, after Mr. Slatter, she would like a gentleman who would open doors for her and stand up when she came into the room. I could see she was proud to be with him. And so I liked him, though I did not like his mouth; his lips were pink and wettish. I did not look at his mouth again for a long time. And because I liked him I was annoyed with my father when he said, after that gymkhana, "Well, I don't know. I don't think I like it after all. He's a bit of a young pup, Cambridge or no Cambridge."

Six months after George Andrews came to the district there was a dance for the young people at the

167

Slatters'. It was the first dance. The two older boys were eighteen and seventeen and they had girls. The two younger boys were fifteen and thirteen and they despised girls. I was fifteen then, and all these boys were too young for me, and the girls of the two older boys were nearly twenty. There were about sixteen of us, and the married people thirty or forty, as usual. The married people sat in the living room and danced in it, and we were on the verandas. Mr. Slatter was dancing with Emmy Pritt, and sometimes another woman; and Mrs. Slatter was busy being a hostess and dancing with George Andrews. I was still in a short dress and unhappy because I was in love with one of the assistants from the farm between the rivers; and I knew very well that until I had a long dress he would not see me. I went into Mrs. Slatter's bedroom latish because it seemed the only room empty, and I looked out of the window at the dark wet night. It was the rainy season, and we had driven over the swollen noisy river and all the way the rain water was sluicing under our tires. It was still raining, and the lamplight gilded streams of rain so that as I turned my head slightly this way and that, the black and the gold rods shifted before me, and I thought (and I had never thought so simply before about these things): "How do they manage? With all these big boys in the house? And they never go to bed before eleven or half-past these days, I bet, and with Mr. Slatter coming home unexpectedly from Emmy Pritt—it must be difficult. I suppose he has to wait until everyone's asleep. It must be horrible, wondering all the time if the boys have noticed something. . . ." I turned from the window and looked from it into the big, low-ceilinged, comfortable room with its big low bed covered over with pink roses, the pillows propped high in pink frilled covers; and although I had been in that room during visits for years of my life, it seemed strange to me, and ugly. I loved Mrs. Slatter. Of all the women in the district she was the kindest, and she had always been good to me. But at that moment I hated her and I despised her.

I started to leave the bedroom, but at the door I stopped, because Mrs. Slatter was in the passage, leaning against the wall, and George Andrews had his arms around her, and his face in her neck. She was saying, "Please don't, George, please don't, please; the boys might see." And he was swallowing her neck and saying nothing at all. She was twisting her face and neck away and pushing him off. He staggered back from her, as though she had pushed him hard, but it was because he was drunk and had no balance, and he said: "Oh, come on into your bedroom a minute. No one will know." She said, "*No*, George. Why should we have to snatch five minutes in the middle of a dance, like—"

"Like what?" he said, grinning. I could see how the light that came down the passage from the big room made his pink lips glisten.

She looked reproachfully at him, and he said: "Molly, this thing is getting a bit much, you know. I have to set my alarm clock for one in the morning, and then I'm dead beat. I drag myself out of my bed, and then you've got your clock set for four, and God knows working for your old man doesn't leave one with much enthusiasm for bouncing about all night." He began to walk off toward the big room where the people were dancing. She ran after him and grabbed at his arm. I retreated toward Mr. Slatter's room, but almost at once she had got him and turned him around and was kissing him. The people in the big room could have seen if they had been interested.

That night Mrs. Slatter had on an electric blue

crêpe dress with diamonds on the straps and in flower patterns on the hips. There was a deep V in front which showed her breasts swinging loose under the crêpe, though usually she wore strong corsets. And the back was cut down to the waist. As the two turned and came along, he put his hand into the front of her dress, and I saw it lift out her left breast, and his mouth was on her neck again. Her face was desperate; but that did not surprise me, because I knew she must be ashamed. I despised her, because her white, long breast, lying in his hand like a piece of limp, floured dough, was not like Mrs. Slatter who called men Mister even if she had known them twenty years, and was really very shy, and there was nothing Mr. Slatter liked more than to tease her because she blushed when he used bad language.

"What did you make such a fuss for?" George Andrews was saying in a drunken sort of way. "We can lock the door, can't we?"

"Yes, we can lock the door," she answered in the same way, laughing.

I went back into the crowd of married people, where the small children also were, and sat beside my mother; and it was only five minutes before Mrs. Slatter came back looking as usual, from one door, and then George Andrews, in at another.

I did not go to the Slatters' again for some months. For one thing, I was away at school; and for another people were saying that Mrs. Slatter was run down and she should get off the altitude for a bit. My father was not mentioning the Slatters by this time, because he had quarreled with my mother over them. I knew they had, because whenever Molly Slatter was mentioned, my mother tightened her mouth and changed the subject.

And so a year went by. At Christmas they had a

dance again, and I had my first long dress, and I went to that dance not caring if it was at the Slatters' or anywhere else. It was my first dance as one of the young people. And so I was on the veranda dancing most of the evening, though sometimes the rain blew in on us, because it was raining again, being the full of the rainy season, and the skies were heavy and dark, with the moon shining out like a knife from the masses of the clouds and then going in again leaving the veranda with hardly light enough to see each other. Once I went down to the steps to say goodbye to some neighbors who were going home early because they had a new baby, and coming back up the steps there was Mr. Slatter and he had Mrs. Slatter by the arm. "Come here, Lady Godiva," he said. "Give us a kiss."

"Oh, go along," she said, sounding goodhumored. "Go along with you and leave me in peace."

He was quite drunk, but not very. He twisted her arm around. It looked like a slight twist but she came up sudden against him, in a bent-back curve, her hips and legs against him, and he held her there. Her face was sick, and she half-screamed, "You don't know your own strength." But he did not slacken the grip, and she stayed there, and the big sky was filtering a little stormy moonlight and I could just see their faces, and I could see his grinning teeth. "Your bloody pride, Lady Godiva," he said. "Who do you think you're doing in? Who do you think is the loser over your bloody locked door?" She said nothing and her eyes were shut. "And now you've frozen out George, too? What's the matter, isn't *he* good enough for you either?" He gave her arm a wrench, and she gasped, but then shut her lips again, and he said: "So now you're all alone in your tidy bed, telling yourself fairy stories in the dark, Sister Theresa, the little flower."

171

He let her go suddenly, and she staggered, so he put out his other hand to steady her, and held her until she was steady. It seemed odd to me that he should care that she shouldn't fall to the ground, and that he should put his hand like that to stop her falling.

And so I left them and went back on to the veranda. I was dancing all the night with the assistant from the farm between the rivers. I was right about the long dress. All those months, at the station or at gymkhanas, he had never seen me at all. But that night he saw me, and I was wanting him to kiss me. But when he did I slapped his face. Because then I knew that he was drunk. I had not thought he might be drunk, though it was natural he was, since everybody was. But the way he kissed me was not at all what I had been thinking. "I beg your pardon I'm sure," he said, and I walked past him into the passage and then into the living room. But there were so many people and my eyes were stinging, so I went through into the other passage, and there, just like last year, as if the whole year had never happened, were Mrs. Slatter and George Andrews. I did not want to see it, not the way I felt.

"And why not?" he was saying, biting into her neck.

"Oh, George, that was all ended months ago, months ago!"

"Oh, come on, Moll, I don't know what I've done. You never bothered to explain."

"No." And then, crying out, "*Mind my arm.*"

"What's the matter with your arm?"

"I fell and sprained it."

So he let go of her, and said, "Well, thanks for the nice interlude, thanks anyway, old girl." I knew that he had been meaning to hurt her, because I could feel what he said hurting me. He went off into the living room by himself, and she went off after him, but to talk to someone else, and I went into her bedroom. It was empty. The lamp was on a low table by the bed, turned down; and the sky through the windows was black and wet and hardly any light came from it.

Then Mrs. Slatter came in and sat on the bed and put her head in her hands. I did not move.

"Oh my God!" she said. "Oh my God, my God!" Her voice was strange to me. The gentleness was not in it, though it was soft, but it was soft from breathlessness.

"Oh my God!" she said, after a long long silence. She took up one of the pillows from the bed, and wrapped her arms around it, and laid her head down on it. It was quiet in this room, although from the big room came the sound of singing, a noise like howling, because people were drunk, or part-drunk, and it had the melancholy savage sound of people singing when they are drunk. An awful sound, like animals howling.

Then she put down the pillow, tidily, in its proper place, and swayed backward and forward and said: "Oh God, make me old soon, make me old. I can't stand this, I can't stand this any longer."

And again the silence, with the howling sound of the singing outside, and the footsteps of the people who were dancing scraping on the cement of the veranda.

"I can't go on living," said Mrs. Slatter, into the dark above the small glow of lamplight. She bent herself up again, double, as if she were hurt physically, her hands gripped around her ankles, holding herself together; and she sat crunched up, her face looking straight in front at the wall, level with the lamplight. So now I could see her face. I did not know that face. It was stone, white stone, but her eyes gleamed out of it black, and with a flicker in them. And her black shining hair that was not gray at all yet had loosened and hung in streaks around the white stone face.

"I can't stand it," she said again. The voice she used was strange to me. She might have been talking to someone. For a moment I even thought she had seen me and was talking to me, explaining herself to me. And then, slowly, she let herself unclench and she went out into the dance again.

I took up the lamp and held it as close as I could to the mirror and bent in and looked at my face. But there was nothing to my face.

Next day I told my father I had heard Mrs. Slatter say she could not go on living. He said, "Oh Lord, I hope it's not because of what I said about her dress"; but I said no, it was before he said he didn't like the dress. "Then if she was upset," he said, "I expect what I said made her feel even worse." And then: "Oh poor woman, poor woman!" He went into the house and called my mother and they talked it over. Then he got onto the telephone and I heard him asking Mrs. Slatter to drop in next time she was going past to the station. And it seemed she was going in that morning, and before lunchtime she was on our veranda talking to my father. My mother was not there, although my father had not asked her in so many words not to be there. As for me, I went to the back of the veranda where I could hear what they said.

"Look, Molly," he said, "we are old friends. You're looking like hell these days. Why don't you tell me what's wrong? You can say anything to me, you know."

After quite a time she said, "Mr. Farquar, there are some things you can't say to anybody. Nobody."

"Ah, Molly," he said, "if there's one thing I've learned—and I learned it early on, when I was a young man and I had a bad time—it's this. Everybody's got something terrible, Molly. Everybody has something awful they have to live with. We all live together and we see each other all the time, and none of us knows what awful thing the other person might be living with."

And then she said, "But, Mr. Farquar, I don't think that's true. I know people who don't seem to have anything private to make them unhappy."

"How do you know, Molly? How do you know?"

"Take Mr. Slatter," she said. "He's a man who does as he likes. But he doesn't know his own strength. And that's why he never seems to understand how other people feel."

"But how do you know, Molly? You can live next to someone for fifty years and still not know. Perhaps he's got something that gives him hell when he's alone, like all the rest of us?"

"No, I don't think so, Mr. Farquar."

"Molly," he said, appealing suddenly, and very exasperated. "You're too hard on yourself, Molly."

She didn't say anything.

He said, "Listen, why don't you get away for a while, get yourself down to the sea? This altitude drives us all quietly crazy. You get down off the altitude for a bit."

She still said nothing, and he lowered his voice, and I could imagine how my mother's face would have gone stiff and cold had she heard what he said: "And have a good time while you're there. Have a good time and let go a bit."

"But, Mr. Farquar, I don't want a good time." The words, a good time, she used as if they could have nothing to do with her.

"If we can't have what we want in this world, then we should take what we can get."

"It wouldn't be right," she said at last, slowly. "I

know people have different ideas, and I don't want to press mine on anyone."

"But *Molly*—" he began, exasperated, or so it sounded, and then he was silent.

From where I sat I could hear the grass chair creaking; she was getting out of it. "I'll take your advice," she said. "I'll get down to the sea and I'll take the children with me. The two younger ones."

"To hell with the kids for once. Take your old man with you and see that Emmy Pritt doesn't go with you this time."

"Mr. Farquar," she said, "if Mr. Slatter wants Emmy Pritt, he can have her. He can have either one or the other of us. But not both. If I took him to the sea he would be over at her place ten minutes after we got back."

"Ah, Molly, you women can be hell. Have some pity on him for once."

"Pity? Mr. Slatter's a man who needs nobody's pity. But thank you for your good advice, Mr. Farquar. You are always very kind, you and Mrs. Farquar."

And she said goodbye to my father, and when I came forward she kissed me and asked me to come and see her soon, and she went to the station to get the stores.

And so Mrs. Slatter went on living. George Andrews bought his own farm and married and the wedding was at the Slatters'. Later on Emmy Pritt got sick again and had another operation and died. It was a cancer. Mr. Slatter was ill for the first time in his life from grief, and Mrs. Slatter took him to the sea, by themselves, leaving the children, because they were grown-up anyway. For this was years later, and Mrs. Slatter's hair had gone gray and she was fat and old, as I had heard her say she wanted to be.

A Road to the Big City

The train left at midnight, not at six. Jansen's flare of temper at the clerk's mistake died before he turned from the counter; he did not really mind. For a week he had been with rich friends, in a vacuum of wealth, politely seeing the town through their eyes. Now, for six hours, he was free to let the dry and nervous air of Johannesburg strike him direct. He went into the station buffet. It was a bare place, with shiny brown walls and tables arranged regularly. He sat before a cup of strong orange-colored tea; and because he was in the arrested, dreamy frame of mind of the uncommitted traveler, he was the spectator at a play that could not hold his attention. He was about to leave, in order to move by himself through the streets, among the people, trying to feel what they were in this city, what they had which did not exist, perhaps, in other big cities—for he believed that in every place there dwelt a demon that expressed itself through the eyes and voices of those who lived there—when he heard someone ask: "Is this place free?" He turned quick, for there was a quality in the voice which could not be mistaken. Two girls stood beside him, and the one who had spoken sat down without waiting for his response; there were many empty tables in the room. She wore a tight, short, black dress, several brass chains, and high-heeled, shiny, black shoes. She was a tall, broad girl with colorless hair ridged tightly round her head, but given a bright surface so that it glinted like metal. She immediately lighted a cigarette and said to her companion, "Sit down, for God's sake." The other girl shyly slid into the chair next to Jansen, averting her face as he gazed at her, which he could not help doing—she was so different from what he expected. Plump, childish, with dull hair bobbing in fat rolls on her neck, she wore a flowered and flounced dress and flat white sandals on bare and sunburned feet. Her face had the jolly friendliness of a little dog. Both girls showed Dutch ancestry in the broad blunt planes of cheek and forehead; both had small blue eyes, though one pair was surrounded by sandy lashes and the other by black varnished fringes.

The waitress came for an order. Jansen was too curious about the young girl to move away. "What will you have?" he asked. "Brandy," said the older one at once. "Two brandies," she added, with another impatient look at her sister—there could be no doubt that they were sisters.

"I haven't never drunk brandy," said the younger with a giggle of surprise. "Except when Mom gave me some sherry at Christmas." She blushed as the older said despairingly, half under her breath: "Oh God preserve me from it!"

"I came to Johannesburg this morning," said the little one to Jansen confidingly. "But Lilla has been here earning a living for a year."

"My God!" said Lilla again. "What did I tell you? Didn't you hear what I told you?" Then, making the best of it, she smiled professionally at Jansen and said, "Green! You wouldn't believe it if I told you. I was green when I came, but compared with Marie. . . ." She laughed angrily.

178

"Have you been to Joburg before this day?" asked Marie in her confiding way.

"You are passing through," stated Lilla, with a glance at Marie. "You can tell easy if you know how to look."

"You're quite right," said Jansen.

"Leaving tomorrow perhaps?" asked Lilla.

"Tonight," said Jansen.

Instantly Lilla's eyes left Jansen and began to rove about her, resting on one man's face and then the next. "Midnight," said Jansen, in order to see her expression change.

"There's plenty time," she said, smiling.

"Lilla promised I could go to the bioscope," said Marie, her eyes becoming large. She looked around the station buffet, and because of her way of looking, Jansen tried to see it differently. He could not. It remained for him a bare, brownish, dirty sort of place, full of badly-dressed and dull people. He felt as one does with a child whose eyes widen with terror or delight at the sight of an old woman muttering down the street, or a flowering tree. What hunched black crone from a fairy tale, what celestial tree does the child see? Marie was smiling with charmed amazement.

"Very well," said Jansen, "let's go to the movies."

For a moment Lilla calculated, her hard blue glance moving from Jansen to Marie. "You take Marie," she suggested, direct to Jansen, ignoring her sister. "She's green, but she's learning." Marie half-rose, with a terrified look. "You can't leave me," she said.

"Oh my God!" said Lilla resignedly. "Oh, all right. Sit down, baby. But I've a friend to see. I told you."

"But I only just came."

"All right, all right. Sit down, I said. He won't bite you."

"Where do you come from?" asked Jansen.

Marie said a name he had never heard.

"It's not far from Bloemfontein," explained Lilla.

"I went to Bloemfontein once," said Marie, offering Jansen this experience. "The bioscope there is big. Not like near home."

"What is home like?"

"It's small," said Marie.

"What does your father do?"

"He works on the railway," Lilla said quickly.

"He's a ganger," said Marie, and Lilly rolled her eyes up and sighed.

Jansen had seen the ganger's cottages, the frail little shacks along the railway lines, miles from any place, where the washing flapped whitely on the lines over patches of garden, and the children ran out to wave to the train that passed shrieking from one wonderful fabled town to the next.

"Mom is old-fashioned," said Marie. She said the word old-fashioned carefully; it was not hers, but Lilla's; she was tasting it, in the way she sipped at the brandy, trying it out, determined to like it. But the emotion was all her own; all the frustration of years was in her, ready to explode into joy. "She doesn't want us to be in Joburg. She says it is wrong for girls."

"Did you run away?" asked Jansen.

Wonder filled the child's face. "How did you guess I ran away?" She said, with a warm admiring smile at Lilla, "My sister sent me the money. I didn't have none at all. I was alone with Mom and Dad, and my brothers are working on the copper mines."

"I see." Jansen saw the lonely girl in the little house by the railway lines, helping with the chickens and the cooking, staring hopelessly at the fashion papers, watching the trains pass, too old now to run out and

180

wave and shout, but staring at the fortunate people at the windows with grudging envy, and reading Lilla's letters week after week: "I have a job in an office. I have a new dress. My young man said to me . . ." He looked over the table at the two fine young South African women, with their broad and capable look, their strong bodies, their health, and he thought: Well, it happens every day. He glanced at his watch and Marie said at once: "There's time for the bioscope, isn't there?"

"You and your bioscope," said Lilla. "I'll take you tomorrow afternoon." She rose, said to Jansen in an offhand way: "Coming?" and went to the door. Jansen hesitated, then followed Marie's uncertain but friendly smile.

The three went into the street. Not far away shone a large white building with film stars kissing between thin borders of colored shining lights. Streams of smart people went up the noble marble steps where splendid men in uniform welcomed them. Jansen, watching Marie's face, was able to see it like that. Lilla laughed and said: "We're going home, Marie. The pictures aren't anything much. There's better things to do than pictures." She winked at Jansen.

They went to a two-roomed flat in a suburb. It was over a grocery store called Mac's Golden Emporium. It had canned peaches, dried fruit, dressed dolls and rolls of cotton goods in the window. The flat had new furniture in it. There was a sideboard with bottles and a radio. The radio played: "Or would you like to swing on a star, carry moonbeams home in a jar, and be better off than you are . . ."

"I like the words," said Marie to Jansen, listening to them with soft delight. Lilla said, "Excuse me, but I have to phone my friend," and went out.

Marie said, "Have a drink." She said it carefully.

She poured brandy, the tip of her tongue held between her teeth, and she spilled the water. She carried the glass to Jansen, and smiled in unconscious triumph as she set it down by him. Then she said: "Wait," and went into the bedroom. Jansen adjusted himself on the juicy upholstery of a big chair. He was annoyed to find himself here. What for? What was the good of it? He looked at himself in the glass over a sideboard. He saw a middle-aged gentleman, with a worn, indulgent face, dressed in a gray suit and sitting uncomfortably in a very ugly chair. But what did Marie see when she looked at him? She came back soon, with a pair of black shiny shoes on her broad feet, and a tight red dress, and a pretty face painted over her own blunt honest face. She sat herself down opposite him, as she had seen Lilla sit, adjusting the poise of her head and shoulders. But she forgot her legs, which lay loosely in front of her, like a schoolgirl's.

"Lilla said I could wear her dresses," she said, lingering over her sister's generosity. "She said today I could live here until I earned enough to get my own flat. She said I'd soon have enough." She caught her breath. "Mom would be mad."

"I expect she would," said Jansen drily, and saw Marie react away from him. She spread her red skirts and faced him politely, waiting for him to make her evening.

Lilla came in, turning her calculating, good-humored eyes from her sister to Jansen, smiled, and said: "I'm going out a little. Oh, keep your hair on. I'll be back soon. My friend is taking me for a walk."

The friend came in and took Lilla's arm; he was a large, handsome sunburned man who smiled with a good-time smile at Marie. She responded with such a passion of admiration in her eyes that Jansen understood at once what she did not see when she looked at

182

himself. "My, my," said this young man with easy warmth to Marie. "You're a fast learner, I can see that."

"We'll be back," said Lilla to Marie. "Remember what I said." Then, to Jansen, like a saleswoman: "She's not bad. Anyhow she can't get herself into any trouble here at home." The young man slipped his arm around her and reached for a glass off the sideboard with his free hand. He poured brandy, humming with the radio: "In a shady nook, by a babbling brook. . . ." He threw back his head, poured the brandy down, smiled broadly at Jansen and Marie, winked and said: "Be seeing you. Don't forget to wind up the clock and put the cat out." Outside on the landing he and Lilla sang, "Carry moonbeams *home* in a jar, be better *off* than you are. . . ." They sang their way down to the street. A car door slammed; an engine roared. Marie darted to the window and said bitterly, "They've gone to the pictures."

"I don't think so," said Jansen. She came back, frowning, preoccupied with responsibility. "Would you like another drink?" she asked, remembering what Lilla had told her. Jansen shook his head and sat still for a moment, weighted with inertia. Then he said, "Marie, I want you to listen to me." She leaned forward dutifully, ready to listen. But this was not as she had gazed at the other man—the warm, generous, laughing, singing young man. Jansen found many words ready on his tongue, disliked them, and blurted: "Marie, I wish you'd let me send you back home tonight." Her face dulled. "No, Marie, you really must listen." She listened politely, from behind her dull resistance. He used words carefully, out of the delicacy of his compassion, and saw how they faded into meaninglessness in the space between him and Marie. Then he grew brutal and desperate, because he had to reach her. He said, "This sort of life isn't as much fun as it looks"; and "Thousands of girls all over the world choose the easy way because they're stupid, and afterward they're sorry." She dropped her lids, looked at her feet in her new high-heeled shoes, and shut herself off from him. He used the words whore and prostitute; but she had never heard them except as swear words and did not connect them with herself. She began repeating, over and over again: "My sister's a typist; she's got a job in an office."

He said angrily, "Do you think she can afford to live like this on a typist's pay?"

"Her gentleman friend gives her things—he's generous, she told me so," said Marie doubtfully.

"How old are you, Marie?"

"Eighteen," she said, turning her broad freckled wrist, where Lilla's bracelet caught the light.

"When you're twenty-five you'll be out on the streets picking up any man you see, taking them to hotels. . . ."

At the word "hotel" her eyes widened; he remembered she had never been in a hotel; they were something lovely on the cinema screen.

"When you're thirty you'll be an old woman."

"Lilla said she'd look after me. She promised me faithfully," said Marie, in terror at his coldness. But what he was saying meant nothing to her, nothing at all. He saw that she probably did not know what the word prostitute meant; that the things Lilla had told her meant only lessons in how to enjoy the delights of this city.

He said, "Do you know what I'm here for? Your sister expects you to take off your clothes and get into bed and. . . ." He stopped. Her eyes were wide open, fastened on him, not in fear, but in the anxious preoccupation of a little girl who is worried she is not behaving properly. Her hands had moved to the buckle of her belt, and she was undoing it.

Jansen got up, and without speaking he gathered clothes that were obviously hers from off the furniture, from off the floor. He went into the bedroom and found a suitcase and put her things into it. "I'm putting you on the train tonight," he said.

"My sister won't let you," she cried out. "She'll stop you."

"Your sister's a bad girl," said Jansen, and saw, to his surprise that Marie's face showed fear at last. Those two words, "bad girl," had had more effect than all his urgent lecturing.

"You shouldn't say such things," said Marie, beginning to cry. "You shouldn't never say someone's a bad girl." They were her mother's words, obviously, and had hit her hard where she could be reached. She stood listless in the middle of the floor, weeping, making no resistance. He tucked her arm under his and led her downstairs. "You'll marry a nice man soon, Marie," he promised. "You won't always have to live by the railway lines."

"I don't never meet no men, except Dad," she said, beginning to tug at his arm again.

He held her tight until they were in a taxi. There she sat crouched on the edge of the seat, watching the promised city sweep past. At the station, keeping a firm hold on her, he bought her a ticket and gave her five pounds, and put her into a compartment and said: "I know you hate me. One day you'll know I'm right, and you'll be glad." She smiled weakly and huddled herself into her seat, like a cold little animal, staring sadly out of the window.

He left her, running, to catch his own train, which already stood waiting on the next platform.

As it drew out of the station he saw Marie waddling

desperately on her tall heels along the platform, casting scared glances over her shoulder. Their eyes met; she gave him an apologetic smile and ran on. With the pound notes clutched loosely in her hand she was struggling her way through the crowds back to the lights, the love, the joyous streets of the promised city.

12

Flight

Above the old man's head was the dovecote, a tall wire-netted shelf on stilts, full of strutting, preening birds. The sunlight broke on their gray breasts into small rainbows. His ears were lulled by their crooning; his hands stretched up toward his favorite, a homing pigeon, a young plump-bodied bird, which stood still when it saw him and cocked a shrewd bright eye.

"Pretty, pretty, pretty," he said, as he grasped the bird and drew it down, feeling the cold coral claws tighten around his finger. Content, he rested the bird lightly on his chest and leaned against a tree, gazing out beyond the dovecote into the landscape of a late afternoon. In folds and hollows of sunlight and shade, the dark red soil, which was broken into great dusty clods, stretched wide to a tall horizon. Trees marked the course of the valley; a stream of rich green grass the road.

His eyes traveled homeward along this road until he saw his granddaughter swinging on the gate underneath a frangipani tree. Her hair fell down her back in a wave of sunlight; and her long bare legs repeated the angles of the frangipani stems, bare, shining brown stems among patterns of pale blossoms.

She was gazing past the pink flowers, past the railway cottage where they lived, along the road to the village.

His mood shifted. He deliberately held out his wrist for the bird to take flight, and caught it again at the moment it spread its wings. He felt the plump shape strive and strain under his fingers; and, in a sudden access of troubled spite, shut the bird into a small box and fastened the bolt. "Now you stay there," he muttered and turned his back on the shelf of birds. He moved warily along the hedge, stalking his granddaughter, who was now looped over the gate, her head loose on her arms, singing. The light happy sound mingled with the crooning of the birds, and his anger mounted.

"Hey!" he shouted, and saw her jump, look back, and abandon the gate. Her eyes veiled themselves, and she said in a pert, neutral voice, "Hullo, Grandad." Politely she moved toward him, after a lingering backward glance at the road.

"Waiting for Steven, hey?" he said, his fingers curling like claws into his palm.

"Any objection?" she asked lightly, refusing to look at him.

He confronted her, his eyes narrowed, shoulders hunched, tight in a hard knot of pain that included the preening birds, the sunlight, the flowers, herself. He said, "Think you're old enough to go courting, hey?"

The girl tossed her head at the old-fashioned phrase and sulked, "Oh, Grandad!"

"Think you want to leave home, hey? Think you can go running around the fields at night?"

Her smile made him see her, as he had every evening of this warm end-of-summer month, swinging hand in hand along the road to the village with that red-handed, red-throated, violent-bodied youth, the son of the postmaster. Misery went to his head and he shouted angrily: "I'll tell your mother!"

"Tell away!" she said, laughing, and went back to the gate.

He heard her singing, for him to hear:

*"I've got you under my skin,
I've got you deep in the heart of . . ."*

"Rubbish," he shouted. "Rubbish. Impudent little bit of rubbish!"

Growling under his breath, he turned toward the dovecote, which was his refuge from the house he shared with his daughter and her husband and their children. But now the house would be empty. Gone all the young girls with their laughter and their squabbling and their teasing. He would be left, uncherished and alone, with that square-fronted, calm-eyed woman, his daughter.

He stooped, muttering, before the dovecote, resenting the absorbed, cooing birds.

From the gate the girl shouted: "Go and tell! Go on, what are you waiting for?"

Obstinately he made his way to the house, with quick, pathetic, persistent glances of appeal back at her. But she never looked around. Her defiant but anxious young body stung him into love and repentance. He stopped. "But I never meant. . . ." he muttered, waiting for her to turn and run to him. "I didn't mean. . . ."

She did not turn. She had forgotten him. Along the road came the young man Steven, with something in his hand. A present for her? The old man stiffened as he watched the gate swing back and the couple embrace. In the brittle shadows of the frangipani tree his granddaughter, his darling, lay in the arms of the postmaster's son, and her hair flowed back over his shoulder.

"I see you!" shouted the old man spitefully. They did not move. He stumped into the little whitewashed house, hearing the wooden veranda creak angrily under his feet. His daughter was sewing in the front room, threading a needle held to the light.

He stopped again, looking back into the garden. The couple were now sauntering among the bushes, laughing. As he watched he saw the girl escape from the youth with a sudden mischievous movement and run off through the flowers with him in pursuit. He heard shouts, laughter, a scream, silence.

"But it's not like that at all," he muttered miserably. "It's not like that. Why can't you see? Running and giggling, and kissing and kissing. You'll come to something quite different."

He looked at his daughter with sardonic hatred, hating himself. They were caught and finished, both of them, but the girl was still running free.

"Can't you *see?*" he demanded of his invisible granddaughter, who was at that moment lying in the thick green grass with the postmaster's son.

His daughter looked at him and her eyebrows went up in tired forbearance.

"Put your birds to bed?" she asked, humoring him.

"Lucy," he said urgently. "Lucy. . . ."

"Well, what is it now?"

"She's in the garden with Steven."

"Now you just sit down and have your tea."

He stumped his feet alternately, thump, thump, on the hollow wooden floor and shouted: "She'll marry him. I'm telling you, she'll be marrying him next!"

His daughter rose swiftly, brought him a cup, set him a plate.

"I don't want any tea. I don't want it, I tell you."

"Now, now," she crooned. "What's wrong with it? Why not?"

"She's eighteen. Eighteen!"

"I was married at seventeen, and I never regretted it."

"Liar," he said. "Liar. Then you should regret it. Why do you make your girls marry? It's you who do it. What do you do it for? Why?"

"The other three have done fine. They've three fine husbands. Why not Alice?"

"She's the last," he mourned. "Can't we keep her a bit longer?"

"Come, now, Dad. She'll be down the road, that's all. She'll be here every day to see you."

"But it's not the same." He thought of the other three girls, transformed inside a few months from charming, petulant, spoiled children into serious young matrons.

"You never did like it when we married," she said. "Why not? Every time, it's the same. When I got married you made me feel like it was something wrong. And my girls the same. You get them all crying and miserable the way you go on. Leave Alice alone. She's happy." She sighed, letting her eyes linger on the sunlit garden. "She'll marry next month. There's no reason to wait."

"You've said they can marry?" he said incredulously.

"Yes, Dad. Why not?" she said coldly and took up her sewing.

His eyes stung, and he went out on to the veranda. Wet spread down over his chin, and he took out a handkerchief and mopped his whole face. The garden was empty.

From around the corner came the young couple; but their faces were no longer set against him. On the wrist of the postmaster's son balanced a young pigeon, the light gleaming on its breast.

191

"For me?" said the old man, letting the drops shake off his chin. "For me?"

"Do you like it?" The girl grabbed his hand and swung on it. "It's for you, Grandad. Steven brought it for you." They hung about him, affectionate, concerned, trying to charm away his wet eyes and his misery. They took his arms and directed him to the shelf of birds, one on each side, enclosing him, petting him, saying wordlessly that nothing would be changed, nothing could change, and that they would be with him always. The bird was proof of it, they said, from their lying happy eyes, as they thrust it on him. "There, Grandad, it's yours. It's for you."

They watched him as he held it on his wrist, stroking its soft, sun-warmed back, watching the wings lift and balance.

"You must shut it up for a bit," said the girl intimately, "until it knows this is its home."

"Teach your grandmother to suck eggs," growled the old man.

Released by his half-deliberate anger, they fell back, laughing at him. "We're glad you like it." They moved off, now serious and full of purpose, to the gate, where they hung, backs to him, talking quietly. More than anything could, their grown-up seriousness shut him out, making him alone; also, it quietened him, took the sting out of their tumbling like puppies on the grass. They had forgotten him again. Well, so they should, the old man reassured himself, feeling his throat clotted with tears, his lips trembling. He held the new bird to his face, for the caress of its silken feathers. Then he shut it in a box and took out his favorite.

"*Now* you can go," he said aloud. He held it poised, ready for flight, while he looked down the garden toward the boy and the girl. Then, clenched in

192

the pain of loss, he lifted the bird on his wrist and watched it soar. A whirr and a spatter of wings, and a cloud of birds rose into the evening from the dove-cote.

At the gate Alice and Steven forgot their talk and watched the birds.

On the veranda, that woman, his daughter, stood gazing, her eyes shaded with a hand that still held her sewing.

It seemed to the old man that the whole afternoon had stilled to watch his gesture of self-command, that even the leaves of the trees had stopped shaking.

Dry-eyed and calm, he let his hands fall to his sides and stood erect, staring up into the sky.

The cloud of shining silver birds flew up and up, with a shrill cleaving of wings, over the dark ploughed land and the darker belts of trees and the bright folds of grass, until they floated high in the sunlight, like a cloud of motes of dust.

They wheeled in a wide circle, tilting their wings so there was flash after flash of light, and one after another they dropped from the sunshine of the upper sky to shadow, one after another, returning to the shadowed earth over trees and grass and field, returning to the valley and the shelter of night.

The garden was all a fluster and a flurry of returning birds. Then silence, and the sky was empty.

The old man turned, slowly, taking his time; he lifted his eyes to smile proudly down the garden at his granddaughter. She was staring at him. She did not smile. She was wide-eyed and pale in the cold shadow, and he saw the tears run shivering off her face.

13

The Day Stalin Died

That day began badly for me with a letter from my aunt in Bournemouth. She reminded me that I had promised to take my cousin Jessie to be photographed at four that afternoon. So I had; and forgotten all about it. Having arranged to meet Bill at four, I had to telephone him to put it off. Bill was a film writer from the United States who, having had some trouble with an un-American Activities Committee, was blacklisted, could no longer earn his living, and was trying to get a permit to live in Britain. He was looking for someone to be a secretary to him. His wife had always been his secretary; but he was divorcing her after twenty years of marriage on the grounds that they had nothing in common. I planned to introduce him to Beatrice.

Beatrice was an old friend from South Africa whose passport had expired. Having been named as a communist, she knew that once she went back she would not get out again, and she wanted to stay another six months in Britain. But she had no money. She needed a job. I imagined that Bill and Beatrice might have a good deal in common; but later it turned out that they disapproved of each other. Beatrice said that Bill was corrupt, because he wrote sexy comedies for TV under another name and acted in bad films. She did not think his justification, namely, that a guy has to eat, had anything in its favor. Bill, for his part, had never been able to stand political women. But I was not to know about the incompatibility of my two dear friends; and I spent an hour following Bill through one switchboard after another, until at last I got him in some studio where he was rehearsing for a film about Lady Hamilton. He said it was quite all right, because he had forgotten about the appointment in any case. Beatrice did not have a telephone, so I sent her a telegram.

That left the afternoon free for cousin Jessie. I was just settling down to work when comrade Jean rang up to say she wanted to see me during lunch hour. Jean was for many years my self-appointed guide or mentor toward a correct political viewpoint. Perhaps it would be more accurate to say she was one of several self-appointed guides. It was Jean who, the day after I had my first volume of short stories published, took the morning off to work to come and see me, in order to explain that one of the stories, I forget which, gave an incorrect analysis of the class struggle. I remember thinking at the time that there was a good deal in what she said.

When she arrived that day at lunch time, she had her sandwiches with her in a paper bag, but she accepted some coffee, and said she hoped I didn't mind her disturbing me, but she had been very upset by something she had been told I had said.

It appeared that a week before, at a meeting, I had remarked that there seemed to be evidence for supposing that a certain amount of dirty work must be going on in the Soviet Union. I would be the first to admit that this remark savored of flippancy.

Jean was a small, brisk woman with glasses, the daughter of a Bishop, whose devotion to the working class was proved by thirty years of work in the Party.

Her manner toward me was always patient and kindly. "Comrade," she said, "intellectuals like yourself are under greater pressure from the forces of capitalist corruption than any other type of party cadre. It is not your fault. But you must be on your guard."

I said I thought I had been on my guard; but nevertheless I could not help feeling that there were times when the capitalist press, no doubt inadvertently, spoke the truth.

Jean tidily finished the sandwich she had begun, adjusted her spectacles, and gave me a short lecture about the necessity for unremitting vigilance on the part of the working class. She then said she must go, because she had to be at her office at two. She said that the only way an intellectual with my background could hope to attain to a correct working-class viewpoint was to work harder in the Party; to mix continually with the working class; and in this way my writing would gradually become a real weapon in the class struggle. She said, further, that she would send me the verbatim record of the Trials in the thirties, and if I read this, I would find my present vacillating attitude toward Soviet justice much improved. I said I had read the verbatim records a long time ago; and I always did think they sounded unconvincing. She said that I wasn't to worry; a really sound working-class attitude would develop with time.

With this she left me. I remember that, for one reason and another, I was rather depressed.

I was just settling down to work again when the telephone rang. It was cousin Jessie, to say she could not come to my flat as arranged, because she was buying a dress to be photographed in. Could I meet her outside the dress shop in twenty minutes? I therefore abandoned work for the afternoon and took a taxi.

On the way the taxi man and I discussed the cost of living, the conduct of the government, and discovered that we had everything in common. Then he began telling me about his only daughter, aged eighteen, who wanted to marry his best friend, aged forty-five. He did not hold with this; had said so; and thereby lost daughter and friend at one blow. What made it worse was that he had just read an article on psychology in the woman's magazine his wife took, from which he had suddenly gathered that his daughter was father-fixated. "I felt real bad when I read that," he said. "It's a terrible thing to come on suddenlike, a thing like that." He drew up smartly outside the dress shop and I got out.

"I don't see why you should take it to heart," I said. "I wouldn't be at all surprised if we weren't all father-fixated."

"That's not the way to talk," he said, holding out his hand for the fare. He was a small, bitter-looking man, with a head like a lemon or like a peanut, and his small blue eyes were brooding and bitter. "My old woman's been saying to me for years that I favored our Hazel too much. What gets me is, she might have been in the right of it."

"Well," I said, "look at it this way. It's better to love a child too much than too little."

"Love?" he said. "Love, is it? Precious little love or anything else these days if you ask me, and Hazel left home three months ago with my mate George and not so much as a postcard to say where or how."

"Life's pretty difficult for everyone," I said, "what with one thing and another."

"You can say that," he said.

This conversation might have gone on for some time, but I saw my cousin Jessie standing on the pavement watching us. I said goodbye to the taxi man and turned, with some apprehension, to face her.

"I saw you," she said. "I saw you arguing with him. It's the only thing to do. They're getting so damned insolent these days. My principle is, tip them sixpence regardless of the distance, and if they argue, let them have it. Only yesterday I had one shouting at my back all down the street because I gave him sixpence. But we've got to stand up to them."

My cousin Jessie is a tall girl, broad-shouldered, aged about twenty-five. But she looks eighteen. She has light brown hair which she wears falling loose around her face, which is round and young and sharp-chinned. Her wide, light blue eyes are virginal and fierce. She is altogether like the daughter of a Viking, particularly when battling with bus conductors, taxi men, and porters. She and my Aunt Emma carry on permanent guerilla warfare with the lower orders; an entertainment I begrudge neither of them, because their lives are dreary in the extreme. Besides, I believe their antagonists enjoy it. I remember once, after a set-to between cousin Jessie and a taxi driver, when she had marched smartly off, shoulders swinging, he chuckled appreciatively and said: "That's a real old-fashioned type, that one. They don't make them like that these days."

"Have you bought your dress?" I asked.

"I've got it on," she said.

Cousin Jessie always wears the same outfit: a well-cut suit, a round-necked jersey, and a string of pearls. She looks very nice in it.

"Then we might as well go and get it over," I said.

"Mummy is coming, too," she said. She looked at me aggressively.

"Oh well," I said.

"But I told her I would *not* have her with me while I was buying my things. I told her to come and pick me up here. I will *not* have her choosing my clothes for me."

"Quite right," I said.

My Aunt Emma was coming toward us from the tearoom at the corner, where she had been biding her time. She is a very large woman, and she wears navy blue and pearls and white gloves like a policeman on traffic duty. She has a big, heavy-jowled, sorrowful face; and her bulldog eyes are nearly always fixed in disappointment on her daughter.

"There!" she said as she saw Jessie's suit. "You might just as well have had me with you."

"What do you mean?" said Jessie quickly.

"I went in to Renée's this morning and told them you were coming, and I asked them to show you that suit. And you've bought it. You see, I do know your tastes as I know my own."

Jessie lifted her sharp battling chin at her mother, who dropped her eyes in modest triumph and began poking at the pavement with the point of her umbrella.

"I think we'd better get started," I said.

Aunt Emma and Cousin Jessie, sending off currents of angry electricity into the air all around them, fell in beside me, and we proceeded up the street.

"We can get a bus at the top," I said.

"Yes, I think that would be better," said Aunt Emma. "I don't think I could face the insolence of another taxi driver today."

"No," said Jessie, "I couldn't either."

We went to the top of the bus, which was empty, and sat side by side along the two seats at the very front.

200

"I hope this man of yours is going to do Jessie justice," said Aunt Emma.

"I hope so too," I said. Aunt Emma believes that every writer lives in a whirl of photographs, press conferences, and publishers' parties. She thought I was the right person to choose a photographer. I wrote to say I wasn't. She wrote back to say it was the least I could do. "It doesn't matter in the slightest anyway," said Jessie, who always speaks in short, breathless, battling sentences, as from an unassuageably painful inner integrity that she doesn't expect anyone else to understand.

It seems that at the boarding house where Aunt Emma and Jessie live, there is an old inhabitant who has a brother who is a TV producer. Jessie had been acting in *Quiet Wedding* with the local Reps. Aunt Emma thought that if there was a nice photograph of Jessie, she could show it to the TV producer when he came to tea with his brother at the boarding house, which he was expected to do any weekend now; and if Jessie proved to be photogenic, the TV producer would whisk her off to London to be a TV star.

What Jessie thought of this campaign I did not know. I never did know what she thought of her mother's plans for her future. She might conform or she might not; but it was always with the same fierce and breathless integrity of indifference.

"If you're going to take that attitude, dear," said Aunt Emma, "I really don't think it's fair to the photographer."

"Oh, Mummy!" said Jessie.

"There's the conductor," said Aunt Emma, smiling bitterly. "I'm not paying a penny more than I did the last time. The fare from Knightsbridge to Little Duchess Street is threepence."

201

"The fares have gone up," I said.

"Not a penny more," said Aunt Emma.

But it was not the conductor. It was two middle-aged people, who steadied each other at the top of the stair and then sat down, not side by side, but one in front of the other. I thought this was odd, particularly as the woman leaned forward over the man's shoulder and said in a loud parrot voice: "Yes, and if you turn my goldfish out of doors once more, I'll tell the landlady to turn *you* out. I've warned you before."

The man, in appearance like a damp, gray, squashed felt hat, looked in front of him and nodded with the jogging of the bus.

She said, "And there's fungus on my fish. You needn't think I don't know where it came from."

Suddenly he remarked in a high insistent voice, "There are all those little fishes in the depths of the sea, all those little fishes. We explode all these bombs at them, and we're not going to be forgiven for that, are we, we're not going to be forgiven for blowing up the poor little fishes."

She said, in an amiable voice, "I hadn't thought of that," and she left her seat behind him and sat in the same seat with him.

I had known that the afternoon was bound to get out of control at some point; but this conversation upset me. I was relieved when Aunt Emma restored normality by saying: "*There.* There never used to be people like *that.* It's the Labor Government."

"Oh, Mummy," said Jessie, "I'm not in the mood for politics this afternoon."

We had arrived at the place we wanted, and we got down off the bus. Aunt Emma gave the bus conductor ninepence for the three of us, which he took without comment. "And they're inefficient as well," she said.

It was drizzling and rather cold. We proceeded up the street, our heads together under Aunt Emma's umbrella.

Then I saw a newsboard with the item: Stalin Is Dying. I stopped and the umbrella went jerking up the pavement without me. The newspaperman was an old acquaintance. I said to him, "What's this, another of your sales boosters?" He said: "The old boy's had it, if you ask me. Well, the way he's lived—the way I look at it, he's had it coming to him. Must have the constitution of a bulldozer." He folded up a paper and gave it to me. "The way I look at it is that it doesn't do anyone any good to live that sort of life. Sedentary. Reading reports and sitting at meetings. That's why I like this job—there's plenty of fresh air."

A dozen paces away Aunt Emma and Jessie were standing facing me, huddled together under the wet umbrella. "What's the matter, dear?" shouted Aunt Emma. "Can't you see, she's buying a newspaper," said Jessie crossly.

The newspaperman said, "It's going to make quite a change, with *him* gone. Not that I hold much with the goings-on out there. But they aren't used to democracy much, are they? What I mean is, if people aren't used to something, they don't miss it."

I ran through the drizzle to the umbrella. "Stalin's dying," I said.

"How do you know?" said Aunt Emma suspiciously.

"It says so in the newspaper."

"They said he was sick this morning, but I expect it's just propaganda. I won't believe it till I see it."

"Oh don't be silly, Mummy. How can you *see* it?" said Jessie.

We went on up the street. Aunt Emma said: "What

203

do you think, would it have been better if Jessie had bought a nice pretty afternoon dress?"

"Oh, Mummy," said Jessie, "can't you see she's upset? It's the same for her as it would be for us if Churchill was dead."

"Oh, my *dear!*" said Aunt Emma, shocked, stopping dead. An umbrella spoke scraped across Jessie's scalp, and she squeaked. "Do put that umbrella down now. Can't you see it's stopped raining?" she said, irritably, rubbing her head.

Aunt Emma pushed and bundled at the umbrella until it collapsed, and Jessie took it and rolled it up. Aunt Emma, flushed and frowning, looked dubiously at me. "Would you like a nice cup of tea?" she said.

"Jessie's going to be late," I said. The photographer's door was just ahead.

"I do hope this man's going to get Jessie's expression," said Aunt Emma. "There's never been one yet that got her *look.*"

Jessie went crossly ahead of us up some rather plushy stairs in a hallway with mauve and gold striped wallpaper. At the top there was a burst of Stravinsky as Jessie masterfully opened a door and strode in. We followed her into what seemed to be a drawing room, all white and gray and gold. The *Rites of Spring* tinkled a baby chandelier overhead; and there was no point in speaking until our host, a charming young man in a black velvet jacket, switched off the machine, which he did with an apologetic smile.

"I do hope this is the right place," said Aunt Emma. "I have brought my daughter to be photographed."

"Of course it's the right place," said the young man. "How delightful of you to come!" He took my Aunt Emma's white-gloved hands in his own and seemed to press her down on to a large sofa; a pressure to which she responded with a confused blush. Then he looked at me. I sat down quickly on another divan, a long way from Aunt Emma. He looked professionally at Jessie, smiling. She was standing on the carpet, hands linked behind her back, like an admiral on the job, frowning at him.

"You don't look at all relaxed," he said to her gently. "It's really no use at all, you know, unless you are really relaxed all over."

"I'm perfectly relaxed," said Jessie. "It's my cousin here who isn't relaxed."

I said, "I don't see that it matters whether I'm relaxed or not, because it's not me who is going to be photographed." A book fell off the divan beside me on the floor. It was *Prancing Nigger* by Ronald Firbank. Our host dived for it, anxiously.

"Do you read our Ron?" he asked.

"From time to time," I said.

"Personally I never read anything else," he said. "As far as I am concerned he said the last word. When I've read him all through, I began again at the beginning and read him through again. I don't see that there's any point in anyone ever writing another word after Firbank."

This remark discouraged me, and I did not feel inclined to say anything.

"I think we could all do with a nice cup of tea," he said. "While I'm making it, would you like the gramophone on again?"

"I can't stand modern music," said Jessie.

"We can't all have the same tastes," he said. He was on his way to a door at the back, when it opened and another young man came in with a tea tray. He was as light and lithe as the first, with the same friendly ease of manner. He was wearing black jeans and a purple sweater, and his hair looked like two irregular glossy black wings on his head.

"Ah, bless you, dear!" said our host to him. Then, to us: "Let me introduce my friend and assistant, Jackie Smith. My name you know. Now if we all have a nice cup of tea, I feel that our vibrations might become just a *little* more harmonious."

All this time Jessie was standing-at-ease on the carpet. He handed her a cup of tea. She nodded toward me, saying, "Give it to her." He took it back and gave it to me. "What's the matter, dear?" he asked. "Aren't you feeling well?"

"I am perfectly well," I said, reading the newspaper.

"Stalin is dying," said Aunt Emma. "Or so they would like us to believe."

"Stalin?" said our host.

"That man in Russia," said Aunt Emma.

"Oh, you mean old Uncle Joe. Bless him."

Aunt Emma started. Jessie looked gruffly incredulous.

Jackie Smith came and sat down beside me and read the newspaper over my shoulder. "Well, well," he said. "Well, well, well, well." Then he giggled and said: "Nine doctors. If there were fifty doctors I still wouldn't feel very safe, would you?"

"No, not really," I said.

"Silly old nuisance," said Jackie Smith. "Should have bumped him off years ago. Obviously outlived his usefulness at the end of the war, wouldn't you think?"

"It seems rather hard to say," I said.

Our host, a teacup in one hand, raised the other in a peremptory gesture, "I don't like to hear that kind of thing," he said. "I really don't. God knows, if there's one thing I make a point of never knowing a thing about, it's politics, but during the war Uncle Joe and

Roosevelt were absolutely my pin-up boys. But absolutely!"

Here Cousin Jessie, who had neither sat down nor taken a cup of tea, took a stride forward and said angrily: "Look, do you think we could get this *damned* business over with?" Her virginal pink cheeks shone with emotion, and her eyes were brightly unhappy.

"But, my *dear!*" said our host, putting down his cup. "But of course. If you feel like that, of course."

He looked at his assistant, Jackie, who reluctantly laid down the newspaper and pulled the cords of a curtain, revealing an alcove full of cameras and equipment. Then they both thoughtfully examined Jessie. "Perhaps it would help," said our host, "if you could give me an idea what you want it for? Publicity? Dust jackets? Or just for your lucky friends?"

"I don't know and I don't care," said Cousin Jessie.

Aunt Emma stood up and said: "I would like you to catch her expression. It's just a little *look* of hers. . . ."

Jessie clenched her fists at her.

"Aunt Emma," I said, "don't you think it would be a good idea if you and I went out for a little?"

"But my *dear.* . . ."

But our host had put his arm around her and was easing her to the door. "There's a duck," he was saying. "You do want me to make a good job of it, don't you? And I never could really do my best, even with the most sympathetic lookers-on."

Again Aunt Emma went limp, blushing. I took his place at her side and took her to the door. As we shut it, I heard Jackie Smith saying: "Music, do you think?" And Jessie: "I *loathe* music." And Jackie again: "We do rather find music helps, you know. . . ."

The door shut and Aunt Emma and I stood at the landing window, looking into the street.

"Has that young man done *you*?" she asked.

"He was recommended to me," I said.

Music started up from the room behind us. Aunt Emma's foot tapped on the floor. "Gilbert and Sullivan," she said. "Well, she can't say she loathes that. But I suppose she would, just to be difficult."

I lit a cigarette. *The Pirates of Penzance* abruptly stopped.

"Tell me, dear," said Aunt Emma, suddenly roguish, "about all the exciting things you are doing."

Aunt Emma always says this; and always I try hard to think of portions of my life suitable for presentation to Aunt Emma. "What have you been doing today, for instance?" I considered Bill; I considered Beatrice; I considered comrade Jean.

"I had lunch," I said, "with the daughter of a Bishop."

"Did you, dear?" she said doubtfully.

Music again: Cole Porter. "That doesn't sound right to me," said Aunt Emma. "It's modern, isn't it?" The music stopped. The door opened. Cousin Jessie stood there, shining with determination. "It's no good," she said. "I'm sorry, Mummy, but I'm not in the mood."

"But we won't be coming up to London again for another four months."

Our host and his assistant appeared behind cousin Jessie. Both were smiling rather bravely. "Perhaps we had better all forget about it," said Jackie Smith.

Our host said, "Yes, we'll try again later, when everyone is really themselves."

Jessie turned to the two young men and thrust out her hand at them. "I'm very sorry," she said, with her fierce virgin sincerity. "I am really terribly sorry."

Aunt Emma went forward, pushed aside Jessie, and shook their hands. "I must thank you both," she said, "for the tea."

Jackie Smith waved my newspaper over the three heads. "You've forgotten this," he said.

"Never mind, you can keep it," I said.

"Oh, bless you, now I can read all the gory details." The door shut on their friendly smiles.

"Well," said Aunt Emma, "I've never been more ashamed."

"I don't care," said Jessie fiercely. "I really couldn't care less."

We descended into the street. We shook each other's hands. We kissed each other's cheeks. We thanked each other. Aunt Emma and Cousin Jessie waved at a taxi. I got on a bus.

When I got home, the telephone was ringing. It was Beatrice. She said she had got my telegram, but she wanted to see me in any case. "Did you know Stalin was dying?" I said.

"Yes, of course. "Look, it's absolutely essential to discuss this business on the Copper Belt."

"Why is it?"

"If we don't tell people the truth about it, who is going to?"

"Oh, well, I suppose so," I said.

She said she would be over in an hour. I set out my typewriter and began to work. The telephone rang. It was comrade Jean. "Have you heard the news?" she said. She was crying.

Comrade Jean had left her husband when he became a member of the Labor Party at the time of the Stalin-Hitler Pact, and ever since then had been living in bed-sitting rooms on bread, butter, and tea, with a portrait of Stalin over her bed.

"Yes, I have," I said.

"It's awful," she said sobbing. "Terrible. They've murdered him."

"Who has? How do you know?" I said.

"He's been murdered by capitalist agents," she said. "It's perfectly obvious."

"He was 73," I said.

"People don't die just like *that*," she said.

"They do at 73," I said.

"We will have to pledge ourselves to be worthy of him," she said.

"Yes," I said, "I suppose we will."

14

Plants and Girls

There was a boy who lived in a small house in a small town in the center of Africa.

Until he was about twelve, this house had been the last in the street, so that he walked straight from the garden, across a railway line, and into the veld. He spent most of his time wandering by himself through the *vleis* and the *kopjes*. Then the town began to grow, so that in the space of a year a new suburb of smart little houses lay between him and the grass and trees. He watched this happening with a feeling of surprised anger. But he did not go through the raw new streets to the *vlei* where the river ran and the little animals moved. He was a lethargic boy, and it seemed to him as if some spell had been put on him, imprisoning him forever in the town. Now he would walk through the new streets, looking down at the hard glittering tarmac, thinking of the living earth imprisoned beneath it. Where the veld trees had been allowed to stay, he stood gazing, thinking how they drew their strength through the layers of rubble and broken brick, direct from the breathing soil and from the invisibly running underground rivers. He would stand there, staring; and it would seem to him that he could see those fresh, subtly running streams of water moving this way and that beneath the tarmac; and he stretched out his fingers like roots toward the earth.

People passing looked away uncomfortably. Children called out: "Moony, moony, mooning again!" Particularly the children from the house opposite laughed and teased him. They were a large, noisy family, solid in the healthy strength of their numbers. He could hardly distinguish one from another; he felt that the house opposite was filled like a box with plump, joyous, brown-eyed people whose noisy, cheerful voices frightened him.

He was a lanky, thin-boned youth whose face was long and unfinished-looking; and his eyes were enormous, blue, wide, staring, with the brilliance of distance in them.

His mother, when he returned to the house, would say tartly: "Why don't you go over and play with the children? Why don't you go into the bush like you used to? Why don't you. . . ."

He was devoted to his mother. He would say vaguely, "Oh, I don't know," and kick stones about in the dust, staring away over the house at the sky, knowing that she was watching him through the window as she sewed, and that she was pleased to have him there, in spite of her tart, complaining voice. Or he would go into the room where she sat sewing, and sit near her, in silence, for hours. If his father came into the room he began to fidget and soon went away. His father spoke angrily about his laziness and his unnatural behavior.

He made the mother fetch a doctor to examine the boy. It was from this time that Frederick took the words "not normal" as his inheritance. He was not normal; well, he accepted it. They made a fact of something he had always known because of the way people looked at him and spoke to him. He was neither surprised nor dismayed at what he was. And when his mother wept over him, after the doctor left, he scarcely heard the noise of her tears; he smiled at her with the warm childish grin that no one else had ever seen, for he knew he could always depend on her.

His father's presence was a fact he accepted. On the surface they made an easy trio, like an ordinary family. At meals they talked like ordinary people. In the evenings his father sometimes read to him, for Frederick found it hard to read, although he was now halfway through his teens; but there were moments when the old man fell silent, staring in unconcealable revulsion at this son he had made; and Frederick would let his eyes slide uncomfortably away, but in the manner of a person who is embarrassed at someone else's shortcomings. His mother accepted him; he accepted himself, that was enough.

When his father died he was sorry and cried with his fists in his eyes like a baby. At the graveside the neighbors looked at this great shambling child, with his colorless locks of hair and the big red fists rubbing at his eyes, and felt relieved at the normal outburst of grief. But afterward it was he and his mother alone in the small suburban house; and they never spoke of the dead father who had vanished entirely from their lives, leaving nothing behind him. She lived for her son, waiting for his return from school, or from his rambles around the streets; and she never spoke of the fact that he was in a class with children five years his junior or that he was always alone at weekends and holidays, never with other children.

He was a good son. He took her tea in the mornings at the time the sun rose and watched her crinkled old face light up from the pillow as he set down the tray by her knees. But he did not stay with her then. He went out again quickly, shutting the door, his eyes turned from the soft, elderly white shoulders, which were not, for him, his mother. This is how he saw her: in her dumpy flowered apron, her brown sinewy arms setting food before him, her round spectacles shining, her warm face smiling. Yet he did not think of her as an old lady. Perhaps he did not see her at all. He would sometimes put out his great lank hand and stroke her apron. Once he went secretly into her bedroom and took her hairbrush off the dressing table and brushed the apron, which was lying on the bed; and he put the apron on and laughed out loud at the sight of himself in the mirror.

Later, when he was seventeen, a very tall, awkward youth with the strange-lighted blue eyes, too old to be put to bed with a story after supper, he wandered about by himself through that area of ugly new houses that seemed to change under the soft brightness of the moon into a shadowy beauty. He walked for hours, or stood still gazing dimly about him at the deep starry sky or at the soft shapes of trees.

There was a big veld tree that stood a short way from their gate in a space between two street lamps, so that there was a well of shadow beneath it which attracted him very much. He stood beneath the tree, listening to the wind moving gently in the leaves and feeling it stir his hair like fingers. He would move slowly in to the tree until his long fingers met the rough bark; and he stroked the tree curiously, learning it, thinking: under this roughness and hardness moves the sap, like rivers under the earth. He came to spend his evenings there, instead of walking among the houses and looking in with puzzled, unenvious eyes through the windows at the other kind of people. One evening an extraordinarily violent spasm shook him, so that he found himself locked about that harsh strong trunk, embracing it violently, his arms and thighs knotted about it, sobbing and muttering angry

214

words. Afterward he slowly went home, entering the small, brightly lighted room shamedly; and his great blue eyes sought his mother's, and he was surprised that she did not say anything, but smiled at him as usual. Always there was this assurance from her; and as time went past, and each night he returned to the tree, caressing and stroking it, murmuring words of love, he would come home simply, smiling his wide childish smile, waiting for her to smile back, pleased with him.

But opposite was still that other house full of people; the children were growing up; and one evening when he was leaning against the tree in deep shadow, his arm loosely about it, as if around a tender friend, someone stopped outside the space of shadow and peered in saying: "Why, Moony, what are you doing here by yourself?" It was one of the girls from that house, and when he did not reply she came toward him, finally putting out her hand to touch his arm. The touch struck cruelly through him, and he moved away; and she said with a jolly laugh: "What's the matter? I won't eat you." She pulled him out into the yellowy light from the street lamp and examined him. She was a fattish, untidy, bright girl, one of the middle children, full of affection for everything in the world; and this odd, silent youth standing there quite still between her hands affected her with amused astonishment, so that she said, "Well, you are a funny boy, aren't you?" She did not know what to do with him, so at last she took him home over the street. He had never been inside her house before, and it was like a foreign country. There were so many people, so much noise and laughter, and the wireless was shouting out words and music. He was silent and smiling in this world which had nothing to do with himself.

His passive smile piqued the girl, and later when he

got up saying: "My mother's waiting for me," she replied, "Well, at any rate you can take me to the movies tomorrow."

He had never taken a girl out; had never been to the movies save with his parents, as a child is taken; and he smiled as at a ridiculous idea. But next evening she came and made him go with her.

"What's the matter, Moony?" she asked, taking his arm. "Don't you like me? Why don't you take girls out? Why do you always stay around your mother? You aren't a baby any longer."

These words he listened to smiling; they did not make him angry, because she could not understand that they had nothing to do with him.

He sat in the theater beside the girl and waited for the picture to be over. He would not have been in the least surprised if the building and the screen and the girl had vanished, leaving him under a tree with not a house in sight, nothing but the veld—the long grasses, the trees, the birds and the little animals. Afterward they walked home, and he listened to her chattering, scolding voice without replying. He did not mind being with her; but he forgot her as soon as she had gone in at her gate. He wandered back across the street to his own gate and looked at the tree standing in its gulf of shadow with the moonlight on its branches. He took two steps toward it and stopped; another step, and stopped again; and finally turned with a bolting movement, as if in fear, and shambled quickly in to his mother. She glanced up at him with a tight, suspicious face; and he knew she was angry, though she did not speak. Soon he went to bed, unable to bear this unspoken anger. He slept badly and dreamed of the tree. And next night he went to it as soon as it was dark, and stood holding the heavy dark trunk in his arms.

The girl from opposite was persistent. Soon he knew, because of the opposition of his mother, that he had a girl, as ordinary young men have girls.

Why did she want him? Perhaps it was just curiosity. She had been brought up in all that noise and warm quarreling and laughter; and so Frederick, who neither wanted her nor did not want her, attracted her. She scolded him and pleaded with him: "Don't you love me? Don't you want to marry me?"

At this he gave her his rambling, confused grin. The word marriage made him want to laugh. It was ridiculous. But to her there was nothing ridiculous in it. In her home, marriages took place between boys and girls, and there were always festivals and lovemaking and new babies.

Now he would take her in his arms beside the tree outside the gate, embracing her as he had embraced the tree, forgetting her entirely, murmuring strangely over her head among the shadows. She hated it and she loved it; for her, it was like being hypnotized. She scolded him, stayed away, returned; and yet he would not say he would marry her.

This went on for some time; though for Frederick it was not a question of time. He did not mind having her in his arms under the tree, but he could not marry her. He was driven, night after night, to the silent lovemaking, with the branches of the tree between him and the moon; and afterward he went straight to his room, so as not to face his mother.

Then she got ill. Instead of going with the girl at night, he stayed at home, making his mother drinks, silently sitting beside her, putting wet handkerchiefs on her forehead. In the mornings the girl looked at him over the hedge and said, "Baby! Baby!"

"But my mother's sick," he said, finding these words with difficulty from the dullness of his mind.

217

At this she only laughed. Finally she left him. It was like a tight string snapping from him, so that he reeled back into his own house with his mother. He watched the girl going in and out of her house with her sisters, her brothers, her friends, her young men; at nights he watched her dancing on the veranda to the gramophone. But she never looked back at him. His mother was still an invalid and kept to her chair; and he understood she was now getting old, but it did not come into his head that she might die. He looked after her. Before going off to the office at the railways, where he arranged luggage under the supervision of another clerk, he would lift his mother from her bed, turn away from her while she painfully dressed herself, support her into a chair by the window, fetch her food, and leave her for the day. At night he returned directly to her from work and sat beside her until it was time to sleep. Sometimes, when the desire for the shadowy street outside became too strong, he would go out for a little time and stand beside his tree. He listened to the wind moving in the branches and thought: It's an old tree. It's too old. If a leaf fell in the darkness he thought: The leaves are falling—it's dying; it's too old to live.

When his mother at last died, he could not understand that she was dead. He stood at her graveside in the efficient, cared-for cemetery of this new town, with its antiseptic look because of the neatness of the rows of graves and the fresh clean sunlight, and gazed down at the oblong hole in the red earth, where the spades had smoothed the steep sides into shares of glistening hardness, and saw the precisely fitting black box at the bottom of the hole, and lifted his head to stare painfully at the neighbors, among whom was the girl from opposite, although he did not see her.

He went home to the empty house that was full of

his mother. He left everything as it was. He did not expand his life to fill the space she had used. He was still a child in the house, while her chair stood empty, and her bed had pillows stacked on it, and her clothes hanging over the foot.

There was very little money. His affairs were managed by a man at the bank in whose custody he had been left, and he was told how much he could spend. That margin was like a safety line around his life; and he liked taking his small notebook where he wrote down every penny he spent at each month's end to the man at the bank.

He lived on, knowing that his mother was dead, but only because people had said she was. After a time he was driven by his pain down to the cemetery. The grave was a mound of red earth. The flowers of the funeral had died long ago. There was a small headstone of granite. A bougainvillea creeper had been planted on the grave; it spread its glossy green branches over the stone in layers of dark shining green and clusters of bleeding purple flowers. The first time he visited the cemetery he stood staring for a long time. Later he would sit by the headstone, fingering the leaves of the plant. Slowly he came to understand that his mother lay underneath where he sat. He saw her folded in the earth, her rough brown forearms crossed comfortably on her breast, her flowered apron pulled down to her fat knees, her spectacles glinting, her wrinkled old face closed in sleep. And he fingered the smooth hard leaves, noting the tiny working veins, thinking: They feed on her. The thought filled him with panic and drove him from the grave. Yet he returned again and again, to sit under the pressure of the heavy yellow sunlight, on the rough warm stone, looking at the red and purple flowers, feeling the leaves between his fingers.

One day, at the grave, he broke off a branch of the bougainvillea plant and returned with it to the house, where he set it in a vase by his bed. He sat beside it, touching and smoothing the leaves. Slowly the branch lost its color and the clusters of flowers grew limp. A spray of stiff, dead, pale leaves stood up out of the vase; and his eyes rested on it, brilliant, vague, spectral, while his face contracted with pain and with wonder.

During the long solitary evenings he began again to stand at his gate, under the stars, looking about him in the darkness. The big tree had been cut down; all the wild trees in that street were gone, because of the danger from the strong old roots to the bricks of the foundations of the houses. The authorities had planted new saplings, domestic and educated trees like bauhinea and jacaranda. Immediately outside his gate, where the old tree had been, was one of these saplings. It grew quickly: one season it was a tiny plant in a little leaning shed of grass; the next it was as high as his head. There was an evening that he went to it, leaning his forehead against it, not thinking, his hands sliding gently and unsurely up and down the long slim trunk. This taut supple thing was nothing he had known; it was strange to him; it was too slight and weak and there was no shadow around it. And yet he stood there night after night, unconscious of the windows about him where people might be looking out, unconscious of passers-by, feeling and fumbling at the tree, letting his eyes stray past to the sky or to the lines of bushy little saplings along the road or to the dusty crowding hedges.

One evening he heard a bright, scornful voice say: "What do you think you're doing?" and he knew it was the girl from opposite. But the girl from opposite had married long ago and was now an untidy, handsome matron with children of her own; she had left him so far behind that she could now nod at him with careless kindness, as if to say: Well, well, so you're still there, are you?

He peered and gawked at the girl in his intense ugly way that was yet attractive because of his enormous lighted eyes. Then, for him, the young and vigorous creature who was staring at him with such painful curiosity became the girl from opposite. She was in fact the other girl's sister, perhaps ten years her junior. She was the youngest of that large, pulsing family, who were all married and gone, and she was the only one who had known loneliness. When people said, with the troubled callousness, the necessary callousness that protects society against its rotten wood: "He's never been the same since the death of his mother; he's quite crazy now," she felt, not merely an embarrassed and fundamentally indifferent pity, but a sudden throb of sympathy. She had been watching Frederick for a long time. She was ready to defend him against people who said, troubled by this attraction of the sick for the healthy, "For God's sake what do you see in him, can't you do better than that?"

As before, he did as she wanted. He would accompany her to the movies. He would come out of his house at her call. He went walking with her through the dark streets at night. And before parting from her he took her into his arms against the sapling that swayed and slipped under their weight and kissed her with a cold persistence that filled her with horror and with desire, so that she ran away from him, sobbing, saying she would never see him again, and returned inevitably the next evening. She never entered his house; she was afraid of the invisibly present old woman. He seemed not to mind what she did. She was driven wild because she knew that if she did not seek him out, the knowledge of loss would never enter him; he would merely return to the lithe young tree, mumbling fierce, thick, reproachful words to it in the darkness.

As he grew to understand that she would always return no matter how she strove and protested, he would fold her against him, not hearing her cries, and as she grew still with chilled fear, she would hear through the darkness a dark sibilant whispering: "Your hair, your hair, your teeth, your bones." His fingers pressed and probed into her flesh. "Here is the bone, under is nothing only bone," and the long urgent fingers fought to defeat the soft envelope of flesh, fought to make it disappear, so that he could grasp the bones of her arm, the joint of her shoulder; and when he had pressed and probed and always found the flesh elastic against his hands, pain flooded along her as teeth closed in on her neck, or while his fist suddenly drove inward, under her ribs, as if the tension of flesh were not there. In the morning she would be bruised. She avoided the eyes of her family and covered up the bruises. She was learning, through this black and savage initiation, a curious strength. She could feel the bones standing erect through her body, a branching, undefeatable tree of strength; and when the hands closed in on her, stopping the blood, half-choking her, the stubborn half-conscious thought remained: You can't do it; you can't do it, I'm too strong.

Because of the way people looked in at them, through the darkness, as they leaned and struggled against the tree, she made him go inside the hedge of the small neglected garden, and there they lay together on the lawn, for hour after hour, with the cold high moon standing over them, sucking the warmth from their flesh, so they embraced in a cold, lethal ecstasy of pain, knowing only the cold, greenish light, feeling the bones of their bodies cleave and knock together while he grasped her so close that she could scarcely draw each breath. One night she fainted, and she came to herself to find him still clasping her, in a cold strong clasp, his teeth bared against her throat, so that a suffocating black pressure came over her brain in wave after wave; and she fought against him, making him tighten his grip and press her into the soil, and she felt the rough grasses driving up into her flesh.

A flame of self-preservation burned up into her brain, and she fought until he came to himself and his grip loosened. She said, "I won't. I won't let you. I won't come back again." He lay still, breathing like a deep sleeper. She did not know if he had heard her. She repeated hurriedly, already uncertain, "I won't let you." He got up and staggered away from her, and she was afraid because of the destructive light in the great eyes that glinted at her in the moonlight.

She ran away and locked herself in her bedroom. For several days she did not return. She watched him from her window as he strode huntedly up and down the street, lurking around the young tree, sometimes shaking it so that the leaves came spinning down around him. She knew she must return; and one evening she drifted across the street and came on him standing under the lithe young tree that held its fine glinting leaves like a spray of tinted water upward in the moonlight over the fine slender trunk.

This time he reached out and grasped her and carried her inside to the lawn. She murmured helplessly, in a dim panic, "You mustn't. I won't."

She saw the hazy brilliant stars surge up behind his black head, saw the greenish moonlight pour down the thin hollows of his cheeks, saw the great crazy eyes immediately above hers. The cages of their ribs

223

ground together; and she heard: "Your hair, dead hair, bones, bones, bones."

The bared desperate teeth came down on her throat, and she arched back as the stars swam and went out.

When people glanced over the hedge in the strong early sunlight of next morning they saw him half-lying over the girl, whose body was marked by blood and by soil; and he was murmuring: "Your hair, your leaves, your branches, your rivers."

15

Wine

A man and woman walked toward the boulevard from a little hotel in a side street.

The trees were still leafless, black, cold; but the fine twigs were swelling toward spring, so that looking upward it was with an expectation of the first glimmering greenness. Yet everything was calm, and the sky was a calm, classic blue.

The couple drifted slowly along. Effort, after days of laziness, semed impossible; and almost at once they turned into a café and sank down, as if exhausted, in the glass-walled space that was thrust forward into the street.

The place was empty. People were seeking the midday meal in the restaurants. Not all: that morning crowds had been demonstrating, a procession had just passed, and its straggling end could still be seen. The sounds of violence, shouted slogans and singing, no longer absorbed the din of Paris traffic; but it was these sounds that had roused the couple from sleep.

A waiter leaned at the door, looking after the crowds, and he reluctantly took an order for coffee.

The man yawned; the woman caught the infection; and they laughed with an affectation of guilt and exchanged glances before their eyes, without regret, parted. When the coffee came, it remained untouched. Neither spoke. After some time the woman yawned again; and this time the man turned and looked at her critically, and she looked back. Desire asleep, they looked. This remained: that while everything which drove them slept, they accepted from each other a sad irony; they could look at each other without illusion, steady-eyed.

And then, inevitably, the sadness deepened in her till she consciously resisted it; and into him came the flicker of cruelty.

"Your nose needs powdering," he said.

"You need a whipping boy."

But always he refused to feel sad. She shrugged, and, leaving him to it, turned to look out. So did he. At the far end of the boulevard there was a faint agitation, like stirred ants, and she heard him mutter, "Yes, and it still goes on. . . ."

Mocking, she said, "Nothing changes, everything always the same. . . ."

But he had flushed. "I remember," he began, in a different voice. He stopped, and she did not press him, for he was gazing at the distant demonstrators with a bitterly nostalgic face.

Outside drifted the lovers, the married couples, the students, the old people. There the stark trees; there the blue, quiet sky. In a month the trees would be vivid green; the sun would pour down heat; the people would be brown, laughing, bare-limbed. No, no, she said to herself, at this vision of activity. Better the static sadness. And, all at once, unhappiness welled up in her, catching her throat, and she was back fifteen years in another country. She stood in blazing tropical moonlight, stretching her arms to a landscape that offered her nothing but silence; and then she was running down a path where small stones glinted sharp underfoot, till at last she fell spent in a swathe of glistening grass. Fifteen years.

It was at this moment that the man turned abruptly and called the waiter and ordered wine.

"What," she said humorously, "already?"

"Why not?"

For the moment she loved him completely and maternally, till she suppressed the counterfeit and watched him wait, fidgeting, for the wine, pour it, and then set the two glasses before them beside the still-brimming coffee cups. But she was again remembering that night, envying the girl ecstatic with moonlight, who ran crazily through the trees in an unsharable desire for—but that was the point.

"What are you thinking of?" he asked, still a little cruel.

"Ohhh," she protested humorously.

"That's the trouble, that's the trouble." He lifted his glass, glanced at her, and set it down. "Don't you want to drink?"

"Not yet."

He left his glass untouched and began to smoke.

These moments demanded some kind of gesture—something slight, even casual, but still an acknowledgment of the separateness of those two people in each of them; the one seen, perhaps, as a soft-staring never-closing eye, observing, always observing, with a tired compassion; the other, a shape of violence that struggled on in the cycle of desire and rest, creation and achievement.

He gave it her. Again their eyes met in the grave irony, before he turned away, flicking his fingers irritably against the table; and she turned also, to note the black branches where the sap was tingling.

"I remember," he began; and again she said, in protest, "Ohhh!"

He checked himself. "Darling," he said drily,

"you're the only woman I've ever loved." They laughed.

"It must have been this street. Perhaps this café—only they change so. When I went back yesterday to see the place where I came every summer, it was a *pâtisserie*, and the woman had forgotten me. There was a whole crowd of us—we used to go around together—and I met a girl here, I think, for the first time. There were recognized places for contacts; people coming from Vienna or Prague, or wherever it was, knew the places—it couldn't be this café, unless they've smartened it up. We didn't have the money for all this leather and chromium."

"Well, go on."

"I keep remembering her, for some reason. Haven't thought of her for years. She was about sixteen, I suppose. Very pretty—no, you're quite wrong. We used to study together. She used to bring her books to my room. I liked her, but I had my own girl, only she was studying something else, I forget what." He paused again, and again his face was twisted with nostalgia, and involuntarily she glanced over her shoulder down the street. The procession had completely disappeared, not even the sounds of singing and shouting remained.

"I remember her because. . . ." And, after a preoccupied silence: "Perhaps it is always the fate of the virgin who comes and offers herself, naked, to be refused."

"What!" she exclaimed, startled. Also, anger stirred in her. She noted it, and sighed. "Go on."

"I never made love to her. We studied together all that summer. Then, one weekend, we all went off in a bunch. None of us had any money, of course, and we used to stand on the pavements and beg lifts, and meet up again in some village. I was with my own girl, but

228

that night we were helping the farmer get in his fruit, in payment for using his barn to sleep in, and I found this girl Marie was beside me. It was moonlight, a lovely night, and we were all singing and making love. I kissed her, but that was all. That night she came to me. I was sleeping up in the loft with another lad. He was asleep. I sent her back down to the others. They were all together down in the hay. I told her she was too young. But she was no younger than my own girl." He stopped; and after all these years his face was rueful and puzzled. "I don't know," he said. "I don't know why I sent her back." Then he laughed. "Not that it matters, I suppose."

"Shameless hussy," she said. The anger was strong now. "You had kissed her, hadn't you?"

He shrugged. "But we were all playing the fool. It was a glorious night—gathering apples, the farmer shouting and swearing at us because we were making love more than working, and singing and drinking wine. Besides, it was that time: the youth movement. We regarded faithfulness and jealousy and all that sort of thing as remnants of bourgeois morality." He laughed again, rather painfully. "I kissed her. There she was, beside me, and she knew my girl was with me that weekend."

"You kissed her," she said accusingly.

He fingered the stem of his wineglass, looking over at her and grinning. "Yes, darling," he almost crooned at her. "I kissed her."

She snapped over into anger. "There's a girl all ready for love. You make use of her for working. Then you kiss her. You know quite well. . . ."

"What do I know quite well?"

"It was a cruel thing to do."

"I was a kid myself. . . ."

"Doesn't matter." She noted, with discomfort, that

229

she was almost crying. "Working with her! Working with a girl of sixteen, all summer!"

"But we all studied very seriously. She was a doctor afterward, in Vienna. She managed to get out when the Nazis came in, but. . . ."

She said impatiently, "Then you kissed her, on *that* night. Imagine her, waiting till the others were asleep, then she climbed up the ladder to the loft, terrified the other man might wake up, then she stood watching you sleep, and she slowly took off her dress and. . . ."

"Oh, I wasn't asleep. I pretended to be. She came up dressed. Shorts and sweater—our girls didn't wear dresses and lipstick—more bourgeois morality. I watched her strip. The loft was full of moonlight. She put her hand over my mouth and came down beside me." Again, his face was filled with rueful amazement. "God knows, I can't understand it myself. She was a beautiful creature. I don't know why I remember it. It's been coming into my mind the last few days." After a pause, slowly twirling the wineglass: "I've been a failure in many things, but not with. . . ." He quickly lifted her hand, kissed it, and said sincerely: "I don't know why I remember it now, when. . . ." Their eyes met, and they sighed.

She said slowly, her hand lying in his: "And so you turned her away."

He laughed. "Next morning she wouldn't speak to me. She started a love affair with my best friend—the man who'd been beside me that night in the loft, as a matter of fact. She hated my guts, and I suppose she was right."

"Think of her. Think of her at that moment. She picked up her clothes, hardly daring to look at you. . . ."

"As a matter of fact, she was furious. She called me

230

all the names she could think of; I had to keep telling her to shut up, she'd wake the whole crowd."

"She climbed down the ladder and dressed again, in the dark. Then she went out of the barn, unable to go back to the others. She went into the orchard. It was still brilliant moonlight. Everything was silent and deserted, and she remembered how you'd all been singing and laughing and making love. She went to the tree where you'd kissed her. The moon was shining on the apples. She'll never forget it, never, never!"

He looked at her curiously. The tears were pouring down her face.

"It's terrible," she said. "Terrible. Nothing could ever make up to her for that. Nothing, as long as she lived. Just when everything was most perfect, all her life, she'd suddenly remember that night, standing alone, not a soul anywhere, miles of damned empty moonlight. . . ."

He looked at her shrewdly. Then, with a sort of humorous, deprecating grimace, he bent over and kissed her and said: "Darling, it's not my fault; it just isn't my fault."

"No," she said.

He put the wineglass into her hands; and she lifted it, looked at the small crimson globule of warming liquid, and drank with him.

16

He

"Goodness! You gave me a start, Mary. . . ."

Mary Brooke was quietly knitting beside the stove. "Thought I'd drop in," she said.

Annie Blake pulled off her hat and flopped a net of bread and vegetables on the table; at the same time her eyes were anxiously inspecting her kitchen: there was an unwashed dish in the sink, a cloth over a chair. "Everything's in such a mess," she said irritably.

Mary Brooke, eyes fixed on her knitting, said, "Eh, sit down. It's clean as can be."

After a hesitation Annie flopped herself into the chair and shut her eyes. "Those stairs. . . ." she panted. Then: "Like a cuppa tea, Mary?"

Mary quickly pushed her knitting away and said, "You sit still. I'll do it." She heaved up her large, tired body, filled a kettle from the tap, and set it on the flame. Then, following her friend's anxious glance, she hung the dish cloth where it belonged and shut the door. The kitchen was so clean and neat it could have gone on exhibition. She sat down, reached for her knitting, and knitted without looking at it, contemplating the wall across the room. "He was carrying on like anything last night," she observed.

Annie's drooping lids flew open, her light body straightened. "Yes?" she murmured casually. Her face was tense.

"What can you expect with that type? She doesn't get the beds made before dinnertime. There's dirt everywhere. He was giving it to her proper. Dirty slut, he called her."

"She won't do for him what I did, that's certain," said Annie bitterly.

"Shouting and banging until nearly morning—we all heard it." She counted purl, plain, purl, and added: "Don't last long, do it? Six months he's been with her now?"

"He never lifted his hand to me, *that's* certain," said Annie victoriously. "Never. I've got my pride, if others haven't."

"That's right, love. Two purl. One plain."

"Nasty temper he's got. I'd be up summer and winter at four, cleaning those offices till ten, then cleaning for Mrs. Lynd till dinnertime. Then if he got home and found his dinner not ready, he'd start to shout and carry on—well, I'd say, if you can't wait five minutes, get home and cook it yourself, I'd say. I bring in as much money as you do, don't I? But he never lifted a finger. Bone lazy. Men are all the same."

Mary gave her friend a swift, searching glance, then murmured, "Eh, you can't tell *me*. . . ."

"I'd have the kids and the cleaning and the cooking, and working all day—sometimes when he was unemployed I'd bring in all the money . . . and he wouldn't even put the kettle on for me. Women's work, he said."

"Two purl, plain." But Mary's kindly face seemed to suggest that she was waiting to say something else. "We know what it is," she agreed at last, patiently.

Annie rose lightly, pulled the shrieking kettle off the flame, and reached for the teapot. Seen from the back, she looked twenty, slim and erect. When she turned with the steaming pot, she caught a glimpse of herself; she set down the pot and went to the mirror. She stood touching her face anxiously. "Look at me!" She pushed a long, sagging curl into position, then shrugged. "Well, who's to care what I look like anyway?"

She began setting out the cups. She had a thin face, sharpened by worry, and small sharp blue eyes. As she sat down, she nervously felt her hair. "I must get the curlers onto my hair," she muttered.

"Heard from the boys?"

Annie's hand fell and clenched itself on the table. "Not a word from Charlie for months. They don't think . . . he'll turn up one fine day and expect his place laid, if I know my Charlie. Tommy's after a job in Manchester, Mrs. Thomas said. But I had a nice letter from Dick. . . ." Her face softened; her eyes were soft and reminiscent. "He wrote about his father. Should he come down and speak to the old so and so for me, he said. I wrote back and said that was no way to speak of his father. He should respect him, I said, no matter what he's done. It's not his place to criticize his father, I said."

"You're lucky in your boys, Annie."

"They're good workers, no one can say they aren't. And they've never done anything they shouldn't. They don't take after their dad, *that's* certain."

At this, Mary's eyes showed a certain tired irony. "Eh, Annie—but we all do things we shouldn't." This gaining no response from the bitter Annie, she added cautiously, "I saw him this morning in the street."

Annie's cup clattered down into the saucer. "Was he alone?"

"No. But he took me aside—he said I could give you a message if I was passing this way—he might be dropping in this evening instead of tomorrow with your money, he said. Thursday *she* goes to her moth-

235

er's—I suppose he thinks while the cat's away. . . ."

Annie had risen, in a panic. She made herself sit down again and stirred her tea. The spoon tinkled in the cup with the quivering of her hand. "He's regular with the money, anyway," she said heavily. "I didn't have to take him into court. He offered. And I suppose he needn't, now the boys are out keeping themselves."

"He still feels for you, Annie. . . ." Mary was leaning forward, speaking in a direct appeal. "He does, really."

"He never felt for anyone but himself," snapped Annie. "Never."

Mary let a sigh escape her. "Oh, well. . . ." she murmured. "Well, I'll be getting along to do the supper." She stuffed her knitting into her carryall and said consolingly: "You're lucky. No one to get after you if you feel like sitting a bit. No one to worry about but yourself. . . ."

"Oh, don't think I'm wasting any tears over *him*. I'm taking it easy for the first time in my life. You slave your life out for your man and your kids. Then off they go, with not so much as a thank you. Now I can please myself."

"I wouldn't mind being in your place," said Mary loyally. At the door she remarked, apparently at random, "Your floor's so clean you could eat off it."

The moment Mary was gone, Annie rushed into her apron and began sweeping. She got down on her knees to polish the floor, and then took off her dress and washed herself at the sink. She combed her dragging wisps of pale hair and did each one up neatly with a pin till her face was surrounded by a ring of little sausages. She put back her dress and sat down at the table. Not a moment too soon. The door opened, and Rob Blake stood there.

He was a thin, rather stooping man, with an air of apology. He said politely, "You busy, Annie?"

"Sit down," she commanded sharply. He stooped loosely in the doorway for a moment, then came forward, minding his feet. Even so she winced as she saw the dusty marks on the gleaming linoleum. "Take it easy," he said with friendly sarcasm. "You can put up with my dust once a week, can't you?"

She smiled stiffly, her blue eyes fastened anxiously on him, while he pulled out a chair and sat down. "Well, Annie?"

To this conciliatory opening she did not respond. After a moment she remarked, "I heard from Dick. He's thinking of getting married."

"Getting married, now? That puts us on the shelf, don't it?"

"*You're* not on any shelf that I can see," she snapped.

"Now—Annie . . ." he deprecated, with an appealing smile. She showed no signs of softening. Seeing her implacable face, his smile faded, and he took an envelope from his pocket and pushed it over.

"Thanks," she said, hardly glancing at it. Then that terrible bitterness came crowding up, and he heard the words: "If you can spare it from *her*."

He let that one pass; he looked steadily at his wife, as if seeking a way past that armor of anger. He watched her, passing the tip of his tongue nervously over his lips.

"Some women know how to keep themselves free from kids and responsibilities. They just do this and that, and take up with anyone they please. None of the dirty work for *them*."

He gave a sigh, and was on the point of getting up, when she demanded, "Like a cuppa tea?"

"I wouldn't mind." He let himself sink back again.

While she worked at the stove, her back to him, he was looking around the kitchen; his face had a look of tired, disappointed irony. An aging man, but with a dogged set to his shoulders. Trying to find the right words, he remarked, "Not so much work for you now, Annie."

But she did not answer. She returned with the two cups and put the sugar into his for him. This wifely gesture encouraged him. "Annie," he began, "Annie—can't we talk this over . . ." He was stirring the tea clumsily, not looking at it, leaning forward. The cup knocked over. "Oh, look what you've done," she cried out. "Just look at the mess." She snatched up a cloth and wiped the table.

"It's only a drop of tea, Annie," he protested at last, shrinking a little aside from her furious energy.

"Only a drop of tea—I can polish and clean half the day, and then in a minute the place is like a pig sty."

His face darkened with remembered irritation.

"Yes, I've heard," she went on accusingly, "she lets the beds lie until dinner, and the place isn't cleaned from one week to the next."

"At least she cares more for me than she does for a clean floor," he shouted. Now they looked at each other with hatred.

At this delicate moment there came a shout: "Rob. Rob!"

She laughed angrily. "She's got you where she wants you—waits and spies on you and now she comes after you."

"Rob! You there, Rob?" It was a loud, confident, female voice.

"She sounds just what she is, a proper . . ."

"Shut up," he interrupted. He was breathing heavily. "You keep that tongue of yours quiet, now."

Her eyes were full of tears, but the blue shone through, bright and vengeful. " 'Rob, Rob'—and off you trot like a little dog."

He got up from the table heavily, as a loud knock came at the door.

Annie's mouth quivered at the insult of it. And *his* first instinct was to stand by her—she could see that. He looked apologetically at her, then went to the door, opened it an inch, and said in a low, furious voice: "Don't you do that now. Do you hear me!" He shut the door, leaned against it, facing Annie. "Annie," he said again, in an awkward appeal. "Annie . . ."

But she sat at her table, hands folded in a trembling knot before her, her face tight and closed against him.

"Oh, all right!" he said at last despairingly, angry. "You've always got to be in the right about everything, haven't you? That's all that matters to you—if you're in the right. Bloody plaster saint, you are." He went out quickly.

She sat quite still, listening until it was quiet. Then she drew a deep breath and put her two fists to her cheeks, as if trying to keep them still. She was sitting thus when Mary Brooke came in. "You let him go?" she said incredulously.

"And good riddance, too."

Mary shrugged. Then she suggested bravely, "You shouldn't be so hard on him, Annie—give him a chance."

"I'd see him dead first," said Annie through shaking lips. Then: "I'm forty-five, and I might as well be on the dust heap." And then, after a pause, in a remote, cold voice: "We've been together twenty-five years. Three kids. And then he goes off with that . . . with that . . ."

"You're well rid of him, and that's a fact," agreed Mary swiftly.

"Yes, I am, and I know it . . ." Annie was swaying from side to side in her chair. Her face was stony, but the tears were trickling steadily down, following a path worn from nose to chin. They rolled off and splashed on to her white collar.

"Annie," implored her friend. "Annie . . ."

Annie's face quivered, and Mary was across the room and had her in her arms. "That's right, love, that's right, that's right, love," she crooned.

"I don't know what gets into me," wept Annie, her voice coming muffled from Mary's large shoulder. "I can't keep my wicked tongue still. He's fed up and sick of that—cow, and I drive him away. I can't help it. I don't know what gets into me."

"There now, love, there now, love." The big, fat, comfortable woman was rocking the frail Annie like a baby. "Take it easy, love. He'll be back, you'll see."

"You think he will?" asked Annie, lifting her face up to see if her friend was lying to comfort her.

"Would you like me to go and see if I can fetch him back for you now?"

In spite of her longing, Annie hesitated. "Do you think it'll be all right?" she said doubtfully.

"I'll go and slip in a word when *she's* not around."

"Will you do that, Mary?"

Mary got up, patting at her crumpled dress. "You wait here, love," she said imploringly. She went to the door and said as she went out: "Take it easy, now, Annie. Give him a chance."

"I go running after him to ask him back?" Annie's pride spoke out of her in a wail.

"Do you want him back or don't you?" demanded Mary, patient to the last, although there was a hint of exasperation now. Annie did not say anything, so Mary went running out.

Annie sat still, watching the door tensely. But vague, rebellious, angry thoughts were running through her head: If I want to keep him, I can't ever say what I think, I can't ever say what's true—I'm nothing to him but a convenience, but if I say so he'll just up and off . . .

But that was not the whole truth; she remembered the affection in his face, and for a moment the bitterness died. Then she remembered her long hard life, the endless work, work, work—she remembered, all at once, as if she were feeling it now, her aching back when the children were small; she could see him lying on the bed reading the newspaper when she could hardly drag herself. . . . It's all very well, she cried out to herself, it's not right, it just isn't right. . . . A terrible feeling of injustice was gripping her; and it was just this feeling she must push down, keep under, if she wanted him. For she knew finally—and this was stronger than anything else—that without him there would be no meaning in her life at all.

17

The Eye of God in Paradise

O—— in the Bavarian Alps is a charming little village. It is no more charming, however, than ten thousand others; although it is known to an astonishing number of people, some of whom have actually been there, while others have savored its attractions in imagination only. Pleasure resorts are like film stars and royalty who—or so one hopes—must be embarrassed by the figures they cut in the fantasies of people who have never met them. The history of O—— is fascinating; for this is true of every village. Its location has every advantage, not least that of being so near to the frontier that when finally located on the map it seems to the exuberant holiday-making fancy that one might toss a stone from it into Austria. This is, of course, not the case, since a high wall of mountains forms a natural barrier to any such adventure, besides making it essential that all supplies for O—— and the ten or a dozen villages in the valley above it must come from Germany. This wall of mountains is in fact the reason why O—— is German, and has always been German; although its inhabitants, or so it would seem from the songs and stories they offer the summer and winter visitors on every possible occasion, take comfort from the belief that Austria is at least their spiritual home. And so those holiday-makers who travel there in the hope of finding the attractions of two countries combined are not so far wrong. And there are those who go there because of the name, which is a homely, simple, gentle name, with none of the associations of, let us say, Berchtesgaden, a place in which one may also take one's ease, if one feels so inclined. O—— has never been famous; never has the spotlight of history touched it. It has not been one of those places that no one ever heard of until woken into painful memory, like Seoul, or Bikini, or, for that matter, this same Berchtesgaden, although that is quite close enough for discomfort.

Two holiday-makers who had chosen O—— out of the several hundred winter resorts that clamored for their patronage were standing in one of the upper streets on the evening of their arrival there. The charming little wooden houses weighted with snow, the delightful little streets so narrow and yet so dignified as to make the great glittering cars seem pretentious and out of place, the older inhabitants in their long dark woolen skirts and heavy clogs, even a sleigh drawn by ribboned horses and full of holiday-makers—all this was attractive, and undeniably what they had come for; particularly as slopes suitable for skiing stretched away on every side. Yet there was no denying that something weighed on them; they were uneasy. And what this thing was does not need to be guessed at, since they had not ceased to express it, and very volubly, since their arrival.

This was a pleasure resort; it existed solely for its visitors. In winter, heavy with snow, and ringing with the shouts of swooping skiers; in summer, garlanded with flowers and filled with the sounds of cowbells—it was all the same: summer and winter dress were nothing but masks concealing the fact that this village had no existence apart from its flux of visitors, which it fed and supplied by means of the single rickety little train that came up from the lowlands of Bavaria, and which in turn it drained of money spent freely on wooden shoes, carved and painted wooden bottles, ironwork, embroidered aprons, ski trousers and sweaters, and those slender curved skis themselves that enabled a thousand earth-plodders to wing over the slopes all through the snow months.

The fact is that for real pleasure a pleasure resort should have no one in it but its legitimate inhabitants, oneself, and perhaps one's friends. Everyone knows it, everyone feels it; and this is the insoluble contradiction of tourism; and perhaps the whole edifice will collapse at that moment when there is not one little town, not one village in the whole of Europe that has not been, as the term is, exploited. No longer will it be possible to drive one's car away into the mountains in search of that unspoiled village, that Old-World inn by the stream; for when one arrives most certainly a professional host will hasten out, offering professional hospitality. What then? Will everyone stay at home?

But what of poor, war-denuded Europe whose inhabitants continue to live, a little sullenly perhaps, under the summer and winter eyes of their visitors, eyes that presumably are searching for some quality, some good, that they do not possess themselves, since otherwise why have they traveled so far from themselves in order to examine the lives of other people?

These were the sort of reflections—which, it must be confessed, could scarcely be more banal—that were being exchanged by our two travelers.

There they stood, outside a little wayside booth, or open shop, that sold, not carved bottles or leather aprons, but real vegetables and butter and cheese. These goods were being bought by a group of American wives who were stationed here with their husbands as

245

part of the army of occupation. Or rather, their husbands were part of the machinery which saw to it that American soldiers stationed all over the American zone of occupation could have pleasant holidays in the more attractive parts of Europe.

Between small, green-painted houses, the snow was pitted and rutted in the narrow street, glazed with the newly frozen heat of tramping feet. In places it was stained yellow and mounded with dark horse droppings, and there was a strong smell of urine mingling with the fresh tang of winter cabbage, giving rise to further reflections about the superiority of automobiles over horses—and even, perhaps, of wide streets over narrow ones, for at every moment the two travelers had to step down off the small pavement into the strong-smelling snow to allow happy groups of skiers to pass by; had to stand back again to make room for the cars that were trying to force a passage up to the big hotels where the American soldiers were holidaying with their wives or girls.

There were so many of the great powerful cars, rocking fast and dangerously up over the slippery snow, that it was hard to preserve the illusion of an unspoiled mountain village. And so the two lifted their eyes to the surrounding forests and peaks. The sun had slipped behind the mountains, but had left their snowfields tinted pink and gold, sentineled by pine groves which, now that the light had gone from them, loomed black and rather sinister, inevitably suggesting wolves, witches, and other creatures from a vanished time—a suggestion, however, tinged with bathos, since it was obvious that wolves or witches would have got short shrift from the mighty creators of those powerful machines. The tinted glitter of the smooth slopes and the black stillness of the woods did their best to set the village in a timelessness not disturbed by the gear and machinery of the traveling cages that lifted clear over intervening valleys to the ledge of a mountain where there was yet another hotel and the amenities of civilization. And perhaps it was a relief, despite all the intrusions of the machinery of domesticity and comfort, to rest one's eyes on those forests, those mountains, whose savagery seemed so innocent. The year was 1951; and, while the inhabitants of the village seemed almost feverishly concerned to present a scene of carefree charm, despite all their efforts the fact which must immediately strike everyone was that most of the people in the streets wore the uniform of the war which was six years past, and that the language most often overheard was American. But it was not possible to stand there, continually being edged this way and that on and off the pavement, with one's eyes fixed determinedly on natural beauty, particularly as the light was going fast and now the houses, shops, and hotels were taking their nocturnal shape and spilling the white pallor of electricity from every door and window, promising warmth, promising certain pleasure. The mountains had massed themselves, black against a luminous sky. Life had left them and was concentrating down in the village. Everywhere came groups of skiers hastening home for the night, and everywhere among them those men and women who proclaimed themselves immediately and at first glance as American. Why? Our two stood there, looking into first one face and then the next, trying to define what it was that set them apart. A good-looking lot, these new policemen of Europe. And well-fed, well-dressed. . . . They were distinguished above all, perhaps, by their assurance! Or was this noisy cheerfulness nothing more than the expression of an inner guilt because the task of policing and preserving order earned such attractive holidays? In which case, it was rather to their credit than not.

But when the four army wives had finished their bargaining at the vegetable and dairy stall and went up the steep street, walking heavily because of their crammed baskets, they so dominated the scene in their well-cut trousers and their bright jackets that the women selling produce and the locals who had been waiting patiently for the four to conclude their shopping seemed almost unimportant, almost like willing extras in a crowd-scene from a film called perhaps *Love in the Alps*, or *They Met in the Snow*.

And six years had been enough to still in the hearts of these Germans—for Germans they were, although Austria was no more than a giant's stone-throw away —all the bitterness of defeat? They were quite happy to provide a homely and picturesque background for whatever nationalities might choose to visit them, even if most were American, and many British—as our two conscientiously added, trying not to dissociate themselves from their responsibilities, even though they felt very strongly that the representatives of *their* country were much too naturally modest and tactful to appropriate a scene simply by the fact that they were in it.

It was hard to believe; and the knowledge of the secret angers, or at the very best, an ironical patience, that must be burning in the breasts of their hosts, the good people of the village of O——, deepened an uneasiness which was almost (and this was certainly irrational) a guilt which should surely have no place in the emotions of a well-deserved vacation.

Guilt about what? It was absurd.

Yet, from the moment they had arrived on the frontier—the word still came naturally to them both —and had seen the signs in German; had heard the language spoken all around them; had passed through towns whose names were associated with the savage hate and terror of headlines a decade old—from that moment had begun in both the complicated uneasiness of which they were so ashamed. Neither had admitted it to the other; both were regretting they had come. Why—they were both thinking—why submit ourselves when we are on vacation and won't be able to afford another one for goodness knows how long, to something that must be unpleasant? Why not say simply and be done with it that, for us, Germany is poisoned? We never want to set foot in it again or hear the language spoken or see a sign in German. We simply do not want to think about it; and if we are unjust and lacking in humanity and reason and good sense then—why not? One cannot be expected to be reasonable about everything.

Yet here they were.

The man remarked, after a long silence, "Last time I was here there was nothing of *that*."

Down the other side of the street, pressed close to the wall to avoid a big car that was going by, came a group of five girls in local peasant costume. All day these girls had been serving behind the counters, or in the restaurants, wearing clothes such as girls anywhere in Europe might wear. Now their individual faces had dwindled behind great white starched headdresses. Their bodies were nothing more than supports for the long-sleeved, long-skirted, extinguishing black dresses. The whole costume had something reminiscent of the prim fantasy of the habits of certain orders of nuns. They were plodding resignedly enough—since after all they were being well paid for doing this—down over the snow toward one of the big hotels where they would regale the tourists with folk songs before slipping home to change into

249

their own clothes in time to spend an hour or so with their young men.

"Well, never mind, I suppose one does like to see it?" The woman slipped her arm through his.

"Oh, I suppose so, why not?"

They began to walk down the street, leaning on each other because of the slipperiness of the rutted snow.

It hung in the balance whether one or other of them might have said something like: Suppose we all stopped coming? Suppose there were no tourists at all; perhaps they would simply cease to exist? Like actors who devote so much of themselves to acting they have no emotions over for their own lives but continue to exist in whatever part they are playing . . .

But neither of them spoke. They turned into the main street of the village, where there were several large hotels and restaurants.

Very easily one of them might have remarked to the other, with a kind of grumbling good humor: It's all very well, all these things we're saying about tourists, but we are tourists ourselves?

Come, come, the other would have replied. Clearly we are tourists on a much higher level than most!

Then they would have both laughed.

But at the same moment they stopped dead, looking at some queer hopping figure that was coming along the pavement over the badly lighted snow. For a moment it was impossible to make out what this great black jumping object could be that was coming fast toward them along the ground. Then they saw it was a man whose legs had been amputated and who was hopping over the snow like a frog, his body swinging and jerking between his heavy arms like the body of some kind of insect.

The two saw the eyes of this man stare up at them as he went hopping past.

At the station that day, when they arrived, two men hacked and amputated by war almost out of humanity, one without arms, his legs cut off at the knee, one whose face was a great scarred eyeless hollow, were begging from the alighting holiday-makers.

"For God's sake," said the man suddenly, as if this were nothing but a continuation of what they had been saying, "for God's sake, let's get out of here."

"Oh, *yes*," she agreed instantly. They looked at each other, smiling, acknowledging in that smile all that they had not said that day.

"Let's go back. Let's find somewhere in France."

"We shouldn't have come."

They watched the cripple lever himself up over a deep doorstep, dragging his body up behind his arms, using the stump of his body as a support while he reached up with long arms to ring the bell.

"What about the money?" she asked.

"We'll go home when it runs out."

"Good, we'll go back tomorrow."

Instantly they felt gay; they were leaving tomorrow.

They walked along the street, looking at the menus outside the hotels. He said, "Let's go in here. It's expensive, but it's the last night."

It was a big, brown, solid-looking hotel called the Lion's Head; and on the old-fashioned gilded sign-board was a great golden lion snarling down at them.

Inside was a foyer, lined with dark, shining wood; there were dark, straight-backed wooden settles around the walls and heavy arrangements of flowers in massive brass tubs. Glass doors opened into the restaurant proper. This was a long room lined with the same gleaming dark wood, and in each corner stood even larger brass tubs crammed with flowers. The tablecloths were heavy white damask; a profusion of cutlery and glass gleamed and glittered. It was a scene of solid middle-class comfort. A waiter showed them to an empty table at one side. The menu was placed between them. They exchanged a grimace, for the place was far too expensive for them, particularly as now they were committed to spending so much of their money on fares away and out of Germany into France—a country where they would feel no compulsion at all to make disparaging and ironical remarks about tourists or tourism.

They ordered their dinner and, while they waited, sat examining the other diners. The Americans were not here. Their hotels were the big, new, modern ones at the top of the village. The clientele here was solidly German. Again the two British tourists were conscious of a secret, half-ashamed unease. They looked from one face to another, thinking: Six years ago, what were you doing? And you—and you? We were mortal enemies then; now we sit in the same room, eating together. You were the defeated.

This last was addressed as a reminder to themselves, for no people could have looked less defeated than these. A more solid, sound, well-dressed, comfortable crowd could not be imagined; and they were eating with the easy satisfaction of those who cannot imagine ever being short of a meal. Yet six years ago. . . .

The waiter brought two plates of soup, very big plates, monogrammed with the sign of the Lion's Head, so full that they asked him to take them away and divide one portion between the two of them. For they had observed that a single portion (served on large metal dishes) of any dish here was enough for two English stomachs. Not that they were not more than willing to do as well as these people around them —the defeated, whose capacity seemed truly incredible. But one day in this country of hearty eaters had not enlarged their stomachs to German capacity; and now that they were leaving, not later than tomorrow, it was too late.

They consumed their half-portions of very strong meat soup, full of vegetables; and pointed out to each other that, even so, their plates held twice as much as they would in England; and continued to dart curious, half-guilty glances at their fellow diners.

Six years ago these people were living amid ruins, in cellars, behind any scrap of masonry that remained standing. They were half-starved, and their clothes were rags. An entire generation of young men were dead. Six years. A remarkable nation, surely.

The jugged hare came and was eaten with appreciation.

They had ordered pastries with cream; but alas, before they could eat them, they had to restore themselves with strong cups of coffee.

Back in France, they told themselves and each other, they would find themselves at home, at table as well as spiritually. By this time tomorrow, they would be in France. And now, with the last meal over and the bill to pay, came the moment of general reckoning, soon over, and in fact accomplished hastily on the back of an envelope.

To take a train, third-class, back to the nearest suitable spot in the French Alps would use up half of their available currency; and it would be a choice of staying out their full three weeks and eating one meal a day—and that a very slender meal—or staying a week and then going home.

They did not look at each other as they reached this final depressing conclusion. They were thinking, of course, that they were mad to leave at all. If to come to Germany was the result of some sort of spiritual quixotry, a symptom of moral philanthropy suitable only for liberal idealists whom—they were convinced —they both despised, then to leave again was simply weak-minded. In fact, their present low-spiritedness was probably due to being overtired, for they had spent two successive nights sitting up on hard wooden train seats, sleeping fitfully on each other's shoulders.

They would have to stay. And now that they reached this conclusion, depression settled on them both; and they looked at the rich Germans who surrounded them with a gloomy hatred which, in their better moments, they would have utterly repudiated.

Just then the waiter came forward, followed by an energetically striding young man apparently fresh from a day's skiing, for his face was flaming scarlet under untidy shags of sandy hair. They did not want him at their table, but the restaurant was now quite full. The waiter left their bill on the tablecloth; and they occupied themselves in finding the right change, under the interested inspection of the young sportsman, who, it seemed, was longing to advise them about money and tips. Resenting his interest, they set themselves to be patient. But the waiter did not return for some time, so busy was he at the surrounding tables; and they watched a party of new arrivals who were settling down at a nearby table that had been reserved for them. There came first a handsome woman in her early middle age, unfastening a shaggy, strong-looking fur coat of the kind worn for winter sports or bad weather outdoors. She flung this open on her chair, making a kind of nest, in which she placed herself, wrapping it closely around her legs. She was wearing a black wool dress, full-skirted and embroidered in bright colors, a dress which flirted with the idea of peasant naïvete. Having arranged herself, she raised her face to greet the rest of her family with a smile that seemed to mock and chide them for taking so long to follow after her. It was a handsome face: she was a fine-looking woman, with her fair curling hair, and a skin bronzed deep with the sun and oil of many weeks of winter sport. Next came a young lad, obviously her son, a very tall, good-looking, attractive youth, who began teasing her because of her hurry to begin eating. He flashed his white strong teeth at her, and his young blue eyes, until she playfully took his arm and shook him. He protested. Then both, with looks of mock concern because this was a public place, desisted, lowered their voices, and sat laughing while the daughter, a delightfully pretty girl of fifteen or so, and the father, a heavy, good-humored gentleman, took the two empty chairs. The family party was complete. The waiter was attentive for their order, which was for four tall glasses of beer, which they insisted on having that moment, before they could order or even think of food. The waiter hurried off to fetch the beer, while they settled down to study the menus. And one could be sure that there would be no half-portions for this family, either for financial reasons or because they suffered from limitations of appetite.

Watching this family, it came home to the couple from Britain that what they were resenting was very likely their sheer capacity for physical enjoyment. Since, like all British people of their type, they spent a great deal of emotional energy on complaining about the inability of their countrymen to experience joy and well-being, they told themselves that what they felt was both churlish and inconsistent. The woman said to the man in a conciliating, apologetic, almost re-signed voice, "They really are extraordinarily good-looking."

To this he responded with a small ironical grimace; and he returned his attention to the family.

Mother, father, and son were laughing over some joke, while the girl turned a very long tapering glass of beer between thumb and forefinger of a thin, tanned hand so that the frost beads glittered and spun. She was staring out of the family group, momentarily lost to it, a fair, dreaming tendril of a girl with an irregular wedge of a little face. Her eyes wandered over the people at the tables, encountered those of our couple, and lingered in open, bland curiosity. It was a gaze of frank unself-consciousness, almost innocence; the gaze of a protected child who knew she might commit no folly on her own individual account, since the family stood between her and the results of folly. Yet, just then, she chose to be out of the family group; or at least, she gazed out of it as one looks through an open door. Her pale, pretty eyes absorbed what she wanted of the British couple, and, at their leisure, moved on to the other diners; and all the time her fingers moved slowly up and down the slim cold walls of her beer glass. The woman, finding in this girl a poetic quality totally lacking from the stolid burghers who filled this room, indicated her to the man by saying: "She's charming." Again he grimaced, as if to say: Every young girl is poetic. And: She'll be her mother in ten years.

Which was true. Already the family had become aware of the infidelity of this, their youngest member; already the handsome mother was leaning over her daughter, rallying her for her dreamy inattention, claiming her by little half-caressing, peremptory exclamations. The solid, kindly father laid his brown and capable hand on the girl's white-wool-covered forearm and bent toward her with solicitude, as if she were sick. The boy put a large forkful of meat into his mouth and ate it ruminantly, watching his sister with an irreverent grin. Then he said in a low tone some word that was clearly an old trumpet for disagreement between them, for she swung her chin toward him petulantly, with a half-reproachful and half-resentful epithet. The brother went on grinning, protective but derisive; the father and mother smiled tenderly at each other because of the brother-and-sister sparring.

No, clearly, this young girl had no chance of escaping from the warm prison of her family; and in a few years she would be a capable, handsome, sensual woman, married to some manufacturer carefully chosen for her by her father. That is, she would be unless another war or economic cataclysm intervened and plunged all her people into the edge-of-disaster hunger-bitten condition from which they had just emerged. Though they did not look as if they had. . . .

Returned full circle to the point of their complicated and irrational dislike, the man and woman raised ironical eyes at each other, and the man said briefly: "Blond beasts."

These two were of another family of mankind from most of the people in the restaurant.

The man was Scotch, small-built, nervous, energetic, with close-springing black hair, white freckled skin, quick, deep blue eyes. He tended to be sarcastic about the English, among whom, of course, he had spent most of his life. He was busy, hard-working, essentially pragmatic, practical, and humane. Yet above and beyond all these admirably useful qualities was something else, expressed in his characteristic little grimace of ironical bitterness, as if he were saying: Well, yes, and then?

As for her, she was small, dark, and watchful, Jewish in appearance and arguably by inheritance, since there had been a Jewish great-grandmother who had escaped from pogrom-loving Poland in the last century and married an Englishman. More potent than the great-grandmother was the fact that her fiancé, a medical student and a refugee from Austria, had been killed in the early days of the war flying over this same country in which they now sat and took their holiday. Mary Parish was one of those people who had become conscious of their claims to being Jewish only when Hitler drew their attention to the possibility they might have some.

She now sat and contemplated the handsome German family and thought: Ten years ago . . . She was seeing them as executioners.

As for the man, who had taken his name, Hamish, from a string of possible names, some of them English, because of another kind of national pride, he had served in his capacity as a doctor on one of the commissions that, after the war, had tried to rescue the debris of humanity the war had left all over Europe.

It was no accident that he had served on this commission. Early in 1939 he had married a German girl, or rather, a Jewish girl, studying in Britain. In July of that year she had made a brave and foolhardy attempt to rescue some of her family who had so far escaped the concentration camps, and had never been heard of since. She had simply vanished. For all Hamish knew, she was still alive somewhere. She might very well be in this village of O——. Ever since yesterday morning when they entered Germany, Mary had been watching Hamish's anxious, angry, impatient eyes moving,

258

preoccupied, from the face of one woman to another: old women, young women; women on buses, trains, platforms; women glimpsed at the end of a street; a woman at a window. And she could feel him thinking: Well, and if I did see her, I wouldn't recognize her.

And his eyes would move back to hers; she smiled; and he gave his small, bitter, ironical grimace.

They were both doctors, both hard-working and conscientious, both very tired because, after all, while living in Britain has many compensations, it is hard work, this business of maintaining a decent level of life with enough leisure for the pursuits that make life worthwhile, or at least to cultivated people, which they both were, and determined to remain. They were above all, perhaps, tired people.

They were tired and they needed to rest. This was their holiday. And here they sat, knowing full well that they were pouring away energies into utterly useless, irrelevant, and above all, unfair, emotions.

The word "unfair" was one they both used without irony.

She said, "I think one week in France would be better than three here. Let's go. I really do think we should."

He said, "Let's go into one of the smaller villages higher up the valley. They are probably just ordinary mountain villages, not tarted-up like this place."

"We'll go tomorrow," she agreed with relief.

Here they both became alert to the fact that the young man who had sat down at their table was watching them, at the same time as he heartily chewed a large mouthful of food, and looked for an inlet into their conversation. He was an unpleasant person. Tall, with an uncoordinated, bony look, his blue eyes met the possibilities of their reaction to him with a steady glare of watchful suspicion out of an ugly face whose skin had a peculiar harsh red texture. The eyes of our couple had been, unknown to them, returning again and again to this remarkable scarlet face, and at the back of their minds they had been thinking professionally: A fool to overheat himself in this strong reflected light up here.

Now, at the same moment, the two doctors realized that the surface of his face was a skin-graft; that the whole highly-colored, shiny, patchy surface, while an extraordinarily skillful reconstruction of a face, was nothing but a mask, and what the face had been before must be guessed at. They saw, too, that he was not a young man, but, like themselves, in early middle age. Instantly pity fought with their instinctive dislike of him; and they reminded themselves that the aggressive glare of the blue eyes was the expression of the pitiful necessity of a wounded creature to defend itself.

He said in stiff but good English, or rather, American: "I must beg your pardon for interrupting your conversation, and beg leave to introduce myself—Dr. Schröder. I wish to place myself at your service. I know this valley well, and can recommend hotels in the other villages."

He was looking at Hamish, as he had from the time he began speaking; though he gave a small, minimal bow when Mary Parrish introduced herself and instantly returned his attention to the man.

Both the British couple felt discomfort; but it was hard to say whether this was because of the man's claim on their pity, because of their professional interest in him, which they must disguise, or because of the impolite insistence of his manner.

"That is very kind of you," said Hamish; and Mary murmured that it was very kind. They wondered whether he had heard his "blond beasts." They wondered what other indiscretions they might have committed.

"As it happens," said Dr. Schröder, "I have a very good buddy who runs a guest house at the top of the valley. I was up there this morning, and she had a dandy room to let."

Once again they indicated that it was very kind of him.

"If it is not too early for you, I shall be taking the 9:30 autobus up the valley tomorrow for a day's skiing, and I shall be happy to assist you."

And now it was necessary to take a stand one way or the other. Mary and Hamish glanced at each other inquiringly; and immediately Dr. Schröder said, with a perceptible increase of tension in his manner, "As you know, at this time in the season, it is hard to find accommodation." He paused, seemed to assure himself of their status by a swift inspection of their clothes and general style, and added: "Unless you can afford one of the big hotels—but they are not of the cheapest."

"Actually," said Mary, trying to make of what he must have heard her say before a simple question of caprice: "Actually we were wondering whether we might not go back to France? We are both very fond of France."

But Dr. Schröder was not prepared to take this from them. "If it is a question of skiing, then the weather report announced today that the snow is not as good in the French Alps as it is with us. And, of course, France is much more expensive."

They agreed that this was so; and he continued to say that if they took the empty room at his buddy's guest house it would cost them much less than it would at a German pension, let alone a French pension. He examined their clothes again and remarked,

"Of course, it must be hard for you to have such unfortunate restrictions with your travel allowance. Yes, it must be annoying. For people of a good salary and position it must be annoying."

For both these two the restrictions of the travel allowance merely confirmed a fact; they could not have afforded more than the allowance in any case. They realized that Dr. Schröder was quite unable to decide whether they were rich and eccentric English people who notoriously prefer old clothes to new clothes, or whether they were rich people deliberately trying to appear poor, or whether they were poor. In the first two cases they would perhaps be eager to do some trade in currency with him? Was that what he wanted?

It seemed it was; for he immediately said that he would be very happy to lend them a modest sum of dough, in return for which he would be glad if they would do the same for him when he visited London, which he intended to do very soon. He fastened the steady glare of his eyes on their faces, or rather, on Hamish's face, and said: "Of course, I am prepared to offer every guarantee." And he proceeded to do so. He was a doctor attached to a certain hospital in the town of S——, and his salary was regular. If they wished to make independent inquiries they were welcome to do so.

And now Hamish intervened to make it clear that they could not afford to spend on this vacation one penny more than the travel allowance. For a long moment Dr. Schröder did not believe him. Then he examined their clothes again and openly nodded.

Now, perhaps, the man would go away?

Not at all. He proceeded to deliver a harangue on the subject of his admiration for Britain. His love for the entire British nation, their customs, their good taste, their sportsmanship, their love of fair play, their history, and their art were the ruling passions of his life. He went on like this for some minutes, while the British couple wondered if they ought to confess that their trade was the same as his. But, if they did, presumably it would let them in for even closer intimacy. And by a hundred of the minute signs which suffice for communication between people who know each other well, they had said that they disliked this man intensely and wished only that he would go away.

But now Dr. Schröder inquired outright what profession his new friend Mr. Anderson pursued; and when he heard that they were both doctors, and attached to hospitals whose names he knew, his expression changed. But subtly. It was not surprise, but rather the look of a prosecutor who has been cross-examining witnesses and at last got what he wants.

And the British couple were beginning to understand what it was Dr. Schröder wanted of them. He was talking with a stiff, brooding passion of resentment about his position and prospects as a doctor in Germany. For professional people, he said, Germany was an unkind country. For the business people—yes. For the artisans—yes. The workers were all millionaires these days, yes sir! Better far to be a plumber or an electrician than a doctor. The ruling dream of his life was to make his way to Britain, and there become an honored—and, be it understood—a well-paid member of his profession.

Here Doctors Anderson and Parrish pointed out that foreign doctors were not permitted to practice in Britain. They might lecture; they might study; but they might not practice. Not unless, added Dr. Parrish, possibly reacting to the fact that not once had this man done more than offer her the barest minimum of politeness until he had recognized that she, as well as Hamish, was a doctor and therefore possibly of use to him—not unless they were refugees, and even then they must take the British examinations.

Dr. Schröder did not react to the word "refugee."

He returned to a close cross-examination about their salaries and prospects, dealing first with Mary's, and then, in more detail, with Hamish. At last, in response to their warning that for him to become a doctor in Britain would be much more difficult than he seemed to think, he replied that in this world everything was a question of pulling strings. In short, he intended they should pull strings for him. It was the most fortunate occurrence of his life that he had happened to meet them that evening, the happiest and the best-timed. . . .

At this, the eyes of the British couple met on a certain suspicion. Ten minutes later in the talk it emerged that he knew the lady who ran the house where they had taken a room, and therefore he probably had heard from her that she had a British doctor as a lodger. Very likely he had arranged with the waiter to be put at their table. For he must know the people of the village well: he had been coming for his winter holidays to O—— since he was a small child—Dr. Schröder held out his hand below table level to show how small. Yes, all those years of winters O—— had known Dr. Schröder, save for the years of war, when he was away serving his country.

There was a small stir in the restaurant. The family were rising, gathering their wraps, and departing. The lady first, her shaggy brown coat slung over her handsome shoulders, her rosy lower lip caught by her white teeth as she searched for belongings she might have forgotten. Then she extended her smile, so white against the clear brown skin, and waited for her son to take her by the shoulder and propel her, while she laughed, protesting, to the door. There, when it opened, she shivered playfully, although it was only the door to the vestibule. Behind her came the pretty, rather languid girl; then the stout authoritative father, shepherding his family away and out to the snow-cold air. The family vanished, leaving their table a mess of empty glasses, plates, broken bread, cheeses, fruit, wine. The waiter cleared the table with a look as if he found it a privilege.

The British couple also rose and said to Dr. Schröder that they would think over his suggestion and perhaps let him know in the morning. His thin-skinned shiny face tilted up at them, and leveled into an affronted mask as he stood up and said, "But I understood all arrangements were made."

And how had they got themselves into this position, where they could not exercise simple freedom of choice without upsetting this extremely dislikable person? But they knew how. It was because he was a wounded man, a cripple; because they knew that his fixed aggression was part of his laudable determination not to let that shockingly raw face drive him into self-pity and isolation. They were doctors, and they were reacting above all to the personality of a cripple. When they said that they were tired and intended to go to bed early, and he replied instantly, insulted, that he would be happy to accompany them to a certain very pleasant place of entertainment, they knew that they could bring themselves to do no more than say they could not afford it.

They knew he would immediately offer to be their host. He did, and they politely refused as they would refuse an ordinary acquaintance, and were answered by the man who could tolerate no refusal, because if he once accepted a refusal, he would be admitting to himself that his face put him outside simple human intercourse.

Dr. Schröder, who had spent all the winter holidays of his life in this valley, naturally knew the proprietor of the hotel where he proposed to take them; and he guaranteed them a pleasant and relaxing evening while he fixed on them a glare of suspicious hate.

They walked together under the snow-weighted eaves of the houses, over snow rutted by the hundred enormous American cars which had rocked over it that day, to the end of the street where there was a hotel whose exterior they had already inspected earlier that day and rejected on the grounds that anything inside it must necessarily be too expensive for them. Immediately outside, on the seared snow, sat the man without legs they had seen earlier. Or rather he stood, his head level with their hips, looking as if he were buried to hip-level in the snow, holding out a cloth cap to them. His eyes had the same bold, watchful glare as those of Dr. Schröder.

Dr. Schröder said, "It's a disgrace that these people should be allowed to behave like this. It makes a bad impression on our visitors." And he led the British couple past the cripple with a look of angry irritation.

Inside was a long room sheltered by glass on two sides from the snow which could be seen spinning down through the areas of yellow light conquered from the black mass of the darkness by the room and its warmth and its noise and its people. It was extraordinarily pleasant to enter this big room, so busy with pleasure, and to see the snow made visible only during its passage through the beams from the big windows, as if the wildness of the mountain valley had been admitted just so far as would give the delight of contrast to the guests who could see savagery as a backdrop of pretty, spinning white flakes.

There was a small band, consisting of piano, clarinet, and drum, playing the kind of jazz that makes a pleasant throb, like a blood-beat, behind conversation.

The family had moved themselves from the table in the restaurant to a table here and sat as before in a close group. The British couple found an empty table near them, which Dr. Schröder approved; and when the waiter came knew they had been right—the drinks were very expensive and this was not a place where one might lightly sip one drink for a whole evening while richer people drank seriously. One was expected to drink; people were drinking, although a small beer cost nearly ten shillings. They saw, too, that Dr. Schröder's boast that he had special privileges here because he was a friend of the proprietor was untrue. His passport here, as everywhere else, was his raw, shiny face. When the proprietor glanced toward him during his hospitable passage among the tables; he did so with a nod and a smile, but it was a smile that had the overkindness of controlled hostility. And his eyes lingered briefly on the British couple who, after this inspection, were forced to feel that everyone else in this place was German. The Americans were in their own rich hotels; the impoverished British in the cheap guest houses; this place was for wealthy Germans. And the British couple wondered at the insistence of Dr. Schröder in bringing them here. Was it possible that he really believed he had a special place in the heart of the proprietor? Yes, it was; he kept smiling and nodding after the turned back of the fat host, as if to say: You see, he knows me; then smiling at them, proud of his achievement. For which he was prepared to pay heavily in actual money. He counted out the price of the drinks with the waiter with a painful care for the small change of currency that they understood very well. What recompense could they possibly give this man; what was he wanting so badly? Was it really only that he wanted to live and work in Britain?

Again Dr. Schröder began to talk, and again of his admiration for their country, leaning across the table, looking into their faces, as if this was a message of incalculable importance to them both.

He was interrupted by the clarinet player who stood up, took a note from the regular ground-throb of the music, and began to develop a theme of his own from it. Couples went onto a small area of shiny floor not occupied by tables, and which was invaded at every moment by the hurrying waiters with their trays of drinks. They were dancing, these people, for the pleasure not of movement, but of contact. A dozen or a score of men and women, seemingly held upright by the pressure of the seated guests around them, idled together, loosely linked, smiling, skeptical, good-natured with the practice of pleasure.

Immediately the dancing was broken up because the group of folk singers had come in at the big glass entrance door, in their demure conventual dress, and now stood by the band waiting.

The woman at the next table gave a large cheerful shrug and said, "This is the fifth time. This is my fifth home-evening." People turned to smile at the words *heimat-abend*, indulgent with the handsome woman and her look of spoiled enjoyment. Already one of the folk singers was moving among the tables to collect their fee, which was high; and already the rich papa was thrusting toward the girl a heap of money, disdaining the change with a shake of his head—change, however, which she did not seem in any urgency to give him. When she reached the table where our couple sat with Dr. Schröder, Hamish paid, and not with good grace. After all, the prices were high enough here without having to pay more for folk songs which one did not necessarily want to listen to at all.

When the girl had made her rounds and collected her money, she rejoined the group, which formed itself together near the band and sang, one after another, songs of the valley, in which yodeling figured often and loudly, earning loud applause.

It was clear that Dr. Schröder, who listened to the group with a look of almost yearning nostalgia, did not feel its intrusion as an irritant at all. Folk songs, his expression said, were something he could listen to all night. He clapped often and glanced at his guests, urging them to share his sentimental enjoyment.

At last the group left; the clarinet summoned the dancers to the tiny floor; and Dr. Schröder resumed his hymn of love for Britain. Tragic, he said, having stated and restated the theme of praise—tragic that these two countries had ever had to fight at all. Tragic that natural friends should have been divided by the machinations of interested and sinister groups. The British couple's eyes met ironically over the unspoken phrase, international Jewry, and even with the consciousness of being pedantic, if not unfair. But Dr. Schröder did not believe in the unstated. He said that international Jewry had divided the two natural masters of Europe, Germany and Britain; and it was his passionate belief that in the future these two countries should work together for the good of Europe and thus, obviously, of the whole world. Dr. Schröder had had good friends, friends who were almost brothers, killed on the fronts where British and German troops had been maneuvered into hostility; and he grieved over them even now as one does for sacrificed victims.

Dr. Schröder paused, fixed them with the glare of his eyes, and said: "I wish to tell you that I, too, was wounded; perhaps you have not noticed. I was wounded on the Russian front. My life was despaired of. But I was saved by the skill of our doctors. My entire face is a witness to the magnificent skill of our German doctors."

The British couple hastened to express their surprise and congratulations. Oddly enough, they felt a lessened obligation toward compassion because of Dr. Schröder's grotesque and touching belief that his face was nearly normal enough to be unnoticed. He said that the surface of his face had burned off when a tank beside him had exploded into pieces, showering him with oil. He had fought for three years with the glorious armies of his country all over the Ukraine. He spoke like a survivor from the Grande Armée to fellow admirers of "The Other," inviting and expecting interested congratulation. "Those Russians," he said, "are savages. Barbarians. No one would believe the atrocities they committed. Unless you had seen it with your own eyes you would not believe the brutality the Russians are capable of."

The British couple, now depressed into silence, and even past the point where they could allow their eyes to meet in ironical support of each other, sat watching the languidly revolving dancers.

Dr. Schröder said insistently, "Do you know that those Russians would shoot at our soldiers as they walked through the streets of a village? An ordinary Russian peasant, if he got the chance, would slaughter one of our soldiers? And even the women—I can tell you cases of Russian women murdering our soldiers after pretending to be buddies with them."

Mary and Hamish kept their peace and wondered how Dr. Schröder had described to himself the mass executions, the hangings, the atrocities of the German army in Russia. They did not wonder long, for he said, "We were forced to defend ourselves. Yes, I can tell you that we had to defend ourselves against the savagery of those people. The Russians are monsters."

Mary Parrish roused herself to say, "Not such monsters, perhaps, as the Jews?" And she tried to catch and hold the fanatic eyes of their host with her own. He said, "Ah, yes, we had many enemies." His eyes, moving fast from Hamish's face to Mary's, paused and wavered. It occurred to him perhaps that they were not entirely in accordance with him. For a second his ugly, blistered mouth twisted in what might have been doubt. He said politely, "Of course, our Führer went too far in his zeal against our enemies. But he understood the needs of our country."

"It is the fate of great men," said Hamish, in the quick sarcastic voice that was the nearest he ever got to expressed anger, "to be misunderstood by the small-minded."

Dr. Schröder was now unmistakably in doubt. He was silent, examining their faces with his eyes, into which all the expression of his scarred face was concentrated, while they suffered the inner diminishment and confusion that happens when the assumptions on which one bases one's life are attacked. They were thinking dubiously that this was the voice of madness. They were thinking that they knew no one in Britain who would describe it as anything else. They were thinking that they were both essentially, self-consciously, of that element in their nation dedicated to not being insular, to not falling into the errors of complacency; and they were, at this moment, feeling something of the despair that people like them had felt ten, fifteen, years ago, watching the tides of madness rise while the reasonable and the decent averted their eyes. At the same time they were feeling an extraordinary but undeniable reluctance to face the fact that

271

Dr. Schröder might represent any more than himself. No, they were assuring themselves, this unfortunate man is simply a cripple, scarred mentally as well as physically, a bit of salvage from the last war.

At this moment the music again stopped, and there was an irregular clapping all over the room; clearly there was to be a turn that the people there knew and expected.

Standing beside the piano was a small, smiling man who nodded greetings to the guests. He was dark, quick-eyed, with an agreeable face that the British couple instinctively described as "civilized." He nodded to the pianist, who began to improvise an accompaniment to his act; he was half-singing, half-talking, the verse of a song or ballad about a certain general whose name the British couple did not recognize. The accompaniment was a steady, military-sounding thump-thump against which the right hand wove fragments of "Deutschland Über Alles" and the "Horst Wessel Song." The refrain was: "And now he sits in Bonn."

The next verse was about an admiral, also now sitting in Bonn.

The British couple understood that the song consisted of the histories of a dozen loyal German militarists who had been overzealous in their devotion to their Führer; had been sentenced by the Allied courts of justice to various terms of imprisonment, or to death; "and now they sat in Bonn."

All that was fair enough. It sounded like a satire on Allied policy in Germany which—so both these conscientious people knew and deplored—tended to be overgenerous to the ex-murderers of the Nazi régime. What could be more heartening than to find their own view expressed there, in this comfortable resort of the German rich? And what more surprising?

They looked at Dr. Schröder and saw his eyes gleaming with pleasure. They looked back at the urbane, ironical little singer, who was performing with the assurance of one who knows himself to be perfectly at one with his audience, and understood that this was the type of ballad adroitly evolved to meet the needs of an occupied people forced to express themselves under the noses of a conqueror. True that the American army was not here, in this room, this evening; but even if they had been, what possible exception could they have taken to the words of this song?

It was a long ballad, and when it was ended there was very little applause. Singer and audience exchanged with each other smiles of discreet understanding, and the little man bowed this way and that. He then straightened himself, looked at the British couple, and bowed to them. It was as if the room caught its breath. Only when they looked at Dr. Schröder's face, which showed all the malicious delight of a child who had thumbed his nose behind teacher's back, did they understand what a demonstration of angry defiance that bow had been. And they understood, with a sinking of the heart, the depths of furious revengeful humiliation which made such a very slight gesture so extremely satisfying to these rich burgesses, who merely glanced discreetly, smiling slightly, at these conquerors in their midst—conquerors who were so much shabbier than they were, so much more worn and tired—and turned away, exchanging glances of satisfaction, to their batteries of gleaming glasses filled with wine and with beer.

And now Mary and Hamish felt that this demonstration, which presumably Dr. Schröder had shared in, perhaps even invited, released them from any obligation to him; and they looked at him with open dislike, indicating that they wished to leave.

Besides, the waiter stood beside them, showing an open insolence that was being observed and admired by the handsome matron and her husband and her son; the girl was, as usual, dreaming some dream of her own and not looking at anyone in particular. The waiter bent over them, put his hands on their still half-filled glasses, and asked what they would have.

Hamish and Mary promptly drank what remained of their beer and rose. Dr. Schröder rose with them. His whole knobbly, ugly body showed agitation and concern. Surely they weren't going? Surely, when the evening was just beginning, and very soon they would have the privilege of hearing again the talented singer who had just retired, but only for a short interval. Did they realize that he was a famous artist from M——, a man who nightly sang to crammed audiences, who was engaged by the management of this hotel, alas, only for two short weeks of the winter season?

This was either the most accomplished insolence or another manifestation of Dr. Schröder's craziness. For a moment the British couple wondered if they had made a mistake and had misunderstood the singer's meaning. But one glance around the faces of the people at the near tables was enough: each face expressed a discreetly hidden smile of satisfaction at the rout of the enemy—routed by the singer, and by the waiter, their willing servant who was nevertheless at this moment exchanging democratic grins of pleasure with the handsome matron.

Dr. Schröder was mad, and that was all there was to it. He both delighted in the little demonstration of hostility and, in some involved way of his own, wanted them to delight in it—probably out of brotherly love for him. And now he was quite genuinely agitated and hurt because they were going.

The British couple went out, past the smiling band, past the conscious waiter, while Dr. Schröder followed. They went down the iced steps of the hotel and stopped by the legless man who was still rooted in the snow like a plant, where Hamish gave him all the change he had, which amounted to the price of another round of drinks had they stayed in the big warm room.

Dr. Schröder watched this and said at once, with indignant reproach, "You should not do this. It is not expected. Such people should be locked away." All his suspicion had returned; they must, obviously, be rich, and they had been lying to him.

Mary and Hamish went without speaking down the snow-soft street, through a faint fall of white snow; and Dr. Schröder came striding behind them, breathing heavily. When they reached the door of the little house where they had a room, he ran around them and stood facing them, saying hurriedly, "And so I shall see you tomorrow at the autobus, nine-thirty."

"We will get in touch with you," said Hamish politely, which, since they did not know his address, and had not asked for it, was as good as dismissing him.

Dr. Schröder leaned toward them, examining their faces with his gleaming, suspicious eyes. He said, "I will attend you in the morning," and left them.

They let themselves in and ascended the shallow wooden stairs to their room in silence. The room was low and comfortable, gleaming with well-polished wood. There were an old-fashioned rose-patterned jug and basin on the washstand and an enormous bed laden with thick eiderdowns. A great, shining, blue-tiled stove filled half a wall. Their landlady had left a note pinned to one of the fat pillows, demanding politely that they should leave, in their turn, a note for her outside their door, saying at what hour they wished to receive their breakfast tray. She was the widow of the pastor. She now lived by letting this room to the summer and winter visitors. She knew this couple were not married because she had had, by regulation, to take down particulars from their passports. She had said nothing of any disapproval she might have felt. The gods of the tourist trade must not be offended by any personal prejudice she might hold; and she must have prejudices, surely, as the widow of a man of God, even against a couple so obviously respectable as this one?

Mary said, "I wish she'd turn us out in a fit of moral indignation. I wish someone would have a fit of moral indignation about something, instead of everything simmering and festering in the background."

To which he replied, with the calm of a practical man, "We will get up extremely early and leave this valley before our friend Dr. Fascist can see us. I don't think I could bear to exchange even one more word with him." He wrote a short note to the widow of the pastor, demanding breakfast for seven o'clock; left it outside the door; and, thus well-organized, invited Mary to come to bed and stop worrying.

They got into bed and lay side by side. This was not a night when their arms could hold any comfort for each other. This was a night when they were not a couple, they were two people. Their dead were in the room with them—if Lise, his wife, could be called dead. For how were they to know? War above all breeds a knowledge of the fantastic, and neither of them heard one of the extraordinary and impossible stories of escape, coincidence, and survival without thinking: Perhaps Lise is alive somewhere after all.

And the possible aliveness of Hamish's dead wife had kept alive the image of the very young medical student who, being a medical student, had no right to risk himself in the air at all; but who had in fact taken wing out of his furious misery and anger because of the Nazis and had crashed in flames a year later. These two, the pretty and vivacious Lise and the gallant and crusading airman, stood by the enormous, eiderdown-weighted bed and said softly: You must include us, you must include us.

And so it was a long time before Mary and Hamish slept.

Both awoke again in the night, aware of the snow-sheen on the windowpanes, listening to the soft noises of the big porcelain stove which sounded as if there were a contented animal breathing beside them in the room. Now they thought that they were leaving this valley because, out of some weakness of character apparently inherent in both of them, they had put themselves in a position where, if they took a room higher up the valley, it would have to be a room chosen for them by Dr. Schröder, since they could not bring themselves to be finally rude to him because of that scarred face of his.

No, they preferred to conclude that Dr. Schröder summed up in his personality and being everything they hated in this country, Germany, the great catalyst and mirror of Europe: summed it up and presented it to them direct and unambiguously, in such a way that they must reject or accept it.

Yet how could they do either? For to meet Dr. Schröder at all made it inevitable that these two serious and conscience-driven people must lie awake and think: One nation is not very different from another. . . . (For if one did not take one's stand on this proposition where did one end?) And therefore it followed that they must think: What in Britain corresponds to Dr. Schröder? What unpleasant forces are this moment simmering in the sewers of our national soul that might explode suddenly into shapes like Dr. Schröder? Well then? And what deplorable depths of complacency there must be in us both that we should feel so superior to Dr. Schröder—that we should wish only that he might be pushed out of sight somewhere, like a corpse in a house full of living people; or masked like a bad smell; or exorcized like an evil spirit?

Were they or were they not on vacation? They were; and therefore exempt by definition from lying awake and thinking about the last war; lying awake and worrying about the possible next war; lying awake and wondering what perverse masochism had brought them here at all.

At the dead and silent hour of four, when not a light glimmered anywhere in the village, they were both awake, lying side by side in the great feather-padded bed, discussing Dr. Schröder in depth. They analyzed him politically, psychologically, and medically—particularly medically—and at such length that when the maid came in with their early breakfast they were extremely reluctant to wake up. But they forced themselves to wake, to eat and to dress, and then went downstairs where their landlady was drinking coffee in her kitchen. They put their problem to her. Yesterday they had agreed to stay with her for a week. Today they wanted to leave. Since it was the height of the season presumably she would let her room today? If not, of course they would be delighted to pay what they were morally bound to do.

Frau Stohr dismissed the subject of payment as irrelevant. At this time of the year her bell rang a dozen times a day with inquiries for rooms by people who

278

had arrived at the station and hoped, usually overoptimistically, to find empty rooms in the village. Frau Stohr was upset that her two guests wished to leave. They were not comfortable? They were badly served?

They hastened to assure her that the place was everything they wanted. At the moment they felt it was. Frau Stohr was the most pleasant sight in an early morning after a night of conscience-searching. She was a thin and elderly lady, her white hair drawn back into a tight knot which was stuck through with stiff utilitarian pins almost the size of knitting needles. Her face was severe, but tranquil and kindly. She wore a long, full, black woolen skirt, presumably a practical descendant of the great woolen skirts of the local peasant costume. She wore a long-sleeved striped woolen blouse fastened high at the throat with a gold brooch.

They found it very hard to say that they wanted to leave the valley the day after arriving in it. The rectitude of this admirable old lady made it difficult. So they said they had decided to take a room farther up the valley where the snow slopes organized for skiing would be closer to the villages. For, above all, they did not want to hurt Frau Stohr's national feelings; they intended to slip quietly down to the station and take the first train away from the place, away and out of Germany into France.

Frau Stohr instantly agreed. She had always thought it more suitable for the serious skiers to find homes farther up the valley. But there were people who came to the winter sports not for the sport, but for the atmosphere of the sport. As for herself she never tired of seeing the young people at their tricks on the snow. Of course, when she had been a girl, it was not a question of tricks at all; skis were simply a means of getting from one place to another quickly . . . but now, of course, all that had changed, and someone like herself who had been almost born on skis, like all the children of the valley, would find it embarrassing to stand on skis again with nothing to show in the way of jumps and turns. Of course, at her age she seldom left the house, and so she did not have to expose her deficiencies. But her two guests, being serious skiers, must be feeling frustrated, knowing that all the long runs, and the big ski lifts were at the head of the valley. Luckily she knew of a lady in the last village of the valley who had a free room and would be just the person to look after them.

Here she mentioned the name of the lady recommended by Dr. Schröder the night before, and it was extraordinary how this name, yesterday associated with every kind of unpleasantness, became attractive and reassuring, simply because it came from the lips of Frau Stohr.

Mary and Hamish exchanged looks and came to a decision without speaking. In the sober light of early morning, all the very sound arguments against leaving the valley returned to them. And after all, Dr. Schröder was staying in O—— itself, and not in the village thirty miles up the valley. At worst he might come and visit them.

Frau Stohr offered to telephone Frau Länge, who was a good woman and an unfortunate one. Her husband had been killed in the last war. Here Frau Stohr smiled at them with the gentle tolerance of the civilized who take it for granted that war between nations need not destroy their common humanity and understanding. Yes, yes, as long as men were so stupid there would be wars and, afterward, widows like poor Frau Lange, who had lost not only her husband

280

but her two sons, and now lived alone with her daughter, taking in lodgers.

Frau Stohr and the British couple, united on the decent common ground of the international humanitarian conscience, smiled at each other, thinking compassionately of Frau Länge. Then Frau Stohr went to the telephone and engaged the room on behalf of her two guests, for whom she was prepared to vouch personally. Then they settled the bill, thanked each other, and separated—Mary and Hamish with their cases in their hands and their skis over their shoulders toward the bus stop, and Frau Stohr to her knitting and her cup of coffee in her big heated kitchen.

It was a clear morning, the sun sparkling pinkly over the slopes of snow where the pine trees stood up, stiff and dark. The first bus of the day was just leaving, and they found places in it. They sat behind two small, pigtailed blonde girls who saw nobody else in the bus, but held each other's hands and sang one folk song after another in small, clear voices. Everyone in the bus turned to smile with affectionate indulgence at them. The bus climbed slowly up and up, along the side of the snow-filled valleys; and as the skiing villages came into sight, one after another, the bus stopped, shedding some passengers and taking on others, but always full; up and up while the two small girls sang, holding hands, looking earnestly into each other's faces, so as to be sure they were keeping time, and never once repeating a song.

The British couple thought it unlikely that they could find, in their own country, two small girls who could sing, without repeating themselves, for two solid hours of a bus journey, even if their British stiff-lippedness would allow them to open their mouths in public in the first place. These two singing children comforted Mary and Hamish quite remarkably. This was the real Germany—rather old-fashioned, a bit sentimental, warm, simple, kindly. Dr. Schröder and what he stood for was an unlucky and not very important phenomenon. Everything they had felt yesterday was the result of being overtired. Now they examined the pleasant villages through which they passed with anticipation, hoping that the one they were committed to would be equally as full of modest wooden chalets and apparently inexpensive restaurants.

It was. At the very head of the valley where the mountain barrier beyond which lay Innsbruck rose tall and impregnable, there was a small village, as charming as all the others. Here, somewhere, was the house of Frau Länge. They made inquiries at a hotel and were directed. A path ran off from the village uphill among the pine woods to a small house about a mile away. The isolation of this house appealed naturally to the instincts of the British couple, who trudged toward it over cushions of glittering snow, feeling grateful to Frau Stohr. The path was narrow, and they had constantly to stand aside while skiers in bright clothes whizzed past them, laughing and waving. The proficiency of the sun-bronzed gods and goddesses of the snowfields discouraged Mary and Hamish, and perhaps half the attraction of that isolated house was that they could make their tame flights over the snow in comparative privacy.

The house was square, small, wooden; built on a low mound of snow in a space surrounded by pine woods. Frau Länge was waiting for them at her front door, smiling. For some reason they had imagined her in the image of Frau Stohr; but she was a good twenty years younger, a robust, straw-headed, red-cheeked woman wearing a tight scarlet sweater and a tight, bright blue skirt. Behind her was a girl, obviously her daughter, a healthy, brown, flaxen-haired girl. Both women occupied themselves with a frank and intensive examination of their new guests for the space of time it took them to cross the snow to the house. The room they were given was at the front of the house, looking away from the village up into a side valley. It was a room like the one they had occupied for the one night at Frau Stohr's: low, large, gleaming with waxed wood, and warmed by an enormous tiled stove. Frau Länge took their passports to write down their particulars, and when she returned them it was with a change of manner which made Mary Parrish and Hamish Anderson know they had been accepted into a freemasonry with their hostess. She said, while her frankly vulgar blue eyes continued a minute examination of them and their belongings, that her dear aunt, Frau Stohr, who was not really her aunt, just a second cousin, called Aunt out of respect for her age and position as widow of the pastor, had spoken for them; that she had every confidence in any person recommended from that quarter. And she had heard, too, from dear Dr. Schröder, who was an old friend, a friend of many years, ah—what a brave man. Did they notice his face? Yes, truly? Did they know that for two years he had lain in hospital while a new face was molded for him and covered with skin taken from his thighs? Poor man. Yes, it was the barbarity of those Russians that was responsible for Dr. Schröder's face. Here she gave an exaggerated sigh and a shrug and left them.

They reminded themselves that they had hardly slept for three nights of their precious holiday, and this doubtless accounted for their present lack of enthusiasm for the idea of putting on skis. They went to sleep and slept the day through; that evening they were served a heavy meal in the living room by Frau Länge herself, who stood chatting to them until they asked her to sit down. Which she did, and proceeded to cross-examine them about the affairs of the British royal family. It was impossible to exaggerate the degree of enthusiasm aroused in Frau Länge by the royal family. She followed every move made by any member of it through a dozen illustrated papers. She knew what they all ate, how they liked things cooked, and how served. She knew the type of corset favored by the Queen, the names of the doctors attending her, the methods of upbringing planned for the royal children, the favorite colors of the two royal Elizabeths and the royal Margaret.

The British couple, who were by temperament republicans and who would have described themselves as such had the word not, at that time, been rather *vieux jeu*, acquired an impressive amount of information about "their" royal family, and felt inadequate, for they were unable to answer any of her questions.

To escape from Frau Länge they went back to their room. They discovered that this house was not at all as isolated as it had seemed during the day when the pine trees had concealed from them buildings farther up the little side valley. Lights sparkled in the trees, and it seemed that there were at least two large hotels less than half a mile away. Music streamed toward them across the dark snow.

In the morning they found there were two American hotels; that is, hotels specifically for the recreation of American troops. Frau Länge used the word American with a mixture of admiration and hatred. And she took it for granted that they, who were after all partners with the Americans (and the Russians of course) in this business of policing the defeated country, should share this emotion with her. It was because they shared with her, Frau Länge, the quality of not being rich.

"Ah," she said, with a false and hearty shrug of her shoulders, a false humility in her voice, "it is a terrible thing, the way they come here and behave as if they owned our country." And she stood at the window, while the British couple ate their breakfast, watching the American soldiers and their wives and their girl friends swooping past down the slopes; and on her face was a bitter envy, an admiring spite, as if she were thinking: Yes? Then wait and see!

Later that day they saw the daughter standing displayed on her doorstep in well-cut ski trousers and sweater, like a girl in a poster, looking at the American soldiers. And they heard her call out, every time a single man went past: "Yank-ee. Yank-ee." The soldier would look up and wave, and she waved back shouting: "I love you, Buddy." At last one came over; and the two went off on skis, down to the village.

Frau Länge, who had seen them watching, said, "Ach, these young girls, I was one myself." She waited until they smiled their tolerant complicity—and waited in such a way they felt they could do no less, seeing that their passports proved they had no right to different standards; and said, "Yes, when one is young one is foolish. I remember how I fell in love with every man I saw. Ach, yes, it was so. I was living in Munich when I was a girl. Yes, youth has no discrimination. I was in love with our Führer, yes, it is true. And before that in love with a Communist leader who lived in our street. And now I tell my Lili it is lucky that she falls in love with the American army, because she is in love with democracy." Frau Länge giggled and sighed.

At all the heavy meals she served them—sausage

285

and *sauerkraut* and potatoes; *sauerkraut*, potatoes, and beef stew—she stood by them, talking, or sat modestly at the other end of the polished wood table, one plump forearm resting before her, one hand stroking and arranging her bright yellow hair, and talked and talked. She told them the history of her life while they ate. Her mother died of hunger in the First World War. Her father was a carpenter. Her elder brother was a political; he was a Social Democrat, and so she had been a Social Democrat, too. And then he had been a Communist; and so she voted for the Communists, God forgive her. And then there came the Führer; and her brother told her he was a good man, and so she became a Nazi. Of course, she was very young and foolish in those days. She told them, giggling, how she had stood in those vast crowds while the Führer spoke, shrieking with enthusiasm. "For my brother was in the uniform, yes, and he was so good-looking, you would never believe it!"

The British couple remembered listening on the radio to the sound of those fanatic crowds roaring and yelling approval to the dedicated, hysterical, drumbeating voice; they watched Frau Länge and imagined her a young girl, sweating and scarlet-faced, yelling with the thousands, arm in arm with her girl friend, who was of course in love with the uniformed brother. Then, afterward cooling her sore throat with beer in a café, she would perhaps have giggled with the girl friend at the memory of her intoxication. Or perhaps she had not giggled. At any rate, she had married and come here to the mountains and had three children.

And now her man was dead, killed on the front near Stalingrad. And one son had been killed in North Africa, and another at Avranches. And when her Lili leaned out of the window giggling and waving at a passing American soldier she giggled and said, with a glance at the British couple, "Lucky for us we aren't in the Russian zone, because if so Lili would have loved a Russki." And Lili giggled and leaned farther out of the window and waved and called "Buddy, I love you."

Frau Länge, conscious perhaps that the continued politeness of her British guests need not necessarily mean agreement, would sometimes straighten her shoulders into prim self-righteousness, look in front of her with lowered and self-conscious eyelids, and say with a murmuring shocked rectitude: "Yes, Lili, say what you like, but we are lucky this time to have English people as guests. They are people like ourselves who have suffered from this terrible war. And they will go back home and tell their friends what we suffer because our country is divided. For it is clear they are shocked. They did not know of the humiliations we have to undergo."

At this Mary Parrish and Hamish Anderson would say nothing at all, but politely passed each other the salt or the dumplings and shortly afterward excused themselves and went to their room. They were sleeping a good deal, for, after all, they were people kept permanently short of sleep. And they ate heartily if not well. They skied a little and lay often in the sun, acquiring a layer of brown that they would lose within a week of returning to London. They were feeling rested. They were in a lethargy of physical contentment. They listened to Frau Länge, accepted her scolding because of their total ignorance of the manners and habits of the royal families of Europe, watched the daughter go off with this U.S. soldier or that; and when Dr. Schröder arrived one afternoon to take coffee with Frau Länge, they were happy to join the party. Frau Länge had explained to them that it was the dream of Dr. Schröder's life to reach the United States. Unfortunately, every attempt he had made to do this had failed. It was, perhaps, easy for them to arrange a visa for Dr. Schröder from London? No? It was difficult there, too? Ach, if she were a young woman she too would go to the United States; that was the country of the future, was it not? She did not blame Dr. Schröder that he wished so much to go there. And if she were in a position to assist him, they must believe her that she would, for friends should always help each other.

They had decided that it was Frau Länge's plan to marry Lili to the doctor. But it seemed Lili did not share this idea, for although she knew he was coming, she did not appear that evening. And perhaps Frau Länge was not altogether sorry, for while the word flirtation could hardly be used of a relationship like this one, it was extremely amiable. Fraud Länge sighed a great deal, her silly blue eyes fastened on the terrible shining mask of her friend's face, saying, "Ach, mein Gott, mein Gott, mein Gott!" while Dr. Schröder accepted the tribute like a film star bored with flattery, making polite gestures of repudiation with one hand, using the other to eat with. He stayed the night, ostensibly on the old sofa in the kitchen.

In the morning he woke Mary and Hamish at seven to say that unfortunately he was leaving the valley because he was due to take up his duties at the hospital, that he was delighted to have been of service to them, that he hoped they would arrange their return journey so as to pass through the city where his hospital was, and asked for their assurances that they would.

The departure of Dr. Schröder brought it home to them that their own vacation would end in a week and that they were bored, or on the point of becoming bored. They had much better rouse themselves, leave the snow mountains, and go down to one of the cities below, take a cheap room, and make an effort to meet some ordinary people. By this they meant neither the rich industrialists who frequented this valley, nor people like Frau Stohr, who were manifestly something left over from an older and more peaceful time; nor like Frau Länge and her daughter Lili; nor like Dr. Schröder. Saying goodbye to Frau Länge was almost painless for, as she said instantly, a day never passed without at least one person knocking on her door and asking for a room because, as everyone in the village knew, she gave good value for money. This was true; Frau Länge was a natural landlady; she had given them far more than had been contracted for in the way of odd cups of coffee and above all in hours of fraternal conversation. But at last she accepted their plea that they wanted to spend a week in their professional guise, seeing hospitals and making contact with their fellow-doctors. "In that case," she said at once, "it is lucky that you know Dr. Schröder, for there could be no better person to show you everything that you need to see." They said that they would look up Dr. Schröder the moment they arrived, if they should happen to pass through his town, and with this the goodbyes were made.

They made the journey by bus down the long winding valley to the mother village, O——, caught the little rickety train, spent another uncomfortable night sitting up side by side on the hard wooden benches, and at last reached the city of Z——, where they found a small room in a cheap hotel. And now they were pledged to contact ordinary people and widen their view of present-day Germany. They took short walks through the streets of the city, surrounded by ordinary people, looked into their faces, as tourists do, made up stories about them, and

289

got into brief conversation from which they made large generalizations. And, like every earnest tourist, they indulged in fantasies of how they would stop some pleasant-faced person in the street and say: We are ordinary people, completely representative of the people of our country. You are obviously an ordinary person, representative of yours. Please divulge and unfold yourself to us, and we will do the same.

Whereupon this pleasant-faced person would let out an exclamation of delight, strike his forehead with his fist and say: But my friends! There is nothing I would like better. With which he would take them to his house, flat, or room; and a deathless friendship would begin, strong enough to outlast any international misunderstandings, accidents, incidents, wars, or other phenomena totally undesired by the ordinary people on both sides.

They did not contact Dr. Schröder, since they had taken good care not to choose the town he was working in. But from time to time they thought how pleasant it would have been if Dr. Schröder had not been such an utterly disgusting person; if he had been a hard-working, devoted, idealistic doctor like themselves, who could initiate them into the medical life of Germany, or at least, of one city, without politics entering their intercourse at all.

Thinking wistfully along these lines led them into a course of action foreign to their naturally diffident selves. It so happened that about a year before, Dr. Anderson had got a letter from a certain Dr. Kroll who was attached to a hospital just outside the city of Z—— congratulating him on a paper he had published recently and enclosing a paper of his own which dealt with a closely related line of research. Hamish remembered reading Dr. Kroll's paper and diagnosing it as typical of the work put out by elderly and established doctors who are no longer capable of ploughing original furrows in the field of medicine but, because they do not wish to seem as if they have lost all interest in original research, from time to time put out a small and harmless paper which amounts to an urbane comment on the work of other people. In short, Dr. Anderson had despised the paper sent to him by his colleague in Germany and had done no more than write him a brief letter of thanks. Now he remembered the incident and told Mary Parrish about it, and both wondered if they might telephone Dr. Kroll and introduce themselves. When they decided that they should, it was with a definite feeling that they were confessing a defeat. Now they were going to be professional people, nothing more. The "ordinary people" had totally eluded them. Conversations with three workmen (on buses), two housewives (in cafés), a businessman (on a train), two waiters and two maids (at the hotel) had left them dissatisfied. None of these people had come out with the final, pithy, conclusive statement about modern Germany that they so badly needed. In fact none of them had said more than what their counterparts in Britain would have said. The nearest to a political comment any one of them had made was the complaint by one of the maids that she did not earn enough money and would very likely go to England where, she understood, wages were much higher.

No, contact with that real, sound, old-fashioned, healthy Germany, as symbolized by the two little girls singing on the bus, had failed them. But certainly it must be there. Something which was a combination of the rather weary irony of the refugees both had known, the bitter affirmation of the songs of Bertolt Brecht, the fighting passion of a Dimitrov (though of course Dimitrov was not a German); the innocence of the little girls, the crashing chords of Beethoven's Fifth. These qualities were fused in their minds into the image of a tired, skeptical, sardonic, but tough, personage, a sort of civilized philosopher prepared at any moment to pick up a rifle and fight for the good and the right and the true. But they had not met anyone remotely like this. As for the two weeks up in the valley, they had simply wiped them out. After all, was it likely that a valley given up wholly to the pursuit of pleasure, and all the year round at that, could be representative of anything but itself?

They would simply accept the fact that they had failed, and ring up Dr. Kroll, and spend the remaining days of their vacation acquiring information about medicine. They rang up Dr. Kroll who, rather to their surprise, remembered the interesting correspondence he had had with Dr. Anderson and invited them to spend the next morning with him. He sounded not at all like the busy head of a hospital, but more like a host. Having made this arrangement, Doctors Parrish and Anderson were on the point of going out to find some cheap restaurant—for their reserve of money was now very small indeed—when Dr. Schröder was announced to them. He had traveled that afternoon all the way from S—— especially to greet them, having heard from his buddy Frau Länge that they were here. In other words, he must have telephoned or wired Frau Länge, who knew their address since she was forwarding letters for them; his need for them was so great that he had also traveled all the way from S——, an expensive business, as he did not hesitate to point out.

The British couple, once again faced with the scarred face and bitter eyes of Dr. Schröder, once again felt a mixture of loathing and compassion and limply made excuses because they had chosen to stop in this town and not in S——. They said they could not possibly afford to spend the evening, as he wanted to do, in one of the expensive restaurants; refused to go as his guests since he had already spent so much money on coming to meet them; and compromised on an agreement to drink beer with him. This they did in various beer cellars where the cohorts of the Führer used to gather in the old days. Dr. Schröder told them this in a way that could be taken either as if he were pointing out a tourist attraction, or as if he were offering them the opportunity to mourn a lost glory with him. His manner toward them now fluctuated between hostility and a self-abasing politeness. They, for their part, maintained their own politeness, drank their beer, occasionally caught each other's eye, and suffered through an evening which, had it not been for Dr. Schröder, might have been a very pleasant one. From time to time he brought the conversation around to the possibilities of his working in Britain; and they repeated their warnings, until at last, although he had not mentioned the United States, they explained that getting visas to live in that part of the world would be no easier in Britain than it was here. Dr. Schröder was not at all discomposed when they showed that they were aware of his real objective. Not at all; he behaved as if he had told them from the start that the United States was his ideal country. Just as if he had never sung songs of praise to Britain, he now disparaged Britain as part of Europe, which was dead and finished, a parasite on the healthy body of America. Quite obviously all people of foresight would make their way to America—he assumed that they, too, had seen this obvious truth, and had possibly already made their plans? Of course he did not blame anyone for looking after himself first, that was a rule of nature; but friends should help each other.

And who knew but that once they were all in America Dr. Schröder might be in a position to help Doctors Anderson and Parrish? The wheel of chance might very well bring such a thing to pass. Yes, it was always advisable in this world to plan well ahead. As for himself, he was not ashamed to admit that it was his first principle; that was why he was sitting this evening in the city of Z——, at their service. That was why he had arranged a day's leave from his own hospital—not the easiest thing to do, this, since he had just returned from a fortnight's holiday—in order to be their guide around the hospitals of Z——.

Mary and Hamish, after a long stunned silence, said that his kindness to them was overwhelming. But unfortunately they had arranged to spend tomorrow with Dr. Kroll of such-and-such a hospital.

The eyes of Dr. Schröder showed a sudden violent animation. The shiny stretched mask of his face deepened its scarlet and, after a wild angry flickering of blue light at the name Kroll, the eyes settled into a steady, almost anguished glare of inquiry.

It appeared that at last they had hit upon, quite by chance, the way to silence Dr. Schröder.

"Dr. Kroll," he said with the sigh of a man who, after long searching, finds the key. "Dr. Kroll. I see. Yes."

At last he had placed them. It seemed that Dr. Kroll's status was so high, and therefore, presumably, their status also, that he could not possibly aspire to any equality with them. Perfectly understandable that they did not need to emigrate to America, being the close friends of Dr. Kroll. His manner became bitter, brooding, and respectful, and at the most suggested that they might have said, nearly three weeks ago on that first evening in O——, that they were intimates of Dr. Kroll, thereby saving him all this anguish and trouble and expense.

Dr. Kroll, it emerged, was a man loaded with honors and prestige, at the very height of his profession. Of course, it was unfortunate that such a man should be afflicted in the way he was. . . .

And how was Dr. Kroll afflicted?

Why, didn't they know? Surely, they must! Dr. Kroll was for six months in every year a voluntary patient in his own hospital—yes, that was something to admire, was it not?—that a man of such brilliance should, at a certain point in every year, hand over his keys to his subordinates and submit to seeing a door locked upon himself, just as, for the other six months, he locked doors on other people. It was very sad, yes. But of course they must know all this quite well, since they had the privilege of Dr. Kroll's friendship.

Mary and Hamish did not like to admit that they had not known it was a mental hospital that Dr. Kroll administered. If they did, they would lose the advantage of their immunity from Dr. Schröder who had, obviously, already relinquished them entirely to a higher sphere. Meanwhile, since his evening was already wasted, and there was time to fill in, he was prepared to talk.

By the time the evening had drawn to a close in a beer cellar where one drank surrounded by great wooden barrels from which the beer was drawn off direct into giant-sized mugs—the apotheosis of all beer cellars—they had formed an image of Dr. Kroll as a very old, Lear-like man, proud and bitter in the dignified acceptance of his affliction; and although neither of them had any direct interest in the problems of the mentally sick, since Mary Parrish specialized in small children and Hamish Anderson in geriatrics, they were sympathetically looking forward to meeting this courageous old man.

The evening ended without any unpleasantness because of the invisible presence of Dr. Kroll. Dr. Schröder returned them to the door of their hotel, shook their hands, and wished them a happy conclusion to their vacation. The violent disharmony of his personality had been swallowed entirely by the self-abasing humility into which he had retreated, with which he was consoling himself. He said that he would look them up when he came to London, but it was merely conventional. He wished them a pleasant reunion with Dr. Kroll and strode off through the black, cold, blowing night toward the railway station, springing on his long lean legs like a black-mantled grasshopper—a hooded, bitter, energetic shape whirled about by flurries of fine white snow that glittered in the streetlights like blown salt or sand.

Next morning it was still snowing. The British couple left their hotel early to find the right bus stop, which was at the other end of the city in a poor suburb. The snow fell listlessly from a low gray sky, and fine shreds of dingy snow lay sparse on the dark earth. The bombs of the recent war had laid the streets here flat for miles around. The streets were etched in broken outlines, and the newly laid railway lines ran clean and shining through them. The station had been bombed, and there was a wooden shed doing temporary duty until another could be built. A dark-wrapped, dogged crowd stood bunched around the bus stop. Nearby a mass of workmen were busy on a new building that rose fine and clean and white out of the miles of damaged houses. They looked like black and energetic insects at work against the stark white of the walls. The British couple stood hunching their cold shoulders and shifting their cold feet with the

German crowd, and watched the builders. They thought that it was the bombs of their country which had created this havoc; thought of the havoc created in their country by the bombs of the people they now stood shoulder to shoulder with, and sank back slowly into a mood of listless depression. The bus was a long time coming. It seemed to grow colder. From time to time people drifted past to the station shed or added themselves to the end of the bus queues, or a woman went past with a shopping basket. Behind the ruined buildings rose the shapes and outlines of the city that had been destroyed and the outlines of the city that would be rebuilt. It was as if they stood solid among the ruins and ghosts of dead cities and cities not yet born. And Hamish's eyes were at work again on the faces of the people about them, fixed on the face of an old shawled woman who was passing; and it seemed as if the crowd, like the streets, became transparent and fluid, for beside them, behind them, among them stood the dead. The dead of two wars peopled the ruined square and jostled the living, a silent snowbound multitude.

The silence locked the air. There was a low, deep thudding that seemed to come from under the earth. It was from a machine at work on the building site. The machine, low in the dirty snow, lifted black grappling arms like a wrestler or like someone in prayer; and the sound of its laboring traveled like a sensation of movement through the cold earth, as if the soil were hoarsely breathing. And the workmen swarmed and worked around the machine and over the steep sides of the new building. They were like children playing with bricks. Half an hour before a giant of a man in black jackboots had strode past their block building and carelessly kicked it down. Now the children were building it again, under the legs of a striding race of great black-booted giants. At any moment another pair of trampling black legs might come straddling over the building and down it would go, down into ruin, to the accompaniment of crashing thunder and bolts of lightning. All over the soil of patient Europe, soil soaked again and again by blood, soil broken again and again by angry metal, the small figures were at work, building their bright new houses among the shells and the ruins of war; and in their eyes was the shadow from the great marching jackbooted feet, and beside each of them, beside every one of them, their dead, the invisible, swarming, memoried dead.

The crowd continued to wait. The machine kept up its hoarse breathing. From time to time a shabby bus came up, a few people climbed in, the bus went off, and more people came dark-clothed through the thinly falling snow to join the crowd, which was very similar to a British crowd in its stolid disciplined quality of patience.

At last a bus with the number they had been told to look for drew up, and they got into it with a few other people. The bus was half empty. Almost at once it left the city behind. Dr. Kroll's hospital, like so many of the similar hospitals in Britain, was built well outside the city boundaries so that the lives of healthy people might not be disturbed by thoughts of those who had to retreat behind the shelter of high walls. The way was straight on a good narrow road, recently rebuilt, over flat black plains streaked and spotted with snow. The quiet, windless air was full of fine particles of snow that fell so slowly it seemed that the sky was falling, as if the slow weight of the snow dragged the gray covering over the black flat plains down to the earth. They traveled forward in a world without color.

Dr. Kroll's hospital made itself visible a long way off over the plain. It consisted of a dozen or more dark, straight buildings set at regular angles to each other, like the arrangement of the sheds in the concentration camps of the war. Indeed, at a distance, the resemblance to the mechanical order of a concentration camp was very great; but as the bus drew nearer the buildings grew and spread into their real size and surrounded themselves with a regular pattern of lawns and shrubs.

The bus set them down outside a heavy iron gate; and at the entrance of the main building, which was high and square, they were welcomed by a doctor whose enthusiasm was expressly delegated from Dr. Kroll, who was impatiently waiting for them upstairs. They went up several staircases and along many corridors, and thought that whatever bleak impression this place might give from the outside, great care had been given to banishing bleakness from within. The walls were all covered by bright pictures, which there was no time to examine now, as they hurried after their busy guide; flowers stood on high pedestals at every turning of the corridor, and the walls and ceiling and woodwork were painted in clean white and blue. They were thinking sympathetically of the storm-driven Lear whom they were so soon to meet, as they passed through these human and pleasant corridors; they were even thinking that perhaps it was an advantage to have as director of a mental hospital a man who knew what it was like to spend time inside it as a victim. But their guide remarked, "This is, of course, the administrative block and the doctors' quarters. Dr. Kroll will be happy to show you the hospital itself later."

With this he shook them by the hand, nodded a

goodbye and went, leaving them outside the half-open door of what looked like a middle-class living room.

A hearty voice called out that they must come in; and they went into a suite of two rooms, half-divided by sheets of sliding glass, brightly lighted, pleasantly furnished, and with nothing in it reminiscent of an office but a single small desk in the farther of the two rooms. Behind the desk sat a handsome man of late middle age who was rising to greet them. It occurred to them, much too late, that this must be Dr. Kroll; and so their greetings, because they were shocked, were much less enthusiastic than his. His greetings were in any case much more like a host's than a colleague's. He was apparently delighted to see them and pressed them to sit down while he ordered them some coffee. This he did by going to the house telephone on the desk in the room beyond the pane of glass; and the two looked at each other, exchanging surprise, and then, finally, pleasure.

Dr. Kroll was, to begin with, extremely distinguished, and they remembered something Dr. Schröder had said the night before, to the effect that he came from an old and respected family; that he was, in short, an aristocrat. They had to accept the word when looking at Dr. Kroll himself, even though they could not conceivably take it from Dr. Schröder. Dr. Kroll was rather tall and managed to combine heaviness and leanness in a remarkable way, for while he was a man of whom one instinctively wondered how much he must weigh when he stood on a scale, he was not fat, or even plump. But he was heavy; and his face, which had strong and prominent bones, carried a weight of large-pored flesh. Yet one would have said, because of the prominent dome of pale forehead and because of the large, commanding nose, and because of the deep dark lively eyes, that it was a lean face. And his movements were not those of a heavy man; he had quick impatient gestures and his large, handsome hands were in constant movement. He returned, smiling, from giving orders about the coffee, sat down in an easy chair opposite the two British doctors, and proceeded to entertain them in the most urbane and pleasant way in the world. He spoke admirable English, he knew a good deal about Britain, and he now discussed the present state of affairs in Britain with assurance.

His admiration for Britain was immense. And this time the British couple were flattered. This was something very different from hearing praise from that appalling Dr. Schröder. Until the coffee came, and while they were drinking it, and for half an hour afterward, they discussed Britain and its institutions. The British couple listened to a view of Britain that they disagreed with profoundly, but without irritation, since it was natural that a man like this should hold conservative ideas. Dr. Kroll believed that a limited monarchy was the best guarantee against disorder and was, in fact, the reason for the well-known British tolerance, which was a quality he admired more than any other. Speaking as a German, and therefore peculiarly equipped to discuss the dangers of anarchy, he would say that the best thing the Allied Armies could have done would have been to impose upon Germany a royal family, created, if necessary, from the shreds and fragments of the unfortunately dwindling royal families of Europe. Further, he believed that this should have been done at the end of the First World War, at the Treaty of Versailles. When Britain, usually so perspicacious in matters of this kind, had left Germany without a royal safeguard, they had made the worst mistake of their history. For a royal family would have imposed good conduct and respect for institutions and made an upstart like Hitler impossible.

At this point the eyes of the British pair met again, though briefly. There was no doubt that to hear Hitler described as an upstart revived some of the sensations they felt when listening to Dr. Schröder or Frau Länge. A few seconds later they heard him being referred to as a mongrel upstart, and unease definitely set in, beneath the well-being induced by the good coffee and their liking for their host.

Dr. Kroll developed his theme for some time, darting his lively and intelligent glances at them, offering them more coffee, offering them cigarettes, and demanded from them an account of how the Health Service worked in Britain. He took it for granted that neither would approve of a scheme which gave people something for nothing, and he commiserated with them for their subjection to state tyranny. They ventured to point out to him certain advantages they felt it had; and at last he nodded and admitted that a country as stable and well-ordered as their own might very well be able to afford extravagant experiments that would wreck other countries—his own, for instance. But he did feel disturbed when he saw their country, which he regarded as the bulwark of decency against socialism in Europe, giving in to the mob.

Here they suggested that they did not want to take up more of his time than was necessary; he must be very busy. For surely the director of such a large hospital could not possibly afford to devote so much time to every foreign doctor who wished to see over it? Or could it be his devotion to Britain that made him so ready to devote his time to them?

At any rate, he seemed disappointed at being reminded of what they had come for. He even sighed and sat silent a little, so that Dr. Anderson, out of politeness, mentioned the paper he had received from him so that they might, if Dr. Kroll wished it, discuss the subject of their research. But Dr. Kroll merely sighed again and said that these days he had very little time for original work; such was the penalty one must pay for accepting the burdens of administration. He rose, all his animation gone, and invited them to step into the other room beyond the glass panel where he would collect his keys. So the three of them went into the inner drawing room, which was an office because of the desk and the telephone; and there Mary Parrish's attention was drawn to a picture on the wall above the desk. At a distance of six or eight feet it was a gay fresh picture of a cornfield painted from root-vision, or field-mouse view. The sheaves of corn rose startlingly up, bright and strong, mingled with cornflowers and red poppies, as if one were crouching in the very center of a field. But as one walked toward the picture it vanished, it became a confusion of bright paint. It was finger-painted. The surface of the canvas was as rough as a ploughed field. Mary Parrish walked up to it, into the bright paint, took a few steps back, and back again; and, behold, the picture recreated itself, the cornfield strong and innocent, with something of the sensual innocence of Renoir's pictures. She was so absorbed that she started when Dr. Kroll dropped a heavy hand on her shoulder and demanded, Was she fond of painting? Instantly both she and Hamish assured him that they were enthusiastically fond of pictures.

Dr. Kroll dropped back on the surface of his very neat desk—so neat one could not help wondering how much it was used—the very large black bunch of keys he had removed from it; and he stood in front of the cornfield picture, his hand on Mary's shoulder.

"This," he said, "is what I am really interested in. Yes, yes; this, you must agree, is more interesting than medicine."

They agreed, since they had just understood that this was the artist in person. Dr. Kroll proceeded to take out from a large cupboard set into the wall a thick stack of pictures, all finger-painted, all with the rough staring surface of thick paint, all of which created themselves at ten paces into highly organized and original pictures.

Soon both rooms were full of pictures that leaned against chairs, tables, walls and along the sliding glass panels. Dr. Kroll, his fine hands knotted together in anxiety because of their possible reception of his work, followed them around as they gazed at one picture after another. It became evident that the pictures separated themselves into two categories. There were those, like the cornfield, done in bright clear colors, very fresh and lyrical. Then there were those which, close up, showed grim rutted surfaces of dirty black, gray, white, a sullen green and—recurring again and again—a characteristic sullen shade of red—a dark, lightless, rusty red like old blood. These pictures were all extraordinary and macabre, of graveyards and skulls and corpses, of war scenes and bombed buildings and screaming women and houses on fire with people falling from burning windows like ants into flames. It was quite extraordinary how, in the space of a few seconds, these two conventional and pretty rooms had been transformed by these pictures into an exhibition of ghoulishness, particularly as the scenes of the pictures were continually vanishing altogether into areas of thick paint that had been smeared, rubbed, piled, worked all over the canvas an inch or so thick by the handsome fingers of Dr. Kroll. Standing at six feet from one picture, the proper distance to view the work of Dr. Kroll, the picture they had been examining five moments before, and which they had now moved away from, lost its meaning and disintegrated into a surface of jumbled and crusted color. They were continually stepping forward or stepping back from chaos into moments of brief, clear, startling illumination. And they could not help wondering if Dr. Kroll was gifted with a peculiar vision of his own, a vision perhaps of his fingertips, which enabled him to *see* his work as he stood up against it, rubbing and plastering the thick paint on to the canvas; they even imagined him as a monster with arms six feet long, standing back from his canvas as he worked on it like a clambering spider. The quality of these pictures was such that, as they examined them, they could not help picturing the artist as a monster, a maniac, or kind of gifted insect. Yet, turning to look at Dr. Kroll, there he stood, a handsome man who was the very essence of everything that was conservative, correct, and urbane.

Mary, at least, was feeling a little giddy. She sought out the battling blue eyes of her partner, Hamish, and understood that he felt the same. For this was an exact repetition of their encounter with Dr. Schröder with his scarred face that demanded compassion. In saying what they thought of his work to Dr. Kroll, they must remember that they were speaking to a man who gallantly and bravely volunteered to hand the keys of sanity over to a subordinate and retired into madness for six months of the year, when, presumably, he painted these horrible pictures, whose very surfaces looked like the oozing, shredding substance of decomposing flesh.

Meanwhile, there he stood beside them, searching their faces anxiously.

They said, in response to his appeal, that this was

obviously a real and strong talent. They said that his work was striking and original. They said they were deeply impressed.

He stood silent, not quite smiling, but with a quizzical look behind the fine eyes. He was judging them. He knew what they were feeling and was condemning them, in the same way as the initiated make allowances for the innocent.

Dr. Anderson remarked that it must be admitted that the pictures were rather strong? Not to everybody's taste, perhaps? Perhaps rather savage?

Dr. Kroll, smiling urbanely, replied that life tended sometimes to be savage. Yes, that was his experience. He deepened his smile and indicated the cornfield on the wall behind his desk and said that he could see Dr. Anderson preferred pictures like that one?

Dr. Anderson took his stand, and very stubbornly, on the fact that he preferred that picture to any of the others he had seen.

Mary Parrish moved to stand beside Dr. Anderson and joined him in asserting that to her mind this picture was entirely superior to all the others; she preferred the few bright pictures, all of which seemed to her to be loaded with a quality of sheer joy, a sensuous joy, to the others which seemed to her—if he didn't mind her saying so—simply horrible.

Dr. Kroll turned his ironical, dark gaze from one face to the other and remarked: "So." And again, accepting their bad taste: "So."

He remarked, "I am subject to fits of depression. When I am depressed, naturally enough, I paint these pictures." He indicated the lightless pictures of his madness. "And when I am happy again, and when I have time—for, as I have said, I am extremely busy—I paint pictures such as these. . . ." His gesture toward the cornfield was impatient, almost contemptuous. It

306

was clear that he had hung the joyous cornfield on the wall of his reception room because he expected all his guests or visiting colleagues to have the bad taste to prefer it.

"So," he said again, smiling drily.

At which, Mary Parrish—since he was conveying a feeling of total isolation—said quickly, "But we are very interested. We would love to see some more, if you have time."

It seemed tht he needed very much to hear her say this. For the ironical condemnation left his face and was succeeded by the pathetic anxiety of the amateur artist to be loved for his work. He said that he had had two exhibitions of his paintings, that he had been misunderstood by the critics, who had praised the paintings he did not care for, so that he would never again expose himself publicly to the stupidity of critics. He was dependent for sympathy on the understanding minority, some of them chance visitors to his hospital; some of them even—if they did not mind his saying so—inmates of it. He would, for two such delightful guests as his visitors from England, be happy to show more of his work.

With this he invited them to step into a passage behind his office. Its walls were covered from floor to ceiling with pictures. Also the walls of the passage beyond it.

It was terrifying to think of the energy this man must have when he was "depressed." Corridor after corridor opened up, the walls all covered with canvases loaded with thick, crusted paint. Some of the corridors were narrow, and it was impossible to stand far enough back for the pictures to compose themselves. But it seemed that Dr. Kroll was able to see what his hands had done even when he was close against the canvas. He would lean into a big area of

307

thick, dry paint from which emerged fragmentarily a jerky branch that looked like a bombed tree, or a bit of cracked bone, or a tormented mouth, and say: "I call this picture 'Love.'" Or Victory, or Death; for he liked this kind of title. "See? See that house there? See how I've put the church?" And the two guests gazed blankly at the smears of paint and wondered if perhaps this canvas represented the apotheosis of his madness and had no form in it at all. But if they stepped back against the opposite wall as far as they could, and leaned their heads back to gain an extra inch of distance, they could see that there was a house or a church. The house was also a skull; and the dead gray walls of the church oozed rusty blood, or spilled a gout of blood over the sills of its windows, or its door ejected blood like a person's mouth coughing blood.

Depression again weighed on the pair who, following after the dignified back of Dr. Kroll as he led them into yet another picture-filled corridor, instinctively reached for each other's hands, reached for the warm contact of healthy flesh.

Soon their host led them back into the office, where he offered them more coffee. They refused politely but asked to see his hospital. Dr. Kroll carelessly agreed. It was not, his manner suggested, that he did not take his hospital seriously, but that he would much rather, now he had been given the privilege of a visit from these rarely sympathetic people, share with them his much higher interests: his love for their country, his art. But he would nevertheless escort them around the hospital.

Again he took up the great bundle of black keys and went before them down the corridor they had first entered by. Now they saw that the pictures they had noticed then were all by him; these were the pictures he despised and hung for public view. But as they passed through a back door into a courtyard he paused, held up his keys, smiling, and indicated a small picture by the door. The picture was of the keys. From a scramble of whitey-gray paint came out, very black and hard and shining, a great jangling bunch of keys that also looked like bells, and, from certain angles, like staring eyes. Dr. Kroll shared a smile with them as if to say: An interesting subject?

The three doctors went across a courtyard into the first block, which consisted of two parallel very long wards, each filled with small, tidy, white beds that had a chair and a locker beside them. On the beds sat, or leaned, or lay, the patients. Apart from the fact that they tended to be listless and staring, there was nothing to distinguish this ward from the ward of any public hospital. Dr. Kroll exchanged brisk greetings with certain of his patients; discouraged an old man who grasped his arm as he passed and said that he had a momentous piece of news to tell him which he had heard that moment over his private wireless station, and which affected the whole course of history; and passed on smiling through this building into the next. There was nothing new here. This block, like the last, had achieved the ultimate in reducing several hundred human beings into complete identity with each other. Dr. Kroll said, almost impatiently, that if you had seen one of these wards you had seen them all, and took off at a tangent across a courtyard to another of these regular blocklike buildings which was full of women. It occurred to the British pair that the two buildings on the other side of the court had men in them only; and they asked Dr. Kroll if he kept the men in the line of buildings on one side of the court, and the women on the other—for there was a high wire fence down the court, with a door in it that he opened and locked behind him. "Why, that is so," said Dr. Kroll indifferently.

"Do the men and the women meet—in the evenings, perhaps?"

"Meet? No."

"Not at social evenings? At dances perhaps? At some meals during the week?"

Here Dr. Kroll turned and gave his guests a tolerant smile. "My friends," he said, "sex is a force destructive enough even when kept locked up. Do you suggest that we should mix the sexes in a place like this, where it is hard enough to keep people quiet and unexcited?"

Dr. Anderson remarked that in progressive mental hospitals in Britain it was a policy to allow men and women to mix together as much as was possible. For what crime were these poor people being punished, he enquired hotly, that they were treated as if they had taken perpetual vows of celibacy?

Dr. Parrish noted that the word "progressive" fell very flat in this atmosphere. Such was the power of Dr. Kroll's conservative personality that it sounded almost eccentric.

"So?" commented Dr. Kroll. "So the administrators of your English hospitals are prepared to give themselves so much unnecessary trouble?"

"Do the men and the women never meet?" insisted Dr. Parrish.

Dr. Kroll said tolerantly that at night they behaved like naughty schoolchildren and passed each other notes through the wire.

The British couple fell back on their invincible politeness and felt their depression inside them like a fog. It was still snowing lightly through the heavy gray air.

Having seen three buildings all full of women of all ages, lying and sitting about in the listlessness of complete idleness, they agreed with Dr. Kroll it was enough; they were prepared to end their tour of inspection. He said that they must return with him for another cup of coffee, but first he had to make a short visit, and perhaps they would be kind enough to accompany him. He led the way to another building set rather apart from others, whose main door he opened with an enormous key from his bunch of keys. As soon as they were inside it became evident that this was the children's building. Dr. Kroll was striding down the main passage, calling aloud for some attendant who appeared to take instructions.

Meanwhile, Mary Parrish, a doctor who specialized in small children, finding herself at the open door of a ward looked in, and invited Dr. Anderson to do the same. It was a very large room, very clean, very fresh, with barred windows. It was full of cots and small beds. In the center of the room a five-year-old child stood upright against the bars of a cot. His arms were confined by a straitjacket, and because he could not prevent himself from falling, he was tied upright against the bars with a cord. He was glaring around the room, glaring and grinding his teeth. Never had Mary seen such a desperate, wild, suffering little creature as this one. Immediately opposite the child sat a very large towheaded woman, dressed in heavy striped gray material, like a prison dress, knitting as comfortably as if she were in her kitchen.

Mary was speechless with horror at the sight. She could feel Hamish stiff and angry beside her.

Dr. Kroll came back down the passage, saw them, and said amiably: "You are interested? So? Of course, Dr. Parrish, you said children are your field. Come in, come in." He led the way into the room, and the fat

311

woman stood up respectfully as he entered. He glanced at the straitjacketed child and moved past it to the opposite wall, where there was a line of small beds, placed head to foot. He pulled back the coverings one after another, showing a dozen children aged between a year and six years—armless children, limbless children, children with enormous misshapen heads, children with tiny heads and monstrous bodies. He pulled the coverings off, one after another, replacing them as soon as Mary Parrish and Hamish Anderson had seen what he was showing them, and remarked: "Modern drugs are a terrible thing. Now these horrors are kept alive. Before, they died of pneumonia."

Hamish said, "The theory is, I believe, that medical science advances so fast that we should keep even the most apparently hopeless people alive in case we find something that can save them?"

Dr. Kroll gave them the ironical smile they had seen before, and said, "Yes, yes, yes. That is the theory. But for my part. . . ."

Mary Parrish was watching the imprisoned little boy, who glared from a flushed wild face, straining his small limbs inside the thick stuff of the straitjacket. She said, "In Britain straitjackets are hardly ever used. Certainly not for children."

"So?" commented Dr. Kroll. "So? But sometimes it is for the patient's own good."

He advanced toward the boy and stood before the bars of the cot, looking at him. The child glared back like a wild animal into the eyes of the big doctor. "This one bites if you go too near him," commented Dr. Kroll; and with a nod of his head invited them to follow him out.

"Yes, yes," he remarked, unlocking the big door and locking it behind them, "there are things we can-

312

not say in public, but we may agree in private that there are many people in this hospital who would be no worse for a quick and painless death."

Again he asked that they should excuse him, and he strode off to have a word with another doctor who was crossing the court in his white coat, with another big bunch of black keys in his hand.

Hamish said, "This man told us that he has directed this hospital for thirty years."

"Yes, I believe he did."

"So he was here under Hitler."

"The mongrel upstart, yes."

"And he would not have kept his job unless he had agreed to sterilize Jews, serious mental defectives, and communists. Did you remember?"

"No, I'd forgotten."

"So had I."

They were silent a moment, thinking of how much they had liked, how much they still liked, Dr. Kroll.

"Any Jew or mental defective or communist unlucky enough to fall into Dr. Kroll's hands would have been forcibly sterilized. And the very ill would have been killed outright."

"Not necessarily," she objected feebly. "After all, perhaps he refused. Perhaps he was strong enough to refuse."

"Perhaps."

"After all, even under the worst governments there are always people in high places who use their influence to protect weak people."

"Perhaps."

"And he might have been one."

"We should keep an open mind?" he inquired, quick and sarcastic. They stood very close together under the cold snow in a corner of the gray courtyard. Twenty paces away, behind walls and locked doors, a small boy, naked save for a straitjacket and tied to bars like an animal, was grinding his teeth and glaring at the fat knitting wardress.

Mary Parrish said miserably, "We don't know, after all. We shouldn't condemn anyone without knowing. For all we know he might have saved the lives of hundreds of people."

At this point Dr. Kroll came back, swinging his keys.

Hamish inquired blandly, "It would interest us very much to know if Hitler's régime made any difference to you professionally?"

Dr. Kroll considered this question as he strolled along beside them. "Life was easy for no one during that time," he said.

"But as regards medical policy?"

Dr. Kroll gave this question his serious thought, and said, "No, they did not interfere very much. Of course, on certain questions, the gentlemen of the Nazi régime had sensible ideas."

"Such as? For instance?"

"Oh, questions of hygiene? Yes, one could call them questions of social hygiene." He had led them to the door of the main building, and now he said: "You will, I hope, join me in a cup of coffee before you leave? Unless I can persuade you to stay and have a meal with us?"

"I think we should catch our bus back to town," said Hamish, speaking firmly for both of them. Dr. Kroll consulted his watch. "Your bus will not be passing for another twenty minutes." They accompanied him back through the picture-hung corridors to his office.

"And I would like so much to give you a memento of your visit," he said, smiling at them both. "Yes, I

314

would like that. No, wait for one minute, I want to show you something."

He went to the wall cupboard and took out a flat object wrapped in a piece of red silk. He unwrapped the silk and brought forth another picture. He set this picture against the side of the desk and invited them to stand back and look at it. They did so, already prepared to admire it, for it was a product of one of the times when he was not depressed. It was a very large picture, done in clear blues and greens, the picture of a forest—an imaginary forest with clear streams running through it, a forest where impossibly brilliant birds flew, and full of plants and trees created in Dr. Kroll's mind. It was beautiful, full of joy and tranquillity and light. But in the center of the sky glared a large black eye. It was an eye remote from the rest of the picture; and obviously what had happened was that Dr. Kroll had painted his fantasy forest, and then afterward, looking at it during some fit of misery, had painted in that black, condemnatory, judging eye.

Mary Parrish stared back at the eye and said, "It's lovely; it's a picture of paradise." She felt uncomfortable at using the word paradise in the presence of Hamish, who by temperament was critical of words like these.

But Dr. Kroll smiled with pleasure, and laid his heavy hand on her shoulder, and said: "You understand. Yes, you understand. That picture is called *The Eye of God in Paradise*. You like it?"

"Very much," she said, afraid that he was about to present that picture to her. For how could they possibly transport such a big picture all the way back to Britain and what would she do with it when she got there? For it would be dishonest to paint out the black, wrathful eye: one respected, naturally, an artist's conception even if one disagreed with it. And she

315

could not endure to live with that eye, no matter how much she liked the rest of the picture.

But it seemed that Dr. Kroll had no intention of parting with the picture itself, which he wrapped up again in its red silk and hid in the cupboard. He took from a drawer a photograph of the picture and offered it to her, saying, "If you really like my picture —and I can see that you do, for you have a real feeling, a real understanding—then kindly take this as a souvenir of a happy occasion."

She thanked him, and both she and Hamish looked with polite gratitude at the photograph. Of course it gave no idea at all of the original. The subtle blues and greens had gone, were not hinted at; and even the softly-waving grasses, trees, plants, foliage, were obliterated. Nothing remained but a reproduction of crude crusts of paint, smeared thick by the fingers of Dr. Kroll, from which emerged the hint of a branch, the suggestion of a flower. Nothing remained except the black, glaring eye, the eye of a wrathful and punishing God. It was the photograph of a roughly-scrawled eye, as a child might have drawn it—as, so Mary could not help thinking, that unfortunate strait-jacketed little boy might have drawn the eye of God, or of Dr. Kroll, had he been allowed to get his arms free and use them.

The thought of that little boy hurt her; it was still hurting Hamish who stood politely beside her. She knew that the moment they could leave this place and get on to the open road where the bus passed would be the happiest of her life.

They thanked Dr. Kroll profoundly for his kindness, insisted they were afraid they might miss their bus, said goodbye, and promised letters and an exchange of medical papers of interest to them all—promised, in short, eternal friendship.

Then they left the big building and Dr. Kroll and emerged into the cold February air. Soon the bus came and picked them up, and they traveled back over the flat black plain to the city terminus.

The terminus was exactly as it had been four or five hours before. Under the low gray sky lay the black chilled earth, the ruins of streets, the already softening shapes of bomb craters, the big new shining white building covered with energetic shapes of the workers. The bus queue still waited patiently, huddled into dark, thick clothes, while a thin bitter snow drifted down, down, hardly moving, as if the sky itself were slowly falling.

Mary Parrish took out the photograph and held it in her chilly gloved hand.

The black angry eye glared up at them.

"Tear it up," he said.

"No," she said.

"Why not? What's the use of keeping the beastly thing?"

"It wouldn't be fair," she said seriously, returning it to her handbag.

"Oh, *fair*," he said bitterly, with an impatient shrug.

They moved off side by side to the bus stop where they would catch a bus back to their hotel. Their feet crunched sharply on the hard earth. The stillness, save for the small shouts of the men at work on the half-finished building, save for the breathing noise of the machine, was absolute. And this queue of people waited like the other across the square, waited eternally, huddled up, silent, patient, under the snow; listening to the silence, under which seemed to throb from the depths of the earth the memory of the sound of marching feet, of heavy, black-booted, marching feet.

317